Last Diner STANDING

A Rose Strickland Mystery

Terri L. Austin

HENERY PRESS

LAST DINER STANDING
A Henery Press Mystery

First Edition
Trade paperback edition | December 2012

Henery Press
www.henerypress.com

ISBN-13: 978-1-938383-08-3

Printed in the United States of America

To Colter and Austin.
Can't imagine my life without the two of you. I love being your mom.
Thank you for being such great kids.

ACKNOWLEDGEMENTS

Even though writing can be a lonely endeavor, getting a book into the hands of readers is a group effort. So many people have been helpful and supportive as I wrote and edited this book. I thank you all and give you a big, fat, virtual smoocheroo!

To Aaron Pilant—police officer extraordinaire. Thanks for all the chop shop knowledge. You're a crime-fighting super hero!

To Larissa Reinhart—You have become such a great friend and co-conspirator in many a shenanigan. Don't know how I'd get along without you, girl. I'm so glad we met.

To Sara Attebury—Thank you. I heart you in a big fangirl way! You've been so supportive and I can't tell you how much I appreciate it. You rock my Hello Kitty socks off!

To Kathy Collins—A legal genius and a wonderful crit partner. Love you and everything you are. Which is awesome.

To Alta Durrant—An amazing crit partner who doesn't judge my comma issues. And I have many. So thank you! My life is happier with you in it!

To Shannon K. Butcher—You're such a wonderful mentor and friend. Your kindness touches me and I'm so blessed to have you in my life.

To Sarah Skolaut—I love your gracious spirit. You're one of the good ones!

A great big shout out to my Little Read Hens—Larissa Reinhart, Anise Rae, Jennifer Tanner, Susan M. Boyer, and LynDee Walker. Love you ladies! Your support has been invaluable! Glad we're in this together!

To my fellow Henery Press chicks—Larissa Reinhart, Susan M. Boyer, Christina Freeburn, and LynDee Walker. Thank you for your help in getting the word out about the books! You're the best!

To Kendel Flaum—Brilliant editor and cover queen! You've been so patient and gracious. Thank you for holding my hand through the whole process.

To Art Molinares—Henery Press's savvy marketing guru! Thank you for your time and patience. You've been terrific.

And a special thanks to my family—Jeff, Colter, and Austin. Without you guys, my life would be a sad, lonely place. I love you.

Chapter 1

There are some absolutes in this life that are irrefutable. If you leave the house looking like crap, you'll see someone you know, usually an ex-boyfriend. If you're running late for an appointment, you'll hit every red light on the way. And a three a.m. phone call is never good news. Either someone's dead, in the hospital, or you're a drunken booty call. But that Saturday morning, I discovered another reason to avoid the ringing harbinger of bad news.

"'ello," I answered, my eyes still closed.

"Rose, I'm in jail, girl."

I sniffed and sat up on my futon. "Janelle?"

"Of course it's Janelle. Get your shit together. They think I tried to kill Asshat."

Scrubbing a hand over my eyes, I glanced at the clock. "Asshat?"

Janelle lowered her voice. "Rose, wake up and listen. I'm in jail, Asshat's in a coma, and they're saying I tried to kill him. I need help."

Her dilemma finally penetrated my sleep-fogged brain. "Oh my God. Where are the kids?" Janelle had two, Damon, nine, and Sherise, seven. Both so cute you wanted to pinch their little cheeks. But I wouldn't recommend it—that Sherise was a biter.

"They're staying with my cousin, Sondra. But I got to get out of here. If they think I'm spending Christmas in jail then I'm Halle Damn Berry."

"What do you want me to do?"

"Call that fancy lawyer you know. He'll figure it out."

Dane Harker. "I'll call him and come see you in the morning. Will they let me bring you anything?"

"Cigarettes and toiletries. These bitches trade everything for cigarettes. And Rose? Thanks."

Oh my God, my study buddy, Janelle Johnson, was in jail, accused of trying to kill her ex-husband, Asshat. I'd never found out his real name, but his moniker seemed apt. When Janelle found him in her bed one afternoon, diddling another woman while eating a drumstick, the marriage was over and the name Asshat was born.

I flipped on the lamp and stood, stretching my legs. I didn't want to call Dane, especially in the middle of the night. For one thing, we kind of dated until a few weeks ago. But he quickly figured out I was too complicated, and I decided he couldn't handle my kind of awesome. And by awesome, I meant crazy dysfunctional drama.

And then there was the fact that I killed a man. Six weeks and one day ago. That sort of thing tended to wither romantic connections pretty fast.

To be fair, the guy I killed was a psycho stalker who would have killed me first. And I didn't feel guilty about. Really.

I was determined to move past it and return to my regularly scheduled life. I had just aced my finals and signed up for two classes next semester. I showed up for work every morning and hung out with friends on the weekends. And I put that night out of my mind.

Mostly. Okay, sleep was sometimes elusive. Two nights ago, I took a toothbrush to the grout on my bathroom tile. Almost passed out from the bleach fumes, but my bathroom sparkled.

What happened, happened. I was alive and I wasn't going to apologize for it.

I dialed Dane's number. Due to recent events, I'd updated from limited minutes to unlimited with all the texts my fingers could stand. My budget winced in pain, but it was worth it.

He answered on the fifth ring. "Yeah?"

"Dane?"

I heard rustling sounds—sheets shifting around. "Who is this?"

"It's Rose Strickland."

"Rose, what's wrong? Are you in trouble?" He'd gone from sleepy to worried in three seconds flat.

"No, I'm fine. But my friend, Janelle, was arrested for attempted murder."

"There's no such thing as attempted murder in Missouri. Assault with deadly injuries perhaps, the law's differ—"

"She's in jail and we need to get her out."

"When's the bail hearing?"

"I'm not sure."

"Do you know the extent of her charges?"

"Nope."

He sighed. "Does she know I charge four-fifty an hour?"

"I was kind of hoping you could give her a discount. Like a freebie."

I heard some teeth grinding.

"Fine. I'll meet you outside the courthouse at nine. We'll go see your friend together and I'll be able to tell you more then."

"Thanks, Dane."

"Hey. I'm glad you called."

I couldn't go back to sleep, so I went to work a little early—around four-ish. Ma's Diner was an institution in Huntingford. We served breakfast from six to one. That's it. No burgers, fries, or chicken sandwiches. Just breakfast.

Ray, my boss, was already in the kitchen preparing cinnamon rolls and biscuit dough. I loved the warm yeasty smell of the kitchen early in the morning.

He glanced up as I walked in. "No sleep?"

Ray was a man of few words. More of a grunter than a talker. In his early fifties, he was a gentle giant with a protruding brow and blond-turning-gray hair he kept in a hairnet.

"Nope. You need help in here?"

He mumbled and shook his head. In Rayspeak that meant, "No thank you, Rose. I'm fine."

I patted his arm on the way to the dining room where I flipped on the lights and started the coffee. The aroma was sharp and rich and comforting as it filled the small room. Saturdays were always busy, so I hoped Ma didn't mind if I left for a few hours to see Janelle.

I'd finished rolling silverware into paper napkins when Roxy Block, a blue-haired fashion plate and my bestie, walked in from the kitchen, chomping gum. She'd quit smoking almost two months ago and now she and her nicotine gum were inseparable. Her short, black skirt was patterned with kittens and playing cards and yarn balls.

"Couldn't sleep again, huh?" She tied an apron around her waist and headed for the coffeepot.

"Not this time. Janelle's in jail."

Roxy's mouth hung open for so long her gum fell on the floor. "For what?" She bent down and scooped it up, stared at it for a second, as if she might pop it back in her mouth. But with a sigh, she walked to the trash can in the corner and threw it away.

"Asshat's in a coma, the police think Janelle tried to kill him. Dane and I are going over to see her this morning. Cool?"

"Yeah, of course." She poured a cup of coffee and glanced up. "Do we think she's guilty?"

Janelle was capable of many things. Putting sugar in Asshat's gas tank? Naturally. Super gluing his dork to his stomach? Of course. But murder? That just wasn't her style. "No, I can't see her killing anybody. Not even Asshat."

"Me neither," Roxy said. "But I can totally picture her beating the shit out of someone."

"Absolutely."

Our conversation was brought to an end when Ma Ferguson barreled through the connecting door and paused in the doorway, looking like a vengeful goddess in sweatpants. Her short white hair stood on end, her eyes narrowed behind large-framed trifocals.

"That man will regret this, I tell ya."

"What's going on?" I asked.

She stormed the rest of the way into the dining room. I'd only seen her this worked up when she lost the iPod raffle on casino night at St. Mary's. "Two words, girls. Rudy. Jorgenson."

"Rudy of Rudy's Roundup Restaurant?" Roxy asked.

Ma nodded, her lips pressed together. "That's him. He's decided to serve breakfast. He's had that place for twenty years and now all of the sudden he's opening early? He must think I've grown soft, but I'll show him. Breakfast my rump." She marched around the diner, taking mismatched chairs off the pink Formica tables and setting them down with a thump.

Rudy's, a slightly bigger place up the street, served bland spaghetti with Texas toast and chicken fried steak smothered in lumpy gravy at dirt cheap prices. "Ma, so what?" I asked. "He'll never touch Ray's pancakes."

Roxy bobbed her head. "And we have eggnog French toast on the menu. You know that's a favorite."

Ma flipped the open sign. "It's not enough. Maybe we need to start making hoity-toity coffee, like that Starbacks."

"Starbucks," Roxy and I corrected in unison.

"Ma, calm down," I said. "Everything will be fine."

"Oh, yes it will." She grinned, her thin lips exposing her dentures. A vicious smile. "Rudy Jorgenson is going down, girls. And I'm the one who's sending him there."

I really hoped she wasn't being literal. I didn't want to have to visit Ma in jail, too.

I met Dane outside the police station at nine on the dot. He looked handsome and professional in a dark suit and pale blue tie. Usually when Dane smiled, cute little dimples popped out on either side of his cheeks. He wasn't dimpling today.

His baby blues swept over me. "How are you, Rose?"

"Great. Things are really great."

He stared at me in uncomfortable silence. "If you ever need to talk—"

"Really, Dane, I'm fine. And just so you know, Janelle's innocent."

He looked like he wanted to say more, but nodded instead. "Okay, let's see if we can help your friend." He placed his hand on the small of my back and led me into the building.

A uniformed officer escorted us into a small room with a table and chairs. Janelle shuffled in wearing white socks and ugly indoor/outdoor slippers. She had smooth cocoa-colored skin and long braids that brushed her apple bottom ass, but her most spectacular feature, her boobs, were now encased in a bright orange jumpsuit and stood out like two gigantic traffic cones.

An officer stood by the door in case she made a run for it. I handed her the bag filled with toiletries and cigs, which had been thoroughly searched, as had my purse and person.

"Thanks, Rose. This that lawyer?"

"Dane, Janelle Johnson. Janelle, Dane Harker."

"Can you get me out of here?" she asked Dane. Janelle didn't look like herself. Free of makeup, her skin was blotchy and her bloodshot eyes were swollen.

"I'll do my best," Dane said. "Tell us what happened."

"Asshat hasn't paid child support for the last year. Not a dime. Word gets back to me that he's going to the strip clubs, flashing bling, making it rain. He can afford an Omega, but he can't pay me?"

Dane leaned toward me. "I'm sorry, but I only got part of that."

Janelle pressed her lips together. "He's been throwing money around, gold rope chains, expensive watches, showering cash on strippers. I dropped the kids at my cousin's, and I went to confront him." She crossed her arms. "Things might have gotten a little heated. I went inside and started throwing some shit out on his front lawn."

"Then what happened?" Dane asked.

"We argued some more. I broke some more shit. Does that fool think he's going to watch a sixty-inch plasma while I can barely afford to get new shoes for my babies? Oh, hells no. It had to go. Then I got in my car and drove home.

"An hour later, there's two cops at my door, arresting me. Asshat's in a coma—someone hit him upside the head. That's all they'll tell me. But I didn't do it." She glanced from me to Dane. "I didn't."

"I believe you, Janelle," I said.

She uncrossed her arms. "You got to get me out of here, Mr. Fancypants Lawyer. I've got two kids to take care of and Christmas is less than three weeks away. I can't be stuck in here." She waved her hand around the room, little rhinestones flashed on her yellow acrylic fingernails.

Dane pulled a paper from his briefcase. "I need you to sign this so I can officially represent you. I'm giving you a discount, since you're Rose's friend." He slid me a look. "But I'll still have to charge one hundred an hour."

Janelle's eyes popped. "Do I look like I have one hundred dollars an hour?"

"Janelle, it's a huge discount," I said. "Maybe she could pay in installments?" I raised my brows at Dane.

He closed his eyes for a second, then nodded. "All right. And you don't have to hire me, Ms. Johnson, but I warn you, court appointed attorneys? You get what you pay for."

She sighed. "Fine. Give me the damn pen." She slashed her signature on the dotted line. "Now what about getting me out of here?"

"You have a bail hearing set for Monday morning. Can you get some money together? You'll need to come up with ten percent, which might be anywhere from ten to fifteen thousand. Depends on the judge."

She threw up her hands. "You got to be fucking kidding me. Is my last name Trump or something?"

"What about Sondra or Tariq?" I asked. Tariq was Janelle's other cousin, the one who danced on the wrong side of legal.

"Yeah, Tariq might have it. Can you call him for me?" She rattled off his number which I put into my phone.

"By the way," I asked, "who told you about Asshat's recent windfall?"

"His sister, Roshanda. We still keep in touch."

We stood to leave, but I glanced back at my friend. "Two questions. Who else wanted Asshat dead and where did he get all that money?"

Janelle stood while the officer placed a hand on her arm. "Anyone who's ever met him and I don't have a clue. Maybe you could check it out for me? When Axton went missing, you found him. Will you find out who put Asshat in a coma?"

I hesitated. I'd had my fill of danger when I went looking for Axton. I was a boring girl now and that's the way I liked it.

"Please, Rose. I got to take care of my kids and I can't do that behind bars."

I looked into her worried eyes. "Okay." How could I say no?

The officer led her away and I felt the weight of Dane's gaze. I knew he had an opinion about my getting involved, but for now he was keeping it to himself and I appreciated his restraint.

"Can you find out exactly what happened last night?" I asked him.

He sighed and squeezed my shoulder. "Sure. After I've examined the police report, I'll call you with the details."

We made our way out of the building and I waved as I walked to my car—an old piece of crap Toyota that was made when 'N Synch ruled the world. One problem. It wasn't there. I looked up and down the street, but my car was gone.

Well, shit.

Chapter 2

I called Ma to let her know my car had vanished, then trudged back into the police station to make a report. After the debacle with Axton two months ago, and Janelle's recent troubles, I had zero confidence in the police. But what else was I going to do?

A very handsome, dark-haired man in a uniform stood at the front desk. The name tag above his right breast pocket read Officer Mike Goedecker. He smiled, his eyes drifting over my face. "May I help you?"

"I hope so. My car was stolen."

His face was a mask of sympathy and he leaned closer to the glass partition that divided us. "That really sucks. Let's see what we can do about that."

I opened my mouth to give him my info when Officer Andre Thomas, or Officer Hard Ass as I not-so-affectionately referred to him, stepped around the corner. When he spotted me, I froze like an ice sculpture with my mouth wide open, and watched, helpless, as he strode toward me like the former military man he probably was.

"Miss Strickland. I can't say I'm surprised to see you here again. What kind of trouble are you in now?"

Officer Goedecker jumped in. "Her car was stolen, sir."

Andre peered at me through frameless glasses, his hazel eyes cold and appraising.

"I know," I held up a hand, "somehow, some way, I brought this on myself."

Ignoring my snark, he pivoted on his heel and strode down the hall. "Follow me," he barked.

I gave one last look of longing at the nice cop and grudgingly straggled behind Officer Hard Ass through a cubicle maze to his depressingly gray corner. I glanced at his padded walls. They were bare except for one framed diploma and a newspaper clipping with a photo of himself and Police Chief Martin Mathers, a handsome, trim man in his fifties, standing side by side at a gala.

Mathers may have sworn to uphold the law in this town, but he was far from squeaky. I'd recently learned he liked illegal gambling. A lot. And owed thousands to the number one criminal in Huntingford.

"When did you last see your car?" He punched at his keyboard.

"An hour ago. Outside the police station."

I pointed at the clipping. "The two of you seem very chummy. Must be nice to have friends in high places."

Officer Thomas glanced up at me. "Make and model?"

"Ninety-seven Toyota Camry."

"Miss a payment?"

I scoffed. "I don't have payments."

"License number?"

I rattled it off.

He tapped away and his printer spit out a form. "Here you go." He handed me a copy of the report.

"You're not even going to look for it, are you?"

"We'll be on the lookout, but most likely you'll never see it again. Older Toyotas are a prime target for choppers. As I'm sure you know, parts for older cars are hard to find."

So I'd never see my crapmobile again. Or the gray hoodie I'd tossed in the backseat. Or the ten dollar bill I'd stuck in the ashtray. "Thanks a bunch, Officer Thomas."

"Sorry I couldn't be more help, Miss Strickland."

As I made my way outside, I called my bud, Axton.

"Hello, Rose. How are you this fine a.m.?"

"Carless. It was stolen right outside the police station."

"Bummer. Want me to pick you up?"

"Will I get you into trouble?"

"Trouble's my middle name," he said. "On my way."

Trouble was not his middle name. Not even close. Axton Fuller Graystone. I kid you not.

The December morning was bright and cold. I shivered in my thrift store wool coat and headed over to the coffee stand on the corner. Lights had been strung up on the lamp poles since Thanksgiving and huge banners that read *Happy Huntingford Holidays* were draped between buildings.

I wasn't feeling very Christmasy this year. Could have been the fact I had very little money to shop with. Maybe I was just in a funk. Or a wacky combination of both, but either way, I was missing the joy of the season. Bah humbug and all that. And my parents' annual Christmas party was tonight. That certainly didn't put me in a yuletide mood.

I ordered a small hot chocolate and paid with my tip money. As I waited for the chocolate to cool, I called Janelle's cousin, Tariq. He told me to meet him at his office on the corner of Oak Tree and Alder after work.

While I waited for Axton, I strolled the streets, glancing in store windows. Pretty party dresses and accessories filled the window of one store. An elaborate train track with bridges and a miniature town filled another. My nephew Scotty would love that.

A blue Honda pulled up beside me. In a nod to the season, Ax had tied a live wreath with a red bow on the front of his car. I hopped in and smiled. "Thanks for the ride."

I handed him my hot chocolate and he took a sip. A black knit cap covered his dishwater blond waves and he'd jauntily tied a neon green scarf around his neck. When he saw me shiver, he turned up the heat.

"No prob, Bob. Not much going on today anyway. Just checking for porn violators." Axton worked in the IT department at Huntingford City College. "Professors are the worst offenders. And you should see the crap they're into. Some of it's creepy and a little weird. So, your car got lifted, huh?"

"Yep."

"What are you gonna do?" He handed the hot chocolate back to me and pulled away from the curb.

Right now, I couldn't afford to replace it. "I'll probably bus pass it for now."

"Waiting for the bus blows. Just take my car."

"Ax—"

"I'll use Stoner Joe's truck. Dude rarely leaves the house. And I can get a ride home from work tonight. No worries."

"Are you sure?" I glanced over and smiled. "Thanks."

"So why were you at the police station in the first place?"

As we drove to the college, I told him about Janelle's situation and Asshat's coma.

"Bummer for Janelle. Hope they catch the real dude soon."

"Me, too." But I wasn't hopeful. Why would the police look for another suspect when they had such a tidy one in Janelle?

At the college, Ax hopped out of the car and I jumped in the driver's seat. "Thanks again, Ax," I called and drove off to the diner.

Inside, every table was full and Roxy ran around, refilling coffee cups, taking orders. When she saw me, she pulled me aside and stuck her pad in her apron pocket. "Your car got stolen outside the police station? The criminals in this town must be trembling."

"I know." I tilted my chin at Ma. "What's up?" Ma sat at the counter with her back to the customers as she scribbled away on a legal pad.

"She's all pissy because Rudy's serving breakfast. She's planning revenge."

Oh dear. I shrugged out of my jacket and tucked it and my purse behind the counter and got to work. When one o'clock rolled around, Roxy flipped the closed sign.

Once our last customer left, Ma lifted her head and peered at us through the bottom half of her glasses. "Listen to this, girls, I've got what they call a marketing plan. We're going to throw some new things on the menu. Hamburgers, chicken fingers, pot roast. And we're going to stay open until three. We'll see how Mr. Rudy likes them apples."

I propped myself against the counter. "Ma, I don't think Rudy's really going to keep up with the breakfast business. And even if he does, I'm sure he won't steal away our loyal customers."

"We're not going to get a chance to find out. This is a dog eat dog business, toots, and I'll be damned if he's going pee on my territory."

"So when do we start?" Roxy asked, moving the wad of gum from one side of her mouth to the other.

"Tomorrow. Rudy's already got a jump on us, girls. We need to catch up."

"What does Ray have to say about all this?" I asked. Ma's son owned half the business and did all the cooking. I had a feeling he wasn't going to like the changes.

"Doesn't matter. Whose name's on the front this place?" She pointed to the door.

Actually, no one's name was on the door. Or the building. No signage at all, in fact.

"Rose, where'd you go this morning? I'm going to need all hands on deck for this new menu plan."

"Janelle's in jail and my car was stolen."

"Right, I forgot. Let me know if she needs anything." She grabbed her legal pad and her purse. "Okay, I'm off to the warehouse store. That Rudy's going to be sorry he decided to tangle with me."

She power-walked out of the diner and Roxy and I commenced with clean up. I scrubbed down and she swept.

"What are you going to do for a car?"

"Axton's letting me borrow his." I swiped a rag over a table and glanced up. "Janelle asked me to look into this situation with Asshat, so I'm meeting Tariq after work. Want to come?" Roxy and Tariq had met once before. It was lust at first sight.

She dropped the broom handle and it clattered against the floor. "Oh my God, why didn't you tell me before now? I'm a mess."

Hands shoved deep in the pockets of his too big jeans, Tariq leaned against the back bumper of his car and watched us drive up. Tariq was a purveyor of used goods. Basically, he sold stolen crap out of his trunk. Today his office was an abandoned gas station in a shabby neighborhood on the south side of town. Huntingford was pretty evenly divided between the have-a-lots and the have-nots. We were in not territory today.

When I pulled to a stop, Tariq walked to Roxy's door and held it open. "My blue-haired princess."

As she climbed out, he grabbed her hand and bending over, kissed the back of it.

"Hey, Tariq," she said. She'd spent thirty minutes in the bathroom, reapplying her makeup and fixing her pigtails. Now her lips were glossy and her eyelids shimmered with metallic shadow.

I walked to his car and peered in the trunk to see what he was selling today. Designer jeans with embroidered back pockets and colorful blouses with recognizable labels.

When I turned back, I found them flirting. Tariq smiled. Roxy coiled her blue hair around one finger and batted her lashes.

"Tariq." I huddled in my jacket. Earlier the sun was out, but now the sky was overcast and I prayed we wouldn't have snow. When he ignored me, I said his name again and strode toward him, jerking one of his many tiny braids.

He frowned and rubbed his head. "What are you doing, Rose? A man's hair is his pride, girl."

"What about Janelle? Can you post bail?"

"How much does she need?"

"Could be up to fifteen thousand."

"Sorry, man. I don't have that kind of money."

"What about your cousin, Sondra? Can she put up her house or something?"

He scoffed. "Sondra doesn't own her house. She rents."

Damn. "So what are we going to do about Janelle?"

"I don't know, man. But if she whacked Asshat, he deserved it."

"Nobody's been whacked. He's just comatose." For now anyway.

My phone vibrated. I looked at the number and my heart stuttered.

Sullivan.

Chapter 3

Thomas Malcolm Sullivan. Criminal numero uno in Huntingford. The man who held markers on the most powerful people in town, including the police chief, Martin Mathers.

Despite the cold, my hands felt clammy as I grasped the phone in one hand. I hadn't seen Sullivan in five weeks, even though he'd called seven times and sent flowers twice. At first, our conversations were short and to the point, but the last two times, we'd spoken for almost half an hour. We never discussed anything too personal, at least he didn't. Now every time I saw his name on my screen, my pulse sped up.

"Hello."

"I hear you're missing a car," he said.

I stepped away from Roxy and Tariq. "Good news travels fast."

"Do you need a ride?" His voice was smooth and rich, like that first cup of coffee early in the morning. My brain went to a whole different kind of ride and got stuck there for a moment.

"Well, I do have band practice after school and an appointment with my orthodontist."

"I'll take that as a no. How've you been holding up?"

"I'm fine and frankly getting pretty tired of people asking me that question every five minutes. I'm not made of glass. I won't break."

Nothing from his end. He liked to pull that crap, long pauses and dramatic silences to make the other person talk first. I waited him out. But I did glance at my phone twice to make sure he hadn't hung up.

"If you need anything," he finally said.

"Thanks." I shoved the phone in my pocket and turned to Tariq and Roxy. He fingered her lacy headband while she giggled.

"Tariq, do you know anyone who's selling a car?" I asked.

He dropped his hand like he'd burned it and his demeanor changed. Gone was the flirtatious, smooth ladies' man and in its place was a businessman who sized me up as a potential customer. "Maybe. What type of car you looking for?"

"One that won't get me pulled over for grand theft auto."

He stroked his jaw. "How much you want to pay?"

"A couple hundred."

He started laughing hysterically. "Shit, Rose. You're funny." Tears filled his eyes. "A couple hundred."

I waited until he sobered a bit. "What can you tell me about Asshat? And what's his real name anyway?"

He wiped his eyes. "Sheik."

I blinked. "Sheik? Sheik Johnson? Really? Who else would want to bash him on the head besides Janelle?"

"How about all his women? All his friends? All his family? Pretty much anyone who's ever met the dude."

Asshat sounded like a real charmer. "What do you mean 'all his women?' I thought he only dated Chicken Licker." She of the infamous eating-a-drumstick-while-getting-it-on-in-Janelle's-bed incident.

Roxy popped her gum. "I thought he was dating someone named Flat Ass for a while."

Janelle was going to have to start using real names instead of physical descriptions.

"Yeah, he fu…dates a lot. He was living with Chicken Licker for a while. But she kicked his ass to the curb."

"Why?" I asked.

"Hell if I know," Tariq said.

I dug a pen and small note pad from my purse. "Okay, Tariq, names please. Let's start with Chicken Licker."

"Destiny Lee. She works at The Bottom Dollar off South Birchwood. Asshat dates a lot of strippers."

"What's Sondra's number and address?" He told me and I jotted it down. "Any other names you want to give me? What about Roshanda?"

"Asshat's sister? I know she lives down by Oakwood Elementary, but I don't have her address or anything."

"Do you know who else Asshat was dating? Or Flat Ass's name?"

He sighed. "I don't keep track of his social life." His eyes took in Roxy, from her platform Mary Janes to her blue hair. "I'm thinking about my own extra-curriculars."

Tariq fenced stolen crap and Roxy used to be a juvenile delinquent. She still missed the thrill of taking things that weren't strictly hers, so I wondered at the wisdom of this Tariq/Roxy matchup. It had fire and gasoline written all over it.

I shoved my hands in the pockets of my jacket and glanced at the gloomy sky once more. I was going to have to invest in some gloves.

"Thanks, Tariq." I tugged on Roxy's sleeve. "Call me if you think of anything that can help Janelle." I pulled her toward the car and we waved at Tariq as I peeled out.

"Want to hit the strip club?" I asked. "I have just enough time before I have to get ready for my parents' party."

"Yep," Roxy said. "So what are these Strickland shindigs like, anyway? Fancy food you can't pronounce and champagne?"

"Pony kegs and beer bongs all the way."

She snorted. "Yeah, I can picture your mom with a funnel tube in her mouth. Seriously, are they any fun at all?"

"Not even a little."

The Bottom Dollar lived down to its hype. A shithole on the wrong side of town with painted windows and a silhouette of a naked woman on the sign. In its former life it had probably been an Italian restaurant, judging from the terra cotta tile floor and the fake stucco walls now painted bright purple.

The bouncer at the door sized us up, his glance lingering on Roxy. "Like the outfit. You here to audition for Freddy?"

"Yeah, where can we find him?" I asked.

He hiked a thumb over his shoulder. After we walked past him, Roxy glared in my direction.

"Audition?"

"Your stripper name could be Sailor Moon."

She scowled. "We don't joke about Sailor Moon, Rose. That's sacred."

"Sorry."

We moved farther into the darkened club. Loud hip hop beat at us from all sides, pulsing its way into my head as a DJ near the stage yelled incoherently into a microphone. Blue and purple glow-in-the-dark swirls covered the carpet, and the place reeked of booze and stale sweat.

The room was two-thirds full of men, all staring at the woman on stage like dieters watching a burger commercial.

I was a little spellbound myself. I nudged Roxy's arm. "Look at her abs. You could bounce a quarter off that six-pack."

"It's takes a lot of muscle to work a pole."

Before I could question her further, a man with a faux hawk stepped out of nowhere. "Hey, I'm Freddy Libra." He wiped a finger under his nose. "You here to audition?" He wore a long-sleeved shiny shirt, the kind I thought they stopped making in the eighties.

"I'm looking for Destiny."

He placed his hand on my shoulder. I stared at it until he removed it. "Why you looking for Des?"

"I'm her cousin. Our aunt's in the hospital. Thought she'd like to know."

He motioned for us to follow him to a tiny office. He closed the door, which muted the music, but the pounding bass still reverberated through me.

"I didn't know Des had family." He pointed to two cheap folding chairs and took a seat behind a metal desk. Roxy and I remained standing.

"We're distant cousins," I said.

Freddy wasn't unattractive with his dark hair and eyes, but he was sleazy. His gaze kept straying from our faces to our boobs.

"You'd do well here, Blue. Get some little nurse's outfit or something. You could pull down some serious cash."

Roxy smacked her gum. "Not interested."

He shrugged. "Suit yourself." He turned his eyes on me. "What about you, Princess? You got little ones, but we could dress you like a school girl. Get you a plaid skirt and some knee socks."

"I need to talk to Destiny."

"If you're her cousin, why are you calling her Destiny instead of Crystal?"

Roxy raised a brow. "Professional courtesy?"

Was Crystal her real name? Seemed like another alias to me. Chicken Licker, Destiny, Crystal. In real life, she was probably something boring like Jane Smith.

"What do you really want with Crystal?" Freddy asked.

Two things I'd learned from Sullivan: stay cool and keep quiet. Whatever you do, don't get defensive and don't start blurting out crap. Of course when I was with Sullivan, that worked more in theory than in practice.

"I told you, our aunt's in the hospital," I said.

"Crystal's not here," he said. "I'd try her at home."

"We'll do that," I said. "By the way, where's the restroom?"

Freddy stood. "Down the hall and to the right. I'll tell Crys you were looking for her. What was your name again?"

"Jane Smith."

I shot Roxy a look as we left the office and walked farther down the hall and into the bathroom. I wanted a chance to talk things over with her. We needed to question the strippers, but I didn't want to have to pay for the privilege.

The woman who'd been on stage stepped out of a stall. She wore a short flowery robe and eight-inch heels. Her long brown hair benefitted from hair extensions and her melon-sized breasts were so firm and round, they couldn't possibly be a gift from Mother Nature.

"You two new?" She walked to the sink and washed her hands.

Roxy leaned against the wall. "Not really."

"Didn't think so. Especially you," she tipped her head in my direction. "You're a civvy all the way."

"Thanks?" Didn't know what she was talking about, wasn't going to ask. "We're looking for Crystal."

Her eyes met mine in the mirror. She would have been pretty if she hadn't worn so much stage makeup. Long fake lashes outlined her deep brown eyes, blue eye shadow highlighted them. "Which Crystal?"

"Destiny."

She grabbed a paper towel from the dispenser and leaned on the counter. "What do you want with that bitch?"

I held out my hand. "My name's Jane, that's Elizabeth." Roxy waved.

The woman shook my hand and left it a little damp. "I'm Jess. Well, my working name is Satin Lace."

"Nice to meet you. Destiny dated a guy named Sheik." Really, these names were all too much. But then my sister and I were named after first ladies, so I had no room to talk.

Jess pinched her lips together. "Yeah, I know him. He's an asshole. He's dated a few girls here, not just Crystal. But then she isn't all lily either, if you know what I mean."

"Are you saying Crystal cheated on Sheik?"

"Yeah, that's what I'm saying. Look, I'm a stripper, but I'm not a whore. Crystal is a whore. She doesn't mind providing extras. And she's stolen more than one dancer's man."

"Extras being…" I asked.

"Billy Joels, Harry James." She waved her hand.

I glanced at Roxy for translation.

"Blow jobs and handies," she said.

I turned my attention back to Jess. "Is that allowed here?"

She smiled, and in that moment she appeared older, harsher, then the smile disappeared and she was back to a pretty young woman with too much makeup. "It's not allowed if you get caught. And sometimes she'd meet up with patrons outside the club. A big no-no, but some girls do it."

"Back to Sheik—"

"We call him Asshat," Roxy said.

"That sounds about right." Jess crossed her arms. "He always wants more than a standard lap dance. Likes to grab."

"He's in a coma, got bashed on the head. His ex-wife didn't do it, so I thought I'd question Crystal."

Little lines appeared on her forehead between her eyes. "He and Crystal did have a huge fight a couple days ago. He comes rolling in here, throwing money around, getting dances from a bunch of the girls. Real generous with the tips, too. Crystal went ape shit. She's yelling at him about owing her money and why is he getting dances from the other girls instead of her. Big production. Freddy threatened to fire her and sent her home for the night. Haven't seen her since."

"So where did Asshat get this money?"

"Don't know."

"Did he come into the club alone or with friends?" Roxy asked.

Jess took a deep breath, tapped her cheek with one manicured, red-tipped finger. "That night by himself, but sometimes he'd come in with a group of guys."

"Do you know their names?"

"I don't remember names. Unless it's a regular. I just call everyone baby." She shrugged and spun toward the mirror. Rubbing her lips together, she smoothed a hand down her long brown hair.

"You don't happen to have Crystal's phone number, do you?" I asked.

"I wouldn't call that bitch if she was on fire."

I narrowed my eyes and tried to work that one out. Nope, didn't get it. "So is Crystal her real name?"

Jess laughed and pushed away from the counter. "Yeah, it is. Crystal Waters."

Chapter 4

I gave Jess my cell number, then Roxy and I made our way to the main room. More men had shown up in our absence, filling the tables near the back. Several of them watched us walk to the door, eyeballing us like a chained Rottweiler stares at his neighbor's cat.

"Why did you call me Elizabeth?" Roxy asked.

"I couldn't sleep the other night so I read Pride and Prejudice," I said.

"I saw that movie. So, Crystal Waters? That can't be her *real* real name."

"It does seem contrived. And it sounds like she was pissed off enough to hit Asshat. Now we just have to find out what she was doing last night. Because according to Jess, she wasn't here."

We stepped outside to thick, gray clouds rolling across the sky. The brisk wind carried a scent of cigarette smoke and Roxy stopped in her tracks.

She clasped my arm. "Can you smell that?" She lifted her nose in the air and wandered around the corner of the building, like a hound dog on a trail.

I hustled to catch up.

She stood beside the DJ I'd seen inside earlier. Clad in a black and white racing jacket, he leaned against the building and puffed. Roxy looked at him longingly.

"Hello," I said.

He took a drag and blew the smoke away from us. "You the new girls?"

"Nope. Looking for Destiny," I said.

In his early thirties, he had pale skin, a healthy five o'clock shadow, and a unibrow. "Haven't seen her in a few days. She got mad at her old man and Freddy kicked her out."

"Do you know where Ass—Sheik—got the money he was throwing around?" Roxy asked.

"Nope, but he was making it rain like a thunderstorm. Must have won the lottery or something, because he didn't have any limits that night."

"What do you mean?" I asked.

"He took six strippers to the VIP room. Was in there for over two hours before Crystal showed up. That kind of entertainment ain't cheap."

Roxy moved closer to him and took a deep breath. "That smoke smells so good."

He smiled. "You want one?"

"She's quitting."

Roxy glared at me, then sighed. "Right."

I leaned my shoulder against the wall and faced him. "So, Destiny—Crystal, had a fight with Sheik. She was mad about the money?"

He laughed and dropped the cigarette on the ground. "Among other things. He was cheating on her. Again. But then she was always getting some on the side, too. Dancers like to bitch and gossip and the word going around was that

Crystal's sugar daddy dumped her. So when Sheik shows up, paying attention to other chicks, she went nuts. Threw a mini bottle of Cristal at his head. Bouncer hauled her into Freddy's office and she stormed out ten minutes later."

"Who was her sugar daddy?" I asked.

Shoving his hands in his pockets, he looked toward the road. "Who did you say you were?"

"I'm Elizabeth," Roxy said. "But you can call me Beth." She was getting into this.

"And I'm Jane. I'm trying to find Crystal. Sheik's in a coma and I have a few questions for her."

"You two detectives or something?"

"Nope," I said. "So who was she seeing and who was Sheik cheating with?"

He laughed. "Crystal was very…generous to her customers. That's why she's the most popular dancer here. Made her quota and then some. But with Sheik, the question isn't who he was cheating with." He leaned toward me and I got the full effect of his cigarette breath. "But who wasn't he cheating with?"

He moved around me and sauntered off.

I hated it when people gave murky answers to very simple questions.

"He could have been more helpful," I said.

"He probably wanted you to tip him. They expect money from the girls to get a good slot, you know."

"How do you know so much about strippers?" I asked.

"I've known a few."

I dropped Roxy off at Ma's and when I got home, I phoned Janelle's cousin, Sondra. Since she wasn't home, I left a message. Not only did I want to quiz her about Asshat, I wanted to check on Janelle's kids. They must be scared to death—their mom in jail, their dad in the hospital. I needed to find some suspects other than Janelle. Maybe then the cops would drop the charges and she could get back home to her kids.

I arrived at my parents' house for pre-party drinks at six. I took one last look at myself in the rearview mirror to make sure I didn't have a hair out of place. Show time.

I walked the paved stone path to the house where my mother answered the door clad in an expensive, beaded black dress. Barbara Strickland is very thin, very flat-chested, very champagne blonde. I inherited my itty bitty titties from her. But my witty personality was all my own.

"Rosalyn, so glad you're on time for a change." She cast a critical eye over my vintage gray dress. Vintage because I bought it at a rummage sale two weeks ago. She sighed. "Is that the best you could come up with?"

Handing my coat off to one of the wait staff, I smiled and stood a little straighter in my secondhand dress. "Sorry. My Dolce is at the cleaners."

White floral arrangements in tall vases were spread throughout the room. The ten foot Christmas tree in the corner filled the space with fragrant, astringent pine. It was trimmed in white lights and ivory ornaments. Gold-wrapped packages strategically dotted the Irish lace tree skirt. I knew from experience those packages were just for show.

"The house looks beautiful, Mom."

"It should. The decorators have been here for the last three days."

My father walked into the foyer and dropped a kiss on my cheek. "You look very pretty."

"Thanks, Dad."

My mother pursed her lips. "Let's have a drink before the guests arrive." She snapped at a waiter. "No, the nuts don't go there. In the living room, please." She pointed toward the formal room across the hall, then made a swath through the wait staff as they darted around the house, lighting tapers and setting out napkins.

My father and I trailed behind, his hand on my shoulder. "Your mother started planning this party in July," he said. "She needs everything to be perfect."

"I know she does."

In the family room, my sister, Jacks, stood next to a smaller Christmas tree trimmed in gold, blown-glass baubles.

"What does she have against color?" I asked out of the side of my mouth.

She turned to me and smiled, pulling me into a hug. My sister was thirty, six years older than me, but we looked the same age. Her blonde hair was shorter than mine, and expertly cut. Her eyes were a little bluer, mine a little greener. But as she pulled back, hers were filled with concern. "I've been worried about you. How are you doing? Really?"

I rubbed the side of my neck. "I'm great."

"If you need to talk—"

"Here you go, ladies." Jacks' husband, Allen, strode over, two glasses of champagne in his hands. With sandy hair and blue eyes, my dad and Allen could be mistaken for father and son. And they were both doctors. Did *I* think Jacks had issues? I had so many of my own I didn't have time to dwell on hers.

Allen's mouth turned down at the corners. "How are you, Rose? You know we're here for you. Anything you need."

I slapped a smile on my face. "I'm just going to powder my nose. Would you please excuse me?"

I calmly walked out of the room, past my mother who was giving a bartender the business about watered down drinks, and into the beige powder room. Leaning against the closed door, I took a deep breath and closed my eyes. I knew they were worried about me, but I wished they would stop talking about it. I was fine, damn it. Just fine.

Guests started arriving around seven. Doctors, lawyers, golf buddies, Junior League members. I smiled and shook hands, always on the move. I usually get three questions from my parents' friends: Am I dating anyone? Am I still in school? Have I found a real job? So I had a strategy this year, I would bob and weave my way through this thing, never landing in one place long enough to answer awkward questions. Make the greetings and move on.

So far, I'd been pretty successful. Then my mother suddenly appeared at my side, her hand wrapped around the bicep of an average-looking man in his thirties.

"James Benchley, I'd like you to meet my youngest daughter, Rosalyn."

"Hello, Rosalyn, it's nice to meet you." He held out his hand.

Oh crap, a set up. I smiled. "You, too, James."

"Your mother tells me you're a student."

I raised my brows. "She did?"

Usually she liked to hide the fact I'd been in school for the past six years and still didn't have my Bachelor's. "Yes," I said, "I am a student."

"I'm a big believer in continuing your education. Going for your doctorate, that's impressive."

I raised a brow at my mother. "Thank you."

Her smile hardened. "I told James how important your studies are to you, dear. James is a financial planner."

"You don't say?"

When a roaming waiter presented us with a tray of salmon and dill covered cucumber slices, James' attention was diverted. My mother leaned closer.

"He's divorced, no kids, and has a decent job. Be nice," she hissed in my ear. "Enjoy the party, James," she said in a loud voice.

With a mouthful of cuke, James smiled and raised his glass to her.

I then spent the next fifteen listening to his complaints about his bitch of an ex-wife and her new boyfriend, Sven, a tennis pro she'd met at the club. They now lived in the house James bought.

When he finally took a breath, I said, "She actually ran over your golf clubs, huh?"

"Yeah, then she backed up and ran over them again. Including my new Titleist irons with steel shafts." He started tearing up. "I loved those clubs."

"James, I am on pins and needles to hear more, but would you excuse me for just a second? I'll be right back."

I squeezed past him and made my way through the crowd to the other side of the room where Jacks nibbled on a cashew.

"Mom told some bitter divorced guy I was working toward my doctorate." I set my glass on a side table and snagged a mint. I was starving.

"Make small talk. Nod and smile and pretend you're listening." She grabbed another glass of wine from a passing waiter. "She used to do the same thing with me. Except she told people I graduated summa cum laude and I was only magna."

"You know you're lucky I love you, right?"

A heavily pregnant woman waddled up to us and began asking Jacks about third trimesters. I moved on.

I tried to remain unobtrusive. And out of my mother's line of sight. I thought I was safe, hiding in a corner with an older couple who told me all about their holiday plans in Costa Rica, when she found me again. Did she have me tagged with a homing beacon?

"Hello, Marie, Donald. I hope you're enjoying the party." She chitchatted with the older couple, then took my hand. "Do you mind if I steal Rosalyn away for a moment. There's someone I want her to meet."

Marie finger waved, Donald raised his glass, and my mother pulled me to her side. "How did things go with James?"

I tried to pull my hand from her grasp, but she tightened her hold. "He spent fifteen minutes telling me about his horrible ex and how angry he is about the divorce."

"Rosalyn, a woman can make a man forget a bad marriage. If she puts her mind to it."

"I don't think so."

She took a deep breath through her nose, then marched through the crowd again, tugging me behind her. In the doorway of the formal dining room, a man in his late twenties nibbled a chicken satay. Although he was attractive in a buttoned-down way, I'd always preferred the bad boys.

Except for Sullivan. Sullivan was all man.

"Tyler, I'd like you to meet Rosalyn."

"Nice to meet you, Tyler."

He juggled his satay and shook my hand.

"You and Tyler have something in common," Barbara said.

"We're both blonds, right?" I asked.

"That, we are," he said with a smile. "But only if you're natural."

Oh God, please let it end.

"No," my mother said, "you have similar jobs." With her smile fixed, she pinned me with a look. "Tyler is a media consultant and you're in public relations," she said, lockjawed. She gazed up at him. "Rosalyn works directly with customers for a small, family-owned firm."

She hated that I was a waitress. In her eyes, I was nothing but a failure. I knew she resented me for letting her down, for not living up to my potential. I should be used to it by now, but sometimes it still got to me.

"You know," Tyler said, "We should get together. Your company could probably benefit from a media push."

"I'm sure we could. Do you have a card?"

As he reached into his pocket to pull out his wallet, I glared at my mother.

She glared right back. "You two enjoy the party." She melted through the crowd.

Tyler, the media consultant, and I did small talk. Then he went in for the kill. "We should have dinner one night this week." He pulled out his phone and checked his schedule. "Does Wednesday work for you?"

Before I could come up with an excuse, my own phone rang. "Whoops. Got to take that. It's probably work. Busy, busy." I slipped past him and down the hall. As I made my way to my father's study, I dug my phone out of my purse and glanced at the screen.

"Hey, Dane. Any news about Janelle?" I shut the office door behind me, closing out the chatter and the Christmas carols as interpreted by a string quartet.

"Sorry to interrupt your evening," he said.

I walked past my dad's desk to the medical books lining the shelves, and let my fingers trail over the spines. "I'm at my parents' Christmas party. Interruptions are welcome."

"I'm afraid I have some bad news. My boss is after me to cut a deal for Janelle. It's a slam dunk for the DA, and as far as my firm's concerned, it's low priority. Plus, I'm not billing her my usual fee, so the firm's losing money."

My hand fell to my side. "What are you saying? You're not going to defend her?"

"I am defending her, but I only took this case as a favor to you, Rose. There's no benefit in dragging this out. Besides, Janelle can't afford months' worth of legal fees."

I felt numb. "What about the other suspects?"

"There are no other suspects."

"Not true. Crystal Waters, Asshat's ex-girlfriend, got into a fight with him a couple days ago. There's a suspect."

"Janelle had an argument with the victim thirty minutes before the police arrived and found him bleeding from a head wound. Her fingerprints are all over the weapon. There's nothing I can do with that kind of evidence."

"What about innocent until proven guilty? Because she's poor, she isn't entitled to a good defense?" He was her lawyer, he should be fixing this, not giving up. "What about a private detective or something?"

"Janelle can't afford it and my boss is breathing down my neck to end this," he said.

"Tell him to go to hell, Dane. There's got to be something you can do. You can't send an innocent woman to jail."

"I'm not the one sending her to jail. I'm telling you, if we take this to a jury, she won't stand a chance. A plea is her best bet."

I stumbled to a chair and sat down. "How much time will she get?"

"If I can persuade the DA to play ball, I'm hoping for two to six years. But if he doesn't make it…"

"She didn't do this. She doesn't deserve to spend two days in jail, let alone two years. And what about her kids?"

"They'll become wards of the state. Most likely they'll go to a relative, but if not, they'll be put into foster care. I'd be doing her a disservice if I didn't try to get her a deal."

Stunned, I gazed at a glass paperweight on my dad's desk. Janelle was in worse trouble than I thought. If I didn't find out who put Asshat in a coma, she wouldn't just miss Christmas with her kids, she'd miss their childhoods.

Chapter 5

I couldn't go back to the party. Not with Janelle sitting in a cell and Dane slacking off on the case.

Frustrated and needing to vent, I called Roxy.

"What the hell," she said. "Dane wants her to take a plea? That's bullshit."

"I'm going to call Janelle's cousin, Sondra, and see if I can stop by."

"Right now? I thought you were at the Strickland Christmastravaganza," she said.

"Yeah, I need to get out of here. My mom's driving me batty."

"Well, I want to go."

"To the party?" I kicked my heels off and curled my toes.

"No, dumbass, to Sondra's," she said.

"Fine, I'll pick you up on the way."

Now the trick was getting out of the house without my mother finding out. And there was only one way to do that. The service entrance.

I grabbed my coat from the rack set up in the spare bedroom and snuck into the kitchen. While the caterers flowed around me, filling trays and clinking empty glasses, I slipped out the back door and trekked around the house to the car.

Roxy was waiting by the curb when I pulled up to the converted Victorian where she rented a room. She hopped in and smacked her gum. "So you survived your mom, huh?"

"Yep." Barely.

I took Apple Tree Boulevard and headed to the poor side of town. The further south you go in Huntingford, the more run down the neighborhood, block by block, until finally, on the southern edge between Huntingford and the city of Glendale, drug related crime, and even gang shootings, weren't uncommon.

Sondra lived somewhere between working class and the hood in a dollhouse-sized saltbox with a one-car garage. I'd never met her, but Janelle talked a lot about her. In her mid-thirties, she was small, bird-like, with dark skin and short hair.

When she answered the door, I smiled and introduced myself. "Hello. I'm Janelle's friend, Rose. This is Roxy."

Sondra's gaze swept over Roxy's cat-card-yarn ball skirt. "Yeah, she's mentioned you. Come in."

The house was cozy with blue furniture and an asymmetrical patterned rug. "Take a seat."

Rox and I parked ourselves on a sofa. "How are you holding up, Sondra? How are the kids?" I asked.

She sank into a chair. "I'm fine. The kids finally fell asleep. They're worried. Especially Damon. He knows Sheik's in the hospital, wants to go see him. Sherise keeps asking for her mama."

"I spoke to Janelle's lawyer. He wants her to take a plea."

She scoffed. "Janelle won't go for that," she said. "You know how stubborn she is. She'll fight to the end."

"What about bail money? Is there any way you can help?" I asked.

Sondra shook her head. "It's all I can do to make ends meet. I work in a dentist's office and it's a good job, but my ex isn't paying child support, either. Frankly, I don't know how I'm going to afford two extra kids."

I pulled the little notebook out of my purse and wrote down my number. "If you need anything, give me a call. Can you think of anyone else who would want to hurt Asshat?"

Sondra laughed. "Everybody. He owes people money, he's a loudmouth, always struts around like some kind stud."

"What was the attraction?" I asked. "I don't see Janelle falling for that type of guy."

"She wasn't always so level-headed. And Sheik's a handsome man. Women do stupid things over pretty men. As soon as Janelle filed for divorce, he quit his job so he wouldn't have to pay child support."

"How does he survive if he doesn't have a job?" Roxy asked.

"My guess is he does some work off the books."

"What did he do when he was on the books?" I asked.

"He worked at that muffler place off the Boulevard."

Little footsteps padded down and hall and Sherise, dressed in a pink nighty with a picture of Dora the Explorer on the front, crept into the room and rubbed her eyes.

"Hey, Sherise, how are you?" I asked. Normally, she ran to me and wanted to play hairdresser whenever I had a study date at Janelle's house, but tonight she looked so sad and young, it broke my heart.

"I miss my mommy." She twisted toward Sondra and buried her head in the woman's shoulder.

Watching her was like a knife in my chest. I couldn't let Janelle sit in jail, I had to do something.

I glanced over at Roxy. She stared at Sherise, but her eyes were unfocused, glazed. I touched her arm. "You ready?"

She jumped a bit. "Yeah."

I stood and waved at Sondra as she cuddled the little girl. I hadn't found out much, but it was a start.

Roxy was silent on the drive home.

"You want to talk about it?" I asked.

"I was like her—Sherise. Alone, without a mom. But at least she has Sondra and isn't going to a stranger."

Roxy had been in and out of foster and group homes most of her life. I knew from the few details she'd dropped that her childhood had been rough.

"You have to find who did this, Rose. You have to get Janelle back home to her kids."

I braked at a stoplight and glanced over at her. "I'll do my best."

"No, that's not good enough. If she didn't do this, you have to find out who did."

I'd been thinking the same thing, but hearing it from Roxy felt overwhelming. I wasn't an investigator, I was just a waitress who took classes on the side. "I promise I'll try."

She stared out the windshield. "Okay."

It was after ten when I got back my apartment and changed into a pair of sweats. I'd just pulled my blanket and pillow from the closet when a knock sounded at the door. I glanced out the peephole at Axton. He held DVD in one hand and a pizza box in the other.

"Figured you were in need some sustenance after a round with your mom," he said when I opened the door.

Ax was the greatest, always there when I needed him with pepperoni and bad sci-fi. I took his coat and hung it on the peg next to the door, my eyes drifting over his t-shirt that read Yoda Knows Best.

"So, how bad was it?" He set the pizza box on the stove and grabbed two plates from the cabinet by the sink.

"Bad enough. Dane called and said Janelle's in deep shit. The evidence is stacked against her."

He slipped two slices onto the plates and handed one to me, then licked the grease off his fingers. "That sucks royally. Are you going to help her?"

I plopped down on the futon while Axton stuck the disk in the machine. "Yeah, I am."

"Good." When he straightened, he gazed around my apartment. "Dude, your place is depressing."

I shrugged. "Looks like it always does."

"Exactly. Where's your Christmas spirit? Where's your tree? It's just sad, man."

"I have no Christmas spirit and it's not sad, it's normal. Maybe I'll boycott Christmas this year. Why force it?"

He waved his plate around the room. "Because Christmas is the time to connect with the child in your soul."

I cocked my head. "Are you high right now?"

"Make fun all you want, but Christmas rocks."

I leaned back and crossed my legs. "Hey, want to do me a favor?"

"I live to do you favors." He sprawled out next to me and ate half the slice of pizza in one bite.

"Asshat was throwing money around a strip club before he went to comasville. I want to know where that money came from. His real name is Sheik Johnson, by the way."

"That's one pimp ass name," Ax said with a full mouth.

"Also, Chicken Licker's real name is Crystal Waters. Maybe. Or that could be another stage name. Anyway, she works at The Bottom Dollar. Can you check her out, too? I need her address. Oh, and some guy named Freddy Libra runs the place."

"Sweet," he said with a full mouth. "Sounds like this project needs some real-time research."

I laughed. "That's my job. You do the computer mojo you do so well and I'll question the strippers."

"You're harsh, man. Want me to look into the strip club while I'm at it?"

"That would be awesome, thank you."

"I would prefer to do it with a lap dance, but..."

"You're the best. What are we watching tonight?"

"*Assignment: Outer Space.* It's Italian."

When I walked into the kitchen the next morning, Ray glowered over his biscuit dough.

"I see Ma told you about staying open for lunch," I said.

"Unh."

"Maybe it won't be so bad."

He shrugged.

"Glad we had this conversation, Ray."

I grabbed an apron and stepped through the swinging door. That delicious, sharp smell of coffee hit me and I poured myself a cup.

I turned and stopped cold when I saw a kid about nineteen or twenty, sitting at the counter, texting. He wore a blue hoodie, baggy jeans, and long brown bangs hid his eyes.

"Who're you?" I asked.

He didn't glance up from his phone.

Roxy, dressed in a short, blue sailor dress, stood with her hands on her hips and stared out the front window. "That's the new busboy and dishwasher. Since we're serving lunch now, Jorge got bumped up to assistant cook."

The new kid didn't acknowledge me. In fact, he hadn't lifted his head or stopped moving his thumbs since I first spotted him.

"Who texts this early in the morning? And what are you watching?" I asked Roxy.

"Ma."

I advanced toward the window. Although it was still dark outside, the restaurant lights illuminated Ma as she wrote on one of those A-frame chalkboards you see outside cafes. LUNCH SPECIAL in hot pink.

Roxy glanced over at me. "What do you think?"

I sighed. "This reminds me of the time she decided we should have cartoon character pancakes. Remember how backed up we got?"

"This will be much worse."

Ma tucked her chalk into a bucket and dusted off her hands. Taking a few steps backward, she stared at the board and nodded. When she opened the front door, all of the cold December wind blew in with her.

"What do you think about my new sign, toots? Snazzy, huh?" She walked over to the counter. "And I got lunch menus printed up. They're not laminated or anything yet, but we can start handing them out."

I took a blue sheet and read it over. "We're serving Pulled Puck?"

"What?" She grabbed the paper from me. "Those damn printers." She wadded it up into a ball. "I'm going to give them a piece of my mind. We'll just have to tell the customers what we're serving." She gathered up her stack of menus and stomped into the kitchen.

"Yeah, this is way worse than cartoon pancakes," I said.

By the time the early crowd started rolling in, I forgot all about the new menu. Ma fluttered from table to table, telling everyone to come back for lunch. The regulars got into lengthy discussions about the change.

New Kid was nowhere to be found, so Roxy and I bussed the tables ourselves. Finally at ten, things slowed down a bit. They'd pick up again once the church crowd descended, but in the meantime, Jorge placed an omelet on the counter and set a cinnamon roll in front of Roxy.

"Ma's going nuts in there." He waved his tattoo-covered arm toward the kitchen. "She made enough pork to serve two hundred people. We only seat forty-five. I don't mind the extra hours though."

"Me, too," I said. I could always use the extra money. And now that I didn't have a freaking car, I needed it more than ever. It still pissed me off someone stole it right across from the police station. That had a certain brass balls quality to it I didn't appreciate. "By the way, congrats on the promotion."

Jorge lifted a shoulder. "It's not much different. That kid hid in the pantry and texted all morning."

Ma hit the swinging door and the tangy smell of barbeque poured out of the kitchen. "Ma's Diner is about to serve lunch for the first time ever, people. Get ready."

My stomach growled and I gobbled up my omelet.

By eleven, people were still ordering breakfast, just like always, but Ma kept pushing the pork. She handed out free samples and even had a few takers. But by one, our usual closing time, we only had two customers left, and they were stragglers who decided to linger over coffee.

"Damn," Ma said. "We've got to get the word out about lunch. I'm going to have to come up with another marketing plan." She stalked back to the kitchen.

I texted Ax and told him to come by the diner. He showed up fifteen minutes later, his ubiquitous backpack balanced on one shoulder.

"You ready for the best pulled puck you've ever had?" I asked.

"Sounds good."

I put in his order brought him a soda. "Any info on Asshat?" Since the diner was empty, I pulled out a chair and sat across from him.

Ax unwrapped his straw and stuck it in his glass. "Divorced from Janelle. No visible means of income. No unemployment checks. And no money trail. Sorry. But I do have his address." He handed me a Post-it note. "And Freddy Libra owns The Bottom Dollar. Pays his taxes on time, owns a three-bedroom home on the decent side of town and a vintage Mustang. Which is pretty awesome. Dude owns a strip club and a Mustang? He must live in poon city, man."

I shuddered. "I'm getting a visual I don't want. Did you find anything on Crystal?"

"She's on my to do list. I'm going to have a hard time calling her Crystal, though. I'm used to Chicken Licker."

"Thanks for helping out, Ax. Let me check on your order." At the pass thru window, I scooped up a plate full of pork, beans, and a thick slice of cornbread covered in melting butter and slid it in front of him.

Ax took a bite and nodded. "This pulled puck rocks."

I grinned. "I'll be sure to tell Ma."

I took care of the stragglers and bussed the tables once they left. Roxy cleaned the restrooms. So far, New Kid had been useless.

When Ax finished eating, I waved the check and handed him a sack of leftover donuts for the road.

"I'll call you when I get more info," he said and left.

By three, the diner was empty and had been for over an hour. Ma was in a snit.

"It's those damn menus. If only I could have passed them out, we'd have had takers, I just know it." She peered at Roxy through her trifocals. "While Rose and I finish clean up, you drive down the street. Go into Rudy's and look at a menu."

I rubbed her shoulder. "Ma, this is ridiculous. Rudy's sucks. We're Ma's Diner. Nobody's going to give Rudy the time of day."

She glared at me. "You don't know the first thing about being a businesswoman, toots. You've got to know your competition. Roxy, get me that menu."

Roxy rolled her eyes and grabbed her coat. "I'm on it."

Chapter 6

After work, Roxy and I decided to check out Asshat's house. Maybe we could find some info about that money he'd been flashing around.

We drove south to a low-rent neighborhood on a dead end street. Asshat's tiny house sat toward the back edge of the property and was surrounded by a chain link fence and overgrown hedges. Brown, patchy bald spots and six cars in various states of disrepair covered the large yard. Some were missing doors and hoods. Three old Pontiacs, two Hondas, and one Toyota sat like my nephew, Scotty's, little toy cars. Except his had wheels.

"What's with the cars?" I asked.

Roxy popped her gum. "Don't know, don't care."

We approached the house and I sidestepped a broken lamp. Roxy jumped over a large wall clock with a silhouette of a naked girl—like the kind you see on mud flaps. And we came to a stop in front of an upside-down coffee table that sat cockeyed near the front porch.

"I think this was Janelle's handiwork," I said.

"She's got some serious upper body strength to flip that coffee table," Roxy said.

As we made our way to the back of the house, I withdrew four latex gloves from my pocket. I'd lifted them from the diner and figured Ma wouldn't mind.

Roxy looked at me with respect. "You came prepared for mischief. I'm impressed."

She pulled an Allen wrench and a bent paperclip out of her purse. The fact that she had these items didn't even faze me. A few weeks ago I'd been wary of Roxy's mad breaking and entering skills. But I'd gotten used to it, just like I had the blue hair and her wacky fashion sense.

"Let's do it," she said with a grin. She loved this shit, lived for it. After jimmying the lock for a few seconds, the door swung open. "How long did that take?"

"I don't know. I wasn't timing you."

"You'd never make it as a criminal, Rose. Timing is everything."

I walked into the house. "Oh, God." I held a hand over my face. The kitchen reeked like old garbage. Dirty dishes piled up in the sink and dried, hardened food was cooked onto the avocado green stovetop.

Roxy wrinkled her nose. "I call dibs on the living room."

As she tromped off, I searched the filthy kitchen. The fridge contained moldy crap and beer. Nothing but a sack of ice in the freezer. The rusty metal cabinets yielded a box of crackers and a jar of peanut butter.

"Nothing in the kitchen." I walked into the living room and took in the broken plasma screen and the leopard print curtains—half torn, half hanging. Janelle must have been beyond pissed to do all this damage.

"Nothing in here, either," Roxy said.

My gaze drifted down to the blood-soaked tan rug where Asshat bled out. Looking at it made me queasy, so I quickly averted my eyes. "I'll hit the bathroom."

Roxy followed me down the hall. "Yep, I'll take the bedroom."

I flipped on the light and almost turned it back off. The bathroom was even more disgusting than the kitchen. Tiny and covered with once-white tile, it held a chipped pedestal sink, a tub full of mildew, and even dirtier toilet.

"Asshat has a real thing for leopard print," Roxy yelled. "Eww, even his underwear."

"Don't want to know," I called back. I popped open the medicine cabinet. Body spray, toiletries, and aspirin. I glanced at the toilet and with one finger, dropped the lid.

I took a deep breath and lifted the lid off the toilet tank. "Rox, I found something."

She stood in the bathroom doorway. "Me, too. Lots of receipts for jewelry—a watch, a gold chain, a man's diamond ring."

I shrugged out of my coat and handed it to her, then shoved up the sleeve of my baby blue t-shirt, and reached into the water, pulling out a Ziploc bag from the bottom of the tank. I tossed it in the sink and stripped the glove from my hand.

Roxy stepped further into the room. "What's in it?"

"Let's find out." I pried the wet bag apart and removed two sheets of paper with precise handwriting and several four by six photos. As I flipped through the pics, my heart thumped in my chest. "Shit."

She peeked over my shoulder. "Who is that?"

"Sullivan."

"Oh, my God. I figured he was hot, but he's *haught*." She grabbed a picture out of my hand.

The photos—there were ten—were taken at different locales. I scanned the handwritten pages. "Look at this, it lists his home address. Monday at home—four a.m. to one p.m. Lunch at Pantorelli's—one-twelve p.m. to two-eighteen p.m. Met with two unidentified men. Left by the back door." On and on it went, giving detailed information of Sullivan's movements for the last two weeks.

I glanced up at Roxy. "Was Asshat following Sullivan? Why?"

"Maybe somebody hired him. Maybe that's where the money came from."

I took another glance around the filthy bathroom. "Let's get out of here."

I dropped Roxy off at Ma's so she could pick up her car, then I went home and changed. I stuck some ramen noodles in the microwave and stood at the counter of my kitchenette, looking over the photos once more. What kind of trouble was Sullivan in? Who would be watching him, recording his every move? My first inclination was to call him and demand some answers, but I knew he'd never give me any. Same old, same old. I needed more info before I talked to him.

My phone rang and I tucked the pictures in my purse before I answered.

"Hey, Jacks. What's up?"

"Just wanted you to know, Mom's on a bit of a tear. She was kind of upset that you sneaked out of the party last night." My sister, mistress of the understatement.

"What else is new?"

"Listen, she's going to call and be all 'grrr,' but I don't want the two of you getting into another kerfuffle."

"Jacks, are you eighty?"

"What?"

"You just used the phrase on a tear and the word kerfuffle. No one under Ma's age uses that word. Ever." I grabbed a spoon from the drawer.

"Just don't get into it with her. Please? It's almost Christmas and I want everyone to be on their best behavior. Think of Scotty."

Right, Christmas. And I did adore Scotty. The little man stole my heart the second he was born. I sighed. "Fine."

"So what's going on with you?" she asked. "We didn't get a chance to talk."

"Well, Janelle's in jail and my car was stolen."

"Is Janelle your friend from school? What's she doing in jail? And why didn't you tell me about your car? You know the same thing happened to my maid, Maria. She came out of the grocery store and her car was gone."

"Yes, I know Janelle from school, but she's innocent. And what kind of car did Maria drive?"

"I don't know. An old, silver car."

"That's not a lot of help, Jacks. I've got to go. I'm cooking." I opened the microwave before it could ding and gave my noodles a stir.

"Call me later? And be nice to Mom. It's Christmas."

The next morning at the diner, Ma was in fine form. Giddy, almost.

"Look at these new menus," Ma said and handed me a laminated bright orange sheet of paper. The color made my eyes water.

"Spaghetti, chicken fried steak, grilled cheese? Did you steal this menu directly from Rudy?" I asked.

"All's fair in love and business. He doesn't have a copyright on Texas toast."

Roxy walked out of the kitchen and tied an apron around her waist. "Who doesn't have a copyright?"

I handed one of the sheets to Roxy. "She stole Rudy's menu and is using it as her own."

"Ma, why the bright orange?" she asked.

"I wanted everybody to see it. It's part of my two-pronged marketing plan."

Again with the marketing plan? "Ma, what about your book club and bunko and casino nights? Isn't all this cooking and marketing going to cut into that?"

"I've been in this business a long time, toots. And nobody is going to horn in on my territory. First it'll be Rudy. He thinks I'm easy pickings because I'm old. Then some fly-by-night place will try the same thing. It's best to end this now. I serve the breakfast in this town." She shoved a finger at her bony chest. "Me and the chain restaurants. Nobody else." She marched back to the kitchen.

Roxy and I exchanged a glance, then got busy prepping the diner. New Kid shuffled around with his hands in his pockets.

"Hey, so like, when do we get a break?" he asked.

"We don't," I said. "If it's busy, we work."

"And if there's a lull, we work," Roxy said.

"Isn't that against my rights or something?"

Roxy stepped into his personal zone. "Don't piss me off, New Kid. Go find something to do."

He sighed and shuffled away.

"Where the hell did Ma dig him up?" I asked.

"No idea."

We flipped the open sign at six, unlocked the door, and let the customers in.

I really needed to see Janelle today, but jail visiting hours were from eight to one. I almost hated to ask Ma for time off, since she was in war mode, but it was important.

"Ma?" I asked tentatively after I filled an order for the table in back. "I was wondering if I could run out and see Janelle this morning?"

"Yeah, but hurry back. I've got a special job for you."

That sounded ominous. "What kind of special job?"

She had a wily smile on her face. "Oh, you'll see, toots. You'll see."

I left at nine and drove to the police station. The weather was cold, but clear. White clouds streaked across a bright blue sky and the brisk wind tossed brown leaves across the street.

I was frisked and walked through a metal detector before being led to the same small room as before. When Janelle shuffled in, she looked worse than ever. She nibbled at her dry, chapped lips, two of her fingernails had popped off, and that orange jumpsuit made her appear washed out. When the officer unlocked her cuffs, she rotated her wrists and sat across from me.

"Have you seen the kids?"

"I saw Sherise Friday night. She misses you, but Sondra's taking good care of them."

"What about bail?" she asked. "Did you talk to Tariq?"

"He doesn't have it. Neither does Sondra."

Janelle dropped her head into her hands. When she looked up, her eyes were red. "I need to get out of here." She flattened her hands on the table. "I need Dane to get me out of here. He says the prosecution has a watertight case. I keep telling him I didn't do it. Rose, I thought he was supposed to help me."

"I'm going to help you." I whipped out my notebook and pen. "Now tell me everything you can about Asshat, who his friends are. I'll question everyone I can. By the way, what do you know about Chicken Licker? Do you know where she lives?"

Janelle raised a brow. "I may have driven by a time or two. And there's your suspect. He was cheating on her, too."

"How do you know?"

"That's what he does. He cheats. He couldn't keep his dick in his pants if somebody paid him."

"Do you know who he was cheating with?"

"No, but ask his brother, Little Donnell. He may know. And his friend, Marcus Walker. But watch out for Marcus. He's shady." She gave me addresses for everyone, but without her phone, which the police had in custody, she couldn't remember phone numbers.

"Don't worry, I'll figure it out," I said. "What about his sister, Roshanda?"

Janelle told me her address. "But you may have an easier time catching her at work. She's a vet tech for Huntingford Animal Clinic. Works from six to six."

As I left the building, I scanned the street and made sure Axton's car was right where I left it.

"Hey," I heard someone shout.

It was the nice cop from the other day. He trotted toward me.

"Are you here about your car?" he asked. He pointed to his badge. "Officer Goedecker. Remember me?"

"Of course I remember. No, Officer Thomas thinks it's gone for good. Chopped into little bits by now."

He stuck his hands in his jacket pockets. "That's probably true."

I shrugged. "It happens, right?"

"Despite our best efforts, it does happen. Sorry."

"Thanks anyway." I left him in front of the station and drove to the diner.

When I got to work, Ma waved me into the back office that housed cleaning supplies, an unused desk, and not much else. "How's your friend, toots?"

"She's not doing well, Ma. She can't make bail and the evidence against her is airtight."

"That's too bad, hon. But all will be well. The truth always comes out in the wash."

I wasn't so sure about that. The longer Janelle sat in jail, the more worried I became. And the police weren't interested in the truth. They had a perfect suspect in Janelle. She was Asshat's unhappy ex and a hothead. Case closed.

"Now," Ma clapped her hands. "I've got a mission for you."

I blinked and focused on the task at hand.

"It's an important one." She opened the bottom drawer of the old faux wood desk and pulled out a stack of flyers. In the middle of the page was a drawing of a yellow chicken and large font pronounced—*Ma's Diner is now open for lunch. Chicken specials every day. Buy one lunch special get one free.*

"This is it, our road into lunch. We offer chicken specials, rotisserie chicken, chicken and dumplings, and chicken soup, in addition to the rest of the menu. We'll be known as chicken central."

I didn't think this idea was any more of a winner winner chicken dinner than the pulled puck. "Why can't New Kid do this?"

"He doesn't have a car and I'm not letting him take Cha Cha." Ma insisted on calling her maroon eighty-seven Buick Le Sabre Cha Cha. Why? That was still a puzzler.

"Go to Rudy's parking lot and put them on every windshield. Hand them out to everyone you see, too."

"Don't you need me here? You know how crowded it gets after eleven."

She hustled me out of the office. "We'll manage. Go on and don't come back until the flyers are gone."

With a sigh, I strode back outside and drove up the road. Rudy's Roundup Restaurant lived in a strip mall off Apple Tree Boulevard with one cut-rate Dollarz store, a Chinese restaurant, an auto parts dealer, a nail salon, and a tropical fish paradise. A larger-than-life, fiberglass black and white cow stood on the roof, gazing out over the parking lot.

Before I got started, I ran into Dollarz and grabbed a pair of hot pink knit gloves. Thin as they were, they wouldn't do much good to ward off the biting chill, but they were better than nothing.

I started at one end of the parking lot and made my way down the rows as fast as I could. I figured the sooner I got rid of the flyers, the sooner I could get back to the diner where it was warm. But I couldn't grab the flyers with my gloved hand, so I had to go barehanded until my fingers were painfully stiff, then rip the glove off the other hand and start all over again.

When I finally got to the cars near the storefronts, a man from the Chinese restaurant wearing a chef's coat and hat pointed at me. He grabbed a flyer off one of the cars and started yelling at me in a language I didn't understand.

Soon, a tiny, gray-haired woman in a black sweater and slacks joined him. "You, go away." She shooed me.

I kept one eye on the couple as I continued to slip flyers under windshield wipers.

"Shoo. Go or I call police," she yelled.

"I'm not doing anything wrong," I said. At least I hoped not. Getting arrested was not on the agenda today.

Without warning, the woman tucked her chin to her chest and charged at me like a Pamplona bull. I was twenty-five feet away, but so shocked, I stood rooted to the sidewalk. I glanced to my left, then my right. As she neared, I spun on my heel and ran as she chased me through the parking lot, losing one of my new crappy gloves in the process.

We must have looked like a couple of loons, me looking over my shoulder, her chasing me and shouting. She was a fast runner, too. She must have had forty years on me, but she was in much better shape. We dodged and weaved. I'd feign to the left and she'd circle to the right. My goal was to get to Axton's car on the far side of the lot. But this crazy woman closed in on me at the opposite end.

She finally trapped me between a car and the busy street in front of the strip mall. When she advanced, I tried to maneuver around the car, but there just wasn't enough room unless I wanted to get squashed by oncoming traffic.

She moved toward me and started slapping at my upper arms. "You go away."

"Ow, stop that." I tried to fend her off with the flyers, but they were slick in my one gloved hand and I lost my hold. In the brisk December breeze, the flyers took flight and scattered all over the ground.

"Look," she yelled. "Look at what you do." Smack, smack.

"Stop it!" I now held up my arms to shield myself.

I supposed *I* could have called the police, but with my luck, Officer Hard Ass would show up. The whole incident would get a write up in the paper and I'd never hear the end of it from my mother.

Tired of the woman's slaps, I finally scampered over the trunk of the car, and running like I was a teenage rock star being chased by twelve-year-old groupies, I forced myself to go faster, even as the muscles in my legs burned. I made it to the Honda and glanced behind me. Standing in front of her restaurant, the crazy lady shook a tiny fist at me. I crammed myself behind the steering wheel and hauled ass out of the parking lot, gulping for air, my heart beating so hard I thought it might burst through my chest.

I parked behind the diner and staggered through the kitchen door.

Chapter 7

The place was hopping as it always was at noon. I grabbed a glass of water and downed it, then tied on an apron, snagged a pad, and got to work.

After one, we hit a wall. No customers, lunch or otherwise. Roxy refilled the ketchup bottles and New Kid sat at the counter and sipped a Coke.

Hands on her hips, Ma glared at me. "Did you put out all those flyers?"

"Most of them, but the Chinese restaurant people threatened to call the police and I had to fight my way out of there."

"That's terrible. It's a free country. You have every right to put out those flyers if you want."

I didn't want.

Roxy and I found some busy work, but after dusting every square inch of the diner and cleaning the windows, we resorted to playing tic-tac-toe with the salt and pepper shakers. It was a relief when Axton came in at two-thirty.

He hopped up on a stool and dropped his backpack on the counter. He glanced over at New Kid. "Who's he?"

"Ma hired him to bus tables. So, what's up?"

"Well, I found out some info on Chicken Licker."

Roxy walked by and lightly punched his arm. "Hey, Axman."

"Hey, Rox. I dig the threads today." She wore a dress with a laced up bodice and extremely short skirt. She paired it with knee high platform boots. Beer garden dominatrix. Quite a showstopper.

"So what's the what on Crystal Waters?" I asked. "Gimme."

He pulled a manila folder out of his bag and handed it to me.

I scanned through the pages and Roxy peered over my shoulder. Two arrests for domestic assault. Her driver's license picture wasn't half bad—long, dark hair, tan skin, lots of creative eye makeup. But her mug shot showed a different side. Dark streaks of mascara and eyeliner had left inky trails down her cheeks and her hair had been pulled into an uneven ponytail.

I laid the pages on the counter. "Domestic assault on a former boyfriend. Another good reason why Crystal is a suspect."

"Crystal has a past history with violence and she was fighting publicly with Asshat in the strip club before he was attacked," Roxy said.

"After work, we're going to drop in on her," I said. "You want come, too, Ax?"

"Sorry, I've got plans tonight."

I leaned on the counter and stared at him. "Plans? You never have plans."

"New game comes out tomorrow—*Target Terminated 2: Target Eliminated.* Joe's been sleeping in a tent in front of the store for the last two days. Told him I'd bring him dinner." Stoner Joe was Axton's wasted roommate. His name said it all.

"Really?" Roxy asked. "Stoner Joe is more important than getting Janelle out of jail?"

"Sorry, but I made a promise."

I sighed. "Fine. Go play your little reindeer games. Roxy and I will do the dirty work." I packaged up the last two donuts and sent him on his way.

Crystal lived in an upscale condo just north of Apple Tree Boulevard. A gift from her rich lover perhaps?

Roxy and I walked into the building and found her unit, 3B. I rang the bell and waited.

Roxy put her ear to the door. "I don't hear anything. Maybe we should check it out."

I glanced around. No one poked their head into the hall to ask what the hell we were doing. Always a good sign. "Here." I dug more gloves out of my purse and handed her a pair.

In seconds she picked the lock and gave me a thumb's up. We slipped into the condo and quietly closed the door.

"Nice digs," Roxy whispered.

Very nice. Apparently stripping and sleeping with rich men made a ton more than waitressing. Who knew? A white leather sofa and love seat were arranged in the small living room. Crystal decorated for the holidays with a mini tree on her coffee table. She forewent the traditional ornaments and draped the whole thing in ropes of fake diamonds. At least I assumed they were fake.

"Do you want to start in here, Rox? Remember to lift the cushions and check the vents."

"You're telling me the drill?"

I left her to it and hit the kitchen. I thought about all those places they say thieves look, like the flour canister—she didn't have one. The freezer—three Lean Cuisines and four bottles of flavored vodka (cotton candy, bacon, whipped cream, and cookie dough). Ugh. I methodically, but quickly, went through every cupboard, her oven, and drawers. The missing money wasn't hiding in her kitchen and I didn't find any evidence she'd bashed in Asshat's head. A written confession would have been nice.

I met Roxy in the hallway. "Nothing. You?"

She shook her head. "You want the bedroom or the bathroom?"

"Bed." I moved down the short hall.

Crystal had one bedroom and it was très cheesy. Black wallpaper with pictures of diamonds covered one wall, the rest were painted eye-popping pink. The bed was a mass of black and pink satin.

I picked up one of the silver frames on the mirrored bedside table. She had a lot of photos of herself, but only one of a tall blond guy with lots of muscles. I studied the photo and put it back where I found it. He didn't look like a sugar daddy.

I yanked open the shallow drawer and found condoms and sex toys and a day planner. Hello, Gorgeous. I stuck the planner in my purse to peruse later at my leisure.

I moved to the bed and lifted the mattress, checked the pillows and beneath the satin dust ruffle. Nothing. The dresser held a profusion of nasty underwear.

I had just started to rifle through an alarming amount of shelf bras when I heard a key slide into the front door. Shit.

"Roxy," I whispered.

She sped into the bedroom and we glanced around for a place to hide. She finally grabbed me and hauled me to the bed and we slid underneath.

My heart beat double time and it seemed like my breathing was really loud. Cold sweat trickled down my forehead. What if Crystal called the police? What if she had a gun?

I heard shuffling, then creaks from the leather furniture in the living room. Footsteps down the hall. Someone entered the room.

"I haven't found it." This had to be Crystal. I assumed she was talking on the phone and not to herself. Her voice was high-pitched and a little squeaky. The closet door opened and closed. "Of course I've looked." She sat on the bed.

I held my breath and prayed she wouldn't look underneath for any reason.

"I know. Okay, bye."

Something thumped against the wall and my whole body tensed. Then she moved off the bed and wandered around the room. I heard drawers opening and closing. I hoped she didn't need her day planner.

After a few minutes, she left the room and the shower turned on. I reached out and squeezed Roxy's hand. She squeezed back.

I lifted the dust ruffle and peeked out from beneath the bed, relieved to see she wasn't in the room. Straining my ears, I listened for any movement other than the water. It was now or never. I scampered from beneath the bed, Roxy right behind me.

We quietly made our way to the bedroom door and I poked my head into the hall. Around the corner, I spotted Crystal's silhouette through the opaque shower door. I nodded at Roxy and we fled the condo, running through the building and out into the parking lot.

With fumbling fingers, I shoved the key into the ignition, and raced off. My heart didn't stop pounding until we were a mile away, parked in a convenience store parking lot.

I glanced over at Roxy. "That was close."

"Way too close."

I jerked my purse onto my lap and dug out the day planner. I paged through it, but there was no appointment for today's date, so I flipped through the last week. Crystal had a very busy life of manicures, salon trips, waxing appointments. Then I saw the name 'Daddy' and flipped the book to show Roxy.

"So, she had lunch with her dad," she said.

"At three on a Wednesday afternoon? There were no pics of him in the place. Strippers tend to have daddy issues." I checked back a few weeks. "Lots of Wednesday afternoons with Daddy."

Roxy glanced at me, her blue eyes wide. "Sugar daddy?"

"That would be my guess." There was no contact info listed in the address part of the book. No personal info on Daddy at all. "But we still don't know who he is."

"Do you think that's who she was talking to on the phone?"

I sighed. "Don't know."

Our next stop was the muffler shop. According to Sondra, Asshat used to work here, and from what Janelle told me this morning, his friend Marcus still did.

I pulled into a lot with at least a dozen other cars. A dark tow truck was parked off to one side. Being here reminded me I needed an oil change. And if I still had my car, I'd totally get one.

I strode into the waiting room and Roxy followed behind. A strong mix of rubber, oil, and gas filled the air. Banging and clanging sounds from the garage echoed through the room. A man in a filthy blue shirt with an embroidered nametag that read 'John' stood behind the counter.

"Is Marcus here?" I asked.

He scratched his cheek with an oil-stained hand. "Who's asking?"

"A friend of Sheik's."

"Just a minute." He left through the glass door that led to the garage. While I waited, I glanced around at the plastic tan chairs, the coin op toy machine, and the empty coffeepot in the corner.

A tall, cute African American man walked through the door, wiping his hands on a dirty rag. "Can I help you?"

"I hope so. We'd like to talk to you about Sheik."

His eyes flicked over me. "Who are you?"

"I'm Jane."

Roxy, who had stuck two quarters in the toy machine and was turning the knob, waved. "I'm Elizabeth."

Marcus looked a little taken aback by her outfit, then lowered his brows. "What do you want to know about Sheik?"

"We're interested in all that money he was throwing around."

"What the hell business is it of yours?" He narrowed his brown eyes and set his fists on the counter, the rag clenched in one hand.

"From what I hear, he's unemployed," I said.

"So where did it come from?" Roxy asked.

"I don't know who the fuck you are—"

"Friends of Janelle's. She'd like a piece of Sheik's pie."

"She's got kids to feed, you know," Roxy said.

The waves of anger coming off him beat at me. "That bitch tried to kill my Holmes. She's lucky she's in jail where I can't touch her."

"She didn't hit Sheik, Marcus. She's innocent."

He scoffed. "If she didn't do it, who the fuck did?"

"Crystal?" I asked.

"Nah, Crystal's got a temper. She'd bitch slap someone, maybe take off her shoe and whack him, but she wouldn't put him in a coma."

"Crystal and Sheik had a big fight at The Bottom Dollar last week," I said.

Roxy walked up to the counter to stand next to me. "And she was arrested for domestic assault twice."

"How do you know that?"

"It's a matter of public record," I said. "Who else was Sheik dating?"

"Sheik doesn't date, he hooks up."

"Who was he hooking up with?"

"It doesn't matter. Janelle's the one who did this. End of story." He strode toward the glass door, jerked it open so hard the handle banged against the wall.

"That guy's got some anger issues."

Roxy held up a rub-on flaming heart tattoo she'd gotten from the machine. "For sure."

We made one more stop at the vet clinic to talk to Sheik's sister, Roshanda. It was after five and the office was surprisingly busy. While Roxy and I waited in line for our turn at the desk, a tan cat pounced on Roxy's feet and made figure eights between her legs.

"Cats love me," she said, reaching down to rub behind its ears.

When I stepped up to the front desk, I asked to speak to Roshanda.

A young woman about my age glanced over her shoulder. "She's really busy."

"I'll just slip on back. I only need to talk to her for a second." She didn't stop us as we darted behind the desk.

I opened a door and was hit with howls, hisses, and whines.

Cages lined opposite walls. Dogs on one side, cats on the other.

A woman in pink scrubs and a short, blond afro sped past us. "Who are you?" She reached into one of the dog cages and pulled out a trembling pug.

"I'm a friend of Janelle's. I need to talk to you about Sheik."

She hooked a leash to the dog's collar and strode toward the front of the office. "Walk with me."

For a second, I didn't know if she was talking to me or the dog.

I ran to catch up. "You're the one who called Janelle and told her that Sheik was throwing money around. Why did you do that?"

She stepped through the door. "Puddles? Owner of Puddles?"

A woman in red slacks and a silk blouse came forward. She leaned down and scooped up the shaking dog. "How's my Puddlewuddles? How's my boy?"

"He's doing better. Doc says feed him soft food and keep an eye on him. If the symptoms come back, take him to the emergency animal clinic." Roshanda spun and side-stepped her way around me.

"I called Janelle because I know she's struggling. If Sheik got a hold of some money, she deserves her share for those kids." She walked back down the hall and I trailed her.

"But how did you find out Sheik had money in the first place?"

She glanced over at me with a raised brow. "Crystal called me, raising hell. Wanted to know where Sheik got the money and demanded half. I told her to blow it out her skinny white ass."

In the back room, Roxy stood next to the cat cages, rubbing the chin of a calico. "Where do you think Sheik got the money?" she asked.

Roshanda stopped and put her hands on her hips. "Who are you girls?"

"I'm Rose, that's Roxy. We're trying to help Janelle. She was arrested, you know."

She sighed. "I know and I can't help but feel responsible. I told her about Sheik and the money. I should have kept it to myself. And no, I have no idea where he got it. But he borrowed three hundred dollars from me last month, and I need it back."

"What about his girlfriends?" I asked.

She walked over the cat cages and opened a door. She whisked a black kitten out and stroked its fur. "I'm not sure. Sheik is like a tomcat, dicking around where he shouldn't be. I try my best to stay out of his love life. I'd need some kind of scorecard to keep up with him, and frankly, I'm just not that interested."

It was close to six by the time I got back to my apartment. I dug out my notebook and started making a list of questions. Top of the list, where did Asshat get that money? Also, why did he have photos of Sullivan hidden in his toilet? If he was following Sullivan, why?

Then I made a list of the players and a little description of each. Muffler Man, Marcus Walker, had been a wash. But Janelle said he was shady. I wondered what she meant by that. I added Freddy Libra, because he owned the club where Asshat spent his money. I still needed to talk to Chicken Licker, as well as Little Donnell, Asshat's brother.

I chewed the end of my pen and tried to decide if anyone else made the cut when my phone rang.

"Rose, this is Sondra, Janelle's cousin. Damon's sick."

Chapter 8

Twenty minutes later, I pulled into her driveway with supplies. When Sondra opened the door, she looked exhausted.

"Thanks for coming. Damon's been throwing up for the last two hours."

Sherise and two little boys huddled around the too loud TV. I followed Sondra through to the kitchen and set the grocery bag on the counter. "Have you called the doctor?"

She shook her head. "No, I don't think it's that bad, but I don't want him to get dehydrated. And I couldn't leave the kids to run to the store."

I stepped into the living room and walked to the sofa where Damon lay, looking tired and drawn. His lips were dry and large purple circles ringed his glassy eyes. "How you doing, kiddo? You want a little 7-UP?"

He shook his head.

"We're going to have to get him to drink," Sondra said. She went to the kitchen and returned with a glass. "I mixed the electrolyte drink with the soda."

"Damon," I said and stroked his forehead. He felt warm to the touch. "I want you to drink a little bit of this, okay?"

He tried to sit up. I held the glass to his mouth and he sipped before letting his head fall back onto the sofa pillow. "I want my mom."

I stroked his short hair. "I know, sweetie." The lights of the Christmas tree in the corner mocked me with their cheery blinking.

"When is she coming home?"

"Soon."

"Promise?"

Those sad brown eyes got to me. It was Christmastime and the kid was sick. He needed his mom. I took a deep breath. "Yeah, Damon, I promise."

Sondra shook her head in disapproval. But I was going to get Janelle out of jail, if I had to break her out myself.

"I need to make a quick call," I said over the blaring cartoons.

"Up the stairs, first bedroom on the right."

"Thanks." I took the short flight of stairs and stepped into a bedroom. The queen bed, with its blue and green striped comforter, took up almost every square inch of space. I shut the door behind me and with a shaky hand dialed Sullivan.

"Hello, Rose."

I took a fortifying breath and blew it out. "I need a favor."

Long pause. "Are you sure?"

No, not at all. "I need ten thousand to get my friend, Janelle, out of jail. One of her kids is sick and they need her. I don't know how I'm going to pay you back." I couldn't even afford to buy a used car right now. Ten thousand? It might as well be a hundred thousand.

Another one of those long ass silences. "All right," he said. "I'll have her out tomorrow."

"Thanks." I hit the end button and wondered if I'd just signed my life away.

I left the bedroom and trotted down the stairs to Sondra and Damon. "I got someone to post bail. She should be out tomorrow."

Sondra stared into my eyes. "What did you do? If it were this easy, she'd be home by now. Who'd you get the money from?"

I smiled. "It's fine. Don't worry about it." I glanced down at Damon. "He finally fell asleep, huh?"

"Yeah, I got some fluid down him. I'll wake him up every thirty minutes and give him a little more."

"You need me to stick around and help out with the kids?"

She hesitated a moment. "If you don't mind."

I spent the evening making macaroni and cheese, reading bedtime stories, and washing a sink full of dishes. As I scrubbed bowls and spoons, my gut clenched in anxiety. I knew I had done the right thing for Janelle, but how was I going to pay back Sullivan?

The next morning I met up with Roxy in the diner parking lot and told her about my debt problem.

"How are you going to come up with ten thousand dollars? Does Sullivan expect you to sex him up?"

"I'm not having sex with him, jeez." At least not for money. I mentally slapped myself.

"Just asking," Roxy said.

When we walked into the kitchen, Ma was waiting for us, looking as excited as a kid on Christmas morning. "Girls, come with me. I've got something to show you."

Exchanging glances, Roxy and I followed Ma through the dining room and into the office. At the green metal storage cabinet, she opened the door and waved her hand with the flourish of a game show hostess. "Ta da!"

"Forget it. I'm not wearing that," I said.

Roxy shook her blue curls. "Me, neither."

"Of course not," Ma said. "It's for Dillon."

I stared at the giant, fuzzy, yellow chicken suit in relief.

"Who's Dillon?" Roxy asked, smacking her gum.

"The busboy." Ma pulled the suit out of the cabinet. "I'd wear it myself, but I'd never be able to get in and out of that thing. Not with my hip. What do you think?"

"I'm sure he'll love it." Poor New Kid. He'd sat around the last two days doing less than nothing, now it was time to pay the piper. Karma was a bitch.

Roxy and I went to work, and by six we had customers waiting. At seven, Dillon stepped out of the office, his face visible through the chicken beak.

The customers stopped eating to gawk as he made his way to the front door. He stopped next to my table. "I'm not getting paid enough for this, man. Being a chicken sucks."

I patted his wing. "Better you than me." Then I whipped out my phone and snapped a picture of him. If he didn't start pulling his weight around here, I'd use it for blackmailing purposes.

We worked steadily until nine when a regular stepped through the door, a newspaper tucked under his arm. "Hey, what's that chicken doing outside?"

I glanced out the window. Ma had given Dillon a sign to hold up to help spread the word about our chicken specials. But New Kid had tossed it aside and was standing on the sidewalk, playing with his phone.

Roxy joined me. "That new kid's a dick."

As the morning progressed, I occasionally checked on him. I'd never seen a chicken flip the bird before. He gave everyone who drove by the one-fingered salute. With both hands. How was this helping business again?

That afternoon, lunch really started to pick up. By noon, people were actually waiting outside the diner for tables. By one, we still had customers, and by three, we had to turn people away.

"See, just like I told you," Ma crowed. Or should I say clucked. "Chicken. That's the answer. And tomorrow's special: chicken pot pie. If business stays this brisk, we may have to hire another cook. Maybe we'll expand the diner. I don't see why we can't stay open for dinner."

Dillon marched himself inside. He had to with those floppy chicken feet. "Look at me. Some idiot poured beer all over my legs."

Roxy stared at his drumsticks. "You better hope it was beer. Could have been pee."

Before I could comment, my phone vibrated. I tugged it from my jeans pocket. Sullivan.

"Hey," I said. I left Roxy and Dillon by the front door and slipped behind the counter. "What's up?"

"Just wanted you to know your friend is out of jail. Henry took her home."

"Thanks. So, how are we going to do this? Do I pay you weekly or something?"

Pause. I wiped down the counter with my free hand and waited him out.

"We can negotiate later."

Now I paused. "I'm not having sex with you."

"I'm going to enjoy proving you wrong." Then he hung up.

Holy freaking cow. He was joking. He had to be. Sex with Sullivan would be...amazing. But it wasn't happening. My legs were firmly closed where that man was concerned. He was a criminal. I had to keep reminding myself that it mattered.

As I stared down at my phone, it vibrated again. This time Janelle.

"Rose, I don't know what you did, girl, but I owe you big time."

"No, we're good. I'm just glad you're out. How's Damon?"

"Better. His fever broke. I'm going to pay you back, I swear. I know you borrowed money from Sullivan. And that Henry's a bad mofo. Scared the bejeezus out of me."

Henry was scary, but I didn't want to her to worry about all this now. She had enough on her plate and if we didn't find out who put Asshat in a coma, she was going back to jail for a long time.

"We can talk about it later. In the meantime, just enjoy being home with your kids."

She sniffed. "I'm going to help you find who did this to Asshat. He wasn't much of a husband. Or man. Or a lover. But he is the kids' dad and he didn't deserve this."

Out of the corner of my eye, I watched Roxy wipe down the tables and Ma snag the empty coffeepot on her way to the kitchen.

"Janelle, let's talk about all this later. I've got to help clean up the diner."

"Come by for dinner tonight. Tariq and Sondra and her kids are coming. It's kind of a welcome home. Six o'clock. Bring Roxy, too."

"You got it."

"Girl, I hate to ask—you've done so much already—but how's it coming? Are you any closer to finding out who hit Asshat?"

"I'm sorry, Janelle, not yet. And I still need to talk to LD."

"You'll find out the truth, Rose. You found Axton, didn't you?"

I wasn't sure if Janelle's faith in me was justified, but I was going to do everything I could to help her. "Yeah. Gotta go."

I walked to the office, grabbed the broom, then Roxy and I commenced with cleanup. New Kid stood out front, smoking and yakking on his phone.

Roxy stood at the window and watched him with longing as she chomped her nicotine gum. "It's official. I hate that kid."

"Hey, Janelle invited us for dinner at six. Tariq will be there."

"Shit, that only gives me two hours to get ready. I don't have a thing to wear."

Chapter 9

I walked into Janelle's house and was treated to the spicy smell of oregano, basil, and garlic. My stomach did a back flip from hunger.

In the living room, a four-foot Christmas tree was completely covered in kids' craft ornaments. I was glad I'd called Sullivan. This was where Janelle belonged.

Damon and his cousins sat on the floor playing video games and Sherise braided Roxy's hair.

"Hey," Roxy said, not moving her head. Looked like she found something to wear: a short black dress edged with pink pom poms and a hot pink Bambi embroidered on the skirt.

"You're hair looks beautiful."

Roxy grinned. "Sherise is the best hairdresser evah."

Sherise bopped Roxy's head. "Hold still."

Sondra waved me into the kitchen where Janelle stood at the stove and stirred a pot of sauce. She looked better than she had in jail, but there were lines of tension around her eyes and mouth.

When she saw me, she handed the long wooden spoon off to Sondra and threw her arms around me. She squeezed until I thought I might pass out. "Thanks for getting me out of jail. My babies needed me." She pulled away.

"You're welcome. Can we talk a minute?"

"I'm so damn glad to be home, I'll give you two." She led me to the master bedroom. A pretty quilt covered the bed and an antique dresser stood against one wall.

"What's up, girl? You look all worried and your ass wasn't even in jail. You nervous about paying Sullivan back? Because I've decided to drop out of school and get a full-time job."

"No, that's not it. Roxy and I broke into Asshat's house and found this." I pulled the pictures of Sullivan and the handwritten pages from my purse.

Her brows lowered as she stared at the photos. "Who's this?"

"Sullivan."

She whistled. "That's Sullivan? Damn. He's one mighty fine piece of ass."

Yes, he was. "Could someone have been paying Asshat to watch Sullivan?"

Janelle scoffed. "Asshat wouldn't know how to do undercover. The man does everything he can to draw attention to himself, like a damn peacock. And this isn't his handwriting." She handed everything back to me.

Well that added a whole new slew of questions, but before I could articulate any of them, my phone vibrated. I held a finger up to Janelle and answered.

"Um, Jane? This is Jess." It was hard to hear her over the loud music.

I wracked my brain. "Jess?"

"You know, Satin Lace, from The Bottom Dollar?"

My brow unfurrowed. The stripper I had talked to in the bathroom. "Right, how are you?"

"Listen, Crystal's here in Freddy's office. Just thought you'd like to know." Then she hung up.

"Who was that?" Janelle asked.

"Jess the stripper. Chicken Licker has been sighted. I'm going to try and catch her."

Janelle hopped off the bed. "Not without me, you're not."

"I don't think that such a goo—"

"I'm not playing with you right now." She pointed a yellow fingernail at me. "Shut up and get your shit."

Janelle, Roxy, and I didn't have to pay a cover to get into the club. Apparently, every night was ladies night at The Bottom Dollar.

The place was packed with men in suits, men in jeans and work jackets, and a group of college-aged guys by the door. Hardly anyone noticed us because all eyes were riveted to the naked woman on stage, shaking her butt in time to the music, or the various women in Santa hats scattered throughout the room riding men's laps like bull riders in a rodeo.

I led Roxy and Janelle to Freddy's office and knocked on the door.

"Come in."

I poked my head inside. Freddy Libra sat behind his desk, his large feet propped on top. When he saw me, he smiled. "Decided to take me up on my offer? Wise choice. And later, you might consider getting implants. I know a doctor. He's good."

Boy, this guy creeped me out and pissed me off at the same time. "Where's Crystal?"

He planted his feet on the floor. "How did you know Crystal was here?"

"Where is she, Freddy?"

He stared at me a moment, then shrugged. "She left a minute ago. You just missed her."

I turned around to Roxy and Janelle. "Go to the parking lot and see if you can find her." Then I entered the office. A Lil Wayne song pounded against the closed door.

"What did she want?" I asked. Crossing my arms, I gave Freddy my meanest stare that mostly involved looking into his eyes and not blinking. I think I ruined the effect when my eyes started watering.

"You're not Crystal's cousin," he said.

"No shit, Sherlock. Now what was she doing here?"

"I don't have to tell you anything." He leaned back in his seat and laced his hands behind his head. "But because it will get you out of my hair, I will. She wanted her job back."

I didn't believe him. Freddy was as bad at lying as he was picking out clothes from this decade.

I turned my death glare into a smile. "Okay, great. Thanks." I walked to the door, my hand on the knob. "Oh, by the way, there are a group of boys out front who are underage—I know a couple of them. Probably got in using fake IDs. I wonder what the cops will think of that." Hey, it could be true. I opened the door.

"Wait."

I turned back around. "Yes?"

He dropped his hands to the desk. "Crystal wanted money. I gave her a couple hundred and she left."

I narrowed my eyes. "Why would you give her money? Because you're such an altruistic person?"

He appeared confused. Note to self: don't use college prep words on a strip club owner.

"Because you're such a generous guy?" I rephrased.

He shrugged. "I felt sorry for the kid. We had to let her go and now she's hurting."

Yeah, Freddy was a really crappy liar. I left without another word and met Roxy and Janelle in the hallway. "Did you find her?"

"That bitch was with Marcus. She hopped into his truck and they hauled ass out of here before we could even think about following them," Janelle said.

"Marcus Walker?" I asked. What was Sheik's friend, the muffler man, doing with Crystal?

Two men in suits entered the hallway from the main room and walked toward us. I knew there wasn't a men's room down this way, so what were they doing? One was older, bald. The other was younger, probably fortyish. He was wiry with weasely features and greased back hair.

They stepped past us and walked into Freddy's office without knocking on the door.

"Clay, you're early," I heard Freddy say before the door slammed shut.

I raised my brows at Roxy. Then I turned and hightailed it to the bathroom.

"Where the hell you going?" Janelle hissed as she followed me.

Roxy trailed behind. "She's trying to see if she can hear anything." She glanced up above the stalls. "There." She pointed at a vent.

"Janelle, you're the tallest. Get up on a toilet and see if you can hear anything."

Janelle walked into the stall and hoisted herself up on the toilet seat, trying to steady herself in the high-heeled boots she wore. Roxy and I crowded around her.

"Well?" Roxy asked.

"Shh," Janelle said and waved her hand.

After a couple of minutes, she looked down from her perch and shook her head. "Can't hear a thing."

Damn. We helped her down and I told the girls I'd meet them at the car. I wanted to see if I could find Jess and ask her a few questions while I was here.

I stepped out of the bathroom, turned right, and walked to the dressing room. The ladies inside were in various states of undress. I'd never seen so many bare breasts and free-wheeling vaginas in my life. I wasn't sure where to look. Plus, the whole room reeked of different perfumes, mingling to combine a truly overwhelming floral, musky, peppery stench. Made me sneeze.

"Hi, ladies. I'm looking for Jess." I addressed my comment toward the ceiling.

"She's on the floor, sweetie, what do you need?"

I lowered my gaze slightly to a tanned blonde who wore lots of eyeliner and not much else. "Oh, hi." I kept my gaze on hers. Naked women flowed around me. One ran into my shoulder. "Did you see Crystal Waters earlier?"

She grabbed a bottle of oil and poured a generous portion into her palm. "God, her. Yeah, I saw her. She and Freddy were having it out. Don't know what the fight was about, but Crystal was pissed." She began oiling herself up like she was turkey getting ready for the oven.

I cast my eyes back to the ceiling. "Nobody overheard anything?"

"Hey," she yelled. The strippers stopped yakking. "Does anybody know why Crystal was fighting with Freddy earlier?"

"Who cares?" a voice asked.

"She probably wanted to see who had the bigger dick, her or Freddy." That garnered quite a few laughs.

"Sorry, sweetie," said Oily McGee.

"Well, thanks." I backed out of the room and shut the door.

Look, I'm fine with nudity. Really. Just not so much of it all at once. Finally, I lowered my eyes from the acoustic ceiling tiles and took a deep breath, my eyes stinging from the perfume cloud.

I walked down the hall and stopped by Freddy's office. I glanced over my shoulder to make sure no one was coming, then I put my ear to the door.

I heard muted male voices, but nothing distinctive over the loud music. The door suddenly opened and the bald man faced me.

"Who are you?" He had hard blue eyes and a bulby nose with huge pores.

"How are you?" I waved like I belonged there and then strolled toward the main room. Once I was out of the hall-way, I wanted to run, but a large group of men—ten or so—stood in a circle and blocked the exit.

I started shoving my way through them, but they shoved back. I used my elbow to jab at them. I jostled through the throng and stumbled into the middle of the cir-cle. Jess wore nothing but the thinnest of g-strings and a pair of reindeer antlers on a headband. She straddled a guy backwards so that she faced me. Reverse cowgirl style.

"Hey," she said, glancing up. "Did you find Crystal?" She didn't stop gyrating.

Jeez Louise, I was going to have to bleach my eyeballs. Too. Much. Boobage. "Nope, she was gone."

Some dude with a bottle of beer tried to push me out of the way for a better view. I stomped on his toe and shoved back. "Do you know why Crystal was fighting with Freddy?"

The guy whose lap she rode stuffed dollar bills into her g-string. His eyes were glazed. "Yeah. I overheard them. She said she wanted money and he told her it didn't belong to her. Said she'd go to the cops about it."

"How did you hear all this?"

She raised her legs and spun around on his lap, shoving her breasts in the guy's face. She glanced over her shoulder. "I was in the hallway and the door was half open."

"Thanks, Jess."

"You bet." She focused on the guy and slapped her own ass.

I needed to get out of here. I fought my way back through the circle of men and staggered to the door and out into the night. Sweet, cold, fresh air with a hint of wood smoke from a fireplace nearby.

Janelle pulled her car up to the building. Roxy rolled down the window.

"Hurry up, I'm hungry."

I climbed into the backseat and told them every salacious, boobtastic detail. "And I can't unsee any of it."

"Who the hell cares about that? What money is Chicken Licker talking about?" Janelle asked. She pulled into traffic.

The roads were always congested this time of year. Christmas shoppers. She honked at the slow car in front of us. "Get your ass moving before I do it for you, pokey."

"Maybe the money Asshat was throwing around?" Roxy asked.

"Exactly," I said. "But where did the money come from? That's the question. And why was Crystal asking Freddy about the money? Are Asshat and Freddy buddies?" I asked Janelle.

"I couldn't tell you," Janelle said. "But his brother, LD, might know."

At Janelle's, Tariq and Roxy flirted their way through dinner, feeding each other bites of meatballs. If they each started sucking a long string of spaghetti à la *Lady and the Tramp*, I was going to gag. Damon still wasn't feeling very well and Janelle had a perpetual worried air. I was glad she was home, but I felt a pressing need to find that money. I was sure it was the key to finding Asshat's assailant.

After dinner, I helped with the dishes and Sondra took her kids home.

"Listen, we should go see LD tonight." Janelle stuck a lid on the plastic container of salad before sticking it in the fridge.

"It's your first night home."

"It won't take that long. Tariq and Roxy can watch the kids. I'll be home before ten."

After we finished cleaning the kitchen, we took Janelle's car. On the drive to LD's apartment, she gave me Sheik's family history.

"Well, LD's the baby of the family and closest to Sheik. They're thick as thieves." That was the first time I'd heard her refer to her ex as anything other than Asshat. "LD has himself a little garage downtown. It's profitable. When Sheik quit the muffler place, Little Donnell gave him side jobs."

"Fixing cars?" I asked. That might explain the graveyard of dismantled vehicles in Asshat's yard.

"Mmm-hmm. Off the books. That way, no child support. I'd always liked LD until then, but he helped Sheik dodge his responsibilities. What kind of a man quits his job so he doesn't have to take care of his children?"

A really terrible one.

She pulled up to the Apple Creek Apartments, not far from my sister's neighborhood.

"This place is beautiful," I said, gazing up at the expansive brick building. "His garage must be doing really well to live here."

"Like I said, off the books. If the IRS ever got a look at what he earned, his ass would be in prison before you could say 'don't drop the soap.'"

We took the elevator to the third floor, then Janelle knocked on the door. When he didn't answer, she knocked again, louder this time. "Donnell, you open this door before I stick my foot up your ass. I know you're home, I saw your Explorer outside."

I heard a lock disengage and the door opened a crack. One big, brown eye framed with long lashes blinked at us.

"Hey, Janelle. Now's not a good time."

Janelle pushed her hefty breasts into the door and shoved him back. "Now's not a good time for my ass to wind up in jail, either, but here we are."

LD sighed and stepped back. A handsome man in his late twenties, he was tall with dark skin and a shaved head. But he also sported a black eye that was almost swollen shut and a dark bruise along his jaw. He wore track pants and no shirt. Judging by his six pack, LD did a lot of crunches.

"Who's this," he nodded, eying me up and down. With his one good eye.

"This here's Rose. You step out of line, I'll put you back in place."

LD held up his hands. "Woman, you're too violent. No wonder they arrested you."

She glared at him. "But we both know I didn't hit Sheik." She marched over to the leather sofa, shrugged out of her coat and sat down. "We've got a few questions to ask."

LD cast me a wary glance. "I don't think we should be talking. The police said it wouldn't be a good idea. Besides, I told you, it's not a good time."

A woman wearing a white t-shirt that almost reached her knees stepped into the room. She was pretty with mocha skin and long, dark, mussed hair. "What's going on LD?"

"Get back in bed. I'll be there in a minute."

She shrugged and returned from whence she came.

"So let me get this straight," Janelle said. "Your brother's in a coma. I'm stuck in jail. And you're getting knobbed?"

"Man, what can I do about any of that? Life is short. You got to live."

"You could've bailed me out of jail."

He crossed his arms over his bare chest. "How would that look, bailing out the woman who put my brother in the hospital?

"I told you, I didn't do it," she said.

"But everyone thinks you did. You two should go."

"No problem," I said. "Come on, Janelle."

She looked at me as if I were crazy. "We're not going anywhere. Not until this fool talks to us."

"We can't force him," I said.

When LD hitched up the waistband of his pants, a large, gold watch slid down his wrist. "That's right," he said. "You can't force me to do anything I don't want to do. I'm a grown ass man."

I glanced around the apartment, took in the thick off-white carpeting, the soft terra cotta walls, the big tan vase filled with twigs in the corner. The furniture looked expensive and the mammoth TV screen rivaled the Jumbotron. Then my eyes met Janelle's. "I wonder what this furniture's worth. And you know, I think the IRS is going to love that watch LD's wearing. Looks expensive."

He held up his hands in protest. "Now wait, that's not funny."

Janelle stood and grabbed her coat. "Yep. And I'm sure they'd be interested in knowing Asshat's getting paid off the books." She walked toward him and reaching up, thumped his black eye with her fingertip.

He cupped it with one hand. "Ow! Goddamn it, Janelle, that hurt."

"Not as much as it's going to, you little fucker." She jabbed his stomach with a long, yellow nail. "Are you going to talk or do I have to call the IRS?"

He dropped his hand. "Fine."

She nodded smugly and poked him once more. "Good." Returning to the sofa, she sank down and pursed her lips. "Rose, ask your questions."

I walked over to where Janelle sat and plopped down next to her. "Tell us the name of the door you ran into."

Chapter 10

He opened his mouth a couple of times as if he was trying to figure out what to say, then finally shook his head. "I'll tell you about Sheik, but not about this." He pointed to his face.

"Fine," Janelle said, "who wanted to hurt Sheik?"

LD sat in the chair across from us. "You know the answer to that."

"Let me guess," I said, "anyone who knew him? According to, well, everyone, Sheik is a ladies man. So who was he dating?"

"What am I, his social secretary?"

Janelle scooted to the edge of her seat. "You know that black eye you got, LD? You're gonna think it feels good when I rip your balls off."

"Shit, woman." He crossed his legs. "I know he was dating some chick named Vi. Works at the Clip N Curl. She's the only name I know besides Crystal."

"Where did the money come from?" I asked.

He shifted uncomfortably in the chair and the leather made farty noises. We all pretended like we didn't hear it. "I don't know."

"Where'd Sheik get the damn money?" Janelle yelled.

He thumped his chest with his palm. "I asked him over and over and he wouldn't tell me. Wouldn't pay what he owed me, either."

"Yeah, I know that feeling," Janelle said.

"Where do you think he got it?" I asked. "You must have some idea."

"I don't know, man.

"Take a guess." I could tell LD knew more than he was letting on. Plus, that black eye he wouldn't talk about made me more than a little suspicious. "How does Sheik make his money?"

Janelle pursed her lips. "I'd like to know that myself."

He rubbed a hand over his bald head and sighed. "Fine. When he needs green, he'll gank off with stuff."

I glanced over at Janelle. "What the hell does that mean?"

"Sheik steals cars, mostly," LD said. "Chops 'em."

"Who does he chop for? You?" I asked.

"Look, man." He spread his hands in front of him. "I'm out there hustling for dollar, just like everybody else. Nothing wrong with that."

"Actually, there are many things wrong with that. Someone just stole my car. And I worked hard for that piece of crap. I take it very personally."

Janelle nudged my shoulder. "Rein it in, girl, this isn't about you."

"Fine. What about Crystal?" I asked.

"She came by the other day." LD glanced at Janelle. "She was pissed that Sheik wasn't throwing any bank her way. Said he owed her, then he goes up in the club like a whale, and she went off."

I held up my hand. "English, please."

"Sheik got some money. From somewhere—"

"You mean he stole it," Janelle said.

He shrugged. "He takes it into The Bottom Dollar like he's the shit and starts getting lap dances from every girl there but Crystal. She starts a fight and gets tossed out on her ass. Then she comes crying to me, like I could do something. Hell man, like I said, Sheik owes me money, too."

"Crystal was in the club tonight asking Freddy Libra about the money. Why would Freddy know anything about it? Were Sheik and Freddy friends?"

"Nah, not that I know of. Look, I can't figure that girl out. She's half crazy."

I eyed LD and his black eye. "How did you feel about Sheik buying bling and strippers instead of paying you?" I asked. Had he been angry enough to bash in Sheik's head? Maybe Sheik hit LD and LD hit back twice as hard.

"I didn't put Sheik in the hospital, if that's what you're asking."

Janelle huffed. "If you see Chicken Licker again, you tell her to fuck off. That money is for my kids and my lawyer fees, you got it?"

"That's not my business. I'm not getting in between you and Crystal. That's suicide, man."

That damn missing money. It always circled back to that. Roxy and I didn't find it at Asshat's house—unless it was so well hidden we missed it. And Crystal didn't have it because she was in the club tonight asking for money. And maybe it was linked to Sullivan and the surveillance stuff I found in Asshat's toilet tank.

"Where do you think the money is now?" I asked him.

"No idea. Seems like it's a lot more trouble than it's worth."

"Is that why you're sporting the shiner? Somebody wanted it and thought you knew where it was?" Sounded like a reasonable explanation to me.

"I told you, I ain't talking about that." He stood. "Y'all need to go."

Janelle and I left the apartment, and as we walked toward the elevator, I glanced over at her. "So, where would Sheik hide a bunch of money?"

She shot me a look. "You're assuming that asshole had any left. Probably spent it all on hoes and fake ass ice. Never gave a dollar to his kids. I wish I had hit him. He wouldn't be in the hospital, he'd be on a slab."

We climbed into her car and she let it warm up before pulling out of the lot.

"I still think Chicken Licker did it," she said.

"Then why did she go to The Bottom Dollar and ask Freddy about the money?"

"Hell, I don't know. But if *I* had any money, I'd put it on her."

After Janelle pulled into her driveway, I climbed out of the passenger seat and waved goodbye, before hopping into Ax's car. While I waited for the heater to kick in, I pulled the pictures of Sullivan and the detailed notes out of my purse. I had a really bad feeling about this. Missing money. Surveillance info. I knew I couldn't keep it to myself any longer.

According to the notes, Sullivan spent the last two Tuesday nights from nine p.m. to two a.m. at Penn's Cigar

Bar. He was going to be pissed I didn't tell him about this right away. Especially after he ponied up for Janelle's bail. But the longer I put it off, the harder it'd be.

I called and told him to expect me in fifteen minutes, then I drove to the one story brick building. With its arched, leaded windows it looked more like a church than a bar. A blazing fire burned in a brick fireplace along one wall and a long bar took up another. Thick, rich cigar smoke hung in the air. Roxy would be in heaven.

It was busy for a Tuesday night. Mostly couples occupied the wooden tables, and a piano player tinkled the ivories in one corner.

Henry, Sullivan's henchman, met me at the door. Henry scared the ever loving crap out of me. He was a giant, close to seven feet. His crooked nose never quite recovered from getting punched a few too many times and a scar stood in relief next to his left eye.

"Follow me," he said.

"I guess we're going to skip the chitchat, huh?" I followed his broad back past the bar, down a hall to the last room on the left. Henry opened the door to an office. A nicely appointed one with no windows and heavy, masculine furniture.

Sullivan sat behind a massive desk. Hotter than a bonfire on the fourth of July. Runner of an illegal gambling operation. Object of more than one erotic dream. He glanced up when the door opened and studied me with his gold eyes.

He was gorgeous. Warm, honeyed skin and strong cheekbones. Black hair brushed away from his flawless face. Yeah, gorgeous almost covered it.

"Hello, Rose."

I barely heard the door close behind me. "Hey."

He stood and walked toward me. He circled me, sliding his hands beneath the back collar of my coat. His long fingers brushed my nape, sending shivers over every part of my body. When he leaned forward, his chest touched my back. "Whatever got you here, it must be important," he said in my ear.

"Kind of, yeah."

"I've been waiting for you to come to me." He slowly pulled the coat from my shoulders and down my arms. I spun to watch him casually toss it over his brown leather desk chair. "Want a drink?" He reached into the bottom drawer and pulled out a nearly empty squat bottle. It carried a fancy foreign label. Snagging two glasses off a shelf, he walked past me to a round table at the other end of the room. He was all lithe grace and smooth moves. "Please, sit."

It wasn't a request.

I walked to the table, slid into a chair. He did the same.

He poured a small amount of liquor into both glasses. Handed me one.

"Is this whiskey?" I sniffed.

"No, I remember you don't like it." His eyes met mine as he leaned back.

I took an experimental sip. It was fiery and burned its way down my throat, but it wasn't unpleasant. "What is it?"

"Brandy."

I took another sip. "Now that's a good stripper name."

He raised a dark brow. "Do you need a stripper name?"

"You don't happen to own The Bottom Dollar, do you?" Sullivan owned a lot of businesses around town, many of them bars like this one.

"Not yet, why?"

"Arrogant."

"It's not arrogance if it's true." He smirked. Arrogantly.

I nibbled my lip. "I've got a story to tell you. No interruptions until I'm through."

He narrowed his eyes a bit and nodded. "All right. It's your show."

"As you know, my friend, Janelle, was accused of putting her ex-husband, Asshat, in a coma."

His lips edged up in the corners.

"Asshat is a ladies man. And a few days before his argument with Janelle, he went to The Bottom Dollar and was throwing money around. But Asshat doesn't have a job." I shook my head. "At least not on the books. So where did he get all that money? Anyway, at the strip club, he got a lap dance from every girl there, except his ex-girlfriend, Chicken Licker."

Sullivan held up a hand. "I have to stop you there. Why Chicken Licker?"

"Because she and Asshat ate chicken and diddled each other in Janelle's bed. At the same time."

He paused. "That's a disturbing image."

I grinned. "You mean you don't eat during sex?" As soon as the teasing words left my mouth, I realized what I had said. I pushed the glass away. No more brandy for me.

"No." His deep voice lowered to a husky timber. He shifted in his chair and leaned his arms on the table. "I'm far too busy putting my mouth to better use."

Oh. My. God. I couldn't talk, could hardly breathe. My gaze tangled with his and my face heated. I licked my dry lips and tried to focus my thoughts.

"Are you going to finish your story?" He raised a brow as he leaned back.

I cleared my throat. "He and Chicken Licker got in a fight. She was thrown out of the club, lost her job. Then Asshat got his head bashed in. And I think Crystal is still looking for the money."

"Are Crystal and Chicken Licker one and the same?"

I nodded. "Yesterday, Roxy and I went to Asshat's house, looking for any clue as to who did this to him, because of course, Janelle's completely innocent."

"Of course," he murmured. He stroked his chin with one finger and watched me.

Bending down to the floor, I grabbed my purse and dug out the papers and pictures. My eyes found his. *Okay, Rose, time to cowboy up.*

"I found these hidden in Asshat's house. Stuffed in his toilet." When I handed them to him, our fingers barely touched. Still, it was enough to feel a sharp tug of attraction in the pit of my stomach.

He read the notes, his jaw tightening with every second that passed. Then he looked at the photos. The skin around his compressed lips turned white.

Like I said. Pissed.

"When did you find these?"

"Sunday," I said, grimacing.

"And you kept this from me?" he ground out.

"Hey, you've kept shit from me before." That was no excuse, but it was true.

He rose from the table so quickly, it startled me. He strode to the door like a large tiger, eating up the short distance before pivoting on his heel and stalking back.

As he moved toward me, I scrambled from my seat and backed myself into a corner. I wanted to get out of his way, but I was out of room unless I climbed the walls. Still he advanced, stopping in front of me, his chest touching mine.

Leaning one hand on the wall behind me, he pressed himself into me. He was breathing hard, almost panting. I focused on the knot in his tie. Real silk, dark teal. He shook the papers with his free hand. "Do you know what this is? Look at me, goddamn it." He never raised his voice, but anger coated his words in ice.

I slowly raised my eyes to his. His pupils had constricted, and his eyes, light gold a moment ago, were dark with rage. Color suffused his cheeks, leaving them ruddy. He let go of the wall and grabbed my chin, tilting my head up further. "Someone's been following me, knows my every fucking move, and you didn't tell me."

I felt an overwhelming sense of guilt. This man had helped me more than once. I owed him, not just money, I owed him my loyalty. He was right, I should have told him, shouldn't have turned this into a game of one-upmanship.

With my fingertips, I touched the back of his hand that gripped my chin. "I'm sorry. I wanted to find out more before I showed you. I was wrong."

In that instant, everything changed between us. The air became charged with a potency that left me breathless and the moment stretched into something more than our usual flirtatious, witty banter. We simply stared into each other's eyes and I felt connected to him somehow.

Then he blinked twice and stepped away, dropping my chin and the connection. Maybe I was the only one who felt it, but I didn't think so.

Taking a deep breath, he turned away from me and strode back to his chair. "Now start again. From the beginning."

I fell into the seat and went over everything again, including Asshat's brother, LD, and Marcus and breaking into Crystal's condo. I told him about my conversation with Jess, the stripper. "And two men went into Freddy Libra's office. A bald man and a skinny guy. Freddy called one of them Clay. Probably Baldy. It seemed like he was in charge."

He stilled.

"Who's Clay?" I asked.

"Finish your story."

"No. I want to know who Clay is."

He leaned forward, his face close, his voice low. "Here's how it's going to work. I give you ten thousand dollars bail money and you answer my questions."

My gaze travelled over his too handsome face. A dark shadow covered his jaw line and being this close I could see a little scar in the shape of a half circle on his chin. "Some guy named Clay waltzed into Freddy Libra's office like he owned it. Someone's been following you and watching your every move. Asshat steals shit, usually cars, and suddenly has a windfall. I think Asshat stole from the wrong person. Found the money and the surveillance pics and the notes. I think you have a hit out on you. Am I right?"

"I think it's likely."

"So who is this Clay guy?"

He stood and removed my coat from his chair. "I'd tell you not to get involved, but we both know you'll do whatever the hell you want." He held the coat out for me.

Well, I guess our special time together was over.

I stood and slipped my arms into the sleeves of my jacket. I faced him, ready to say something snarky before I left, when his arm snaked around my waist and he pulled me close. "Be careful." He leaned down and softly kissed the corner of my mouth. I almost came on the spot. If he could do that with a tiny kiss...

"And if you get in my way," he said, "I'll remove you."

Did I take that threat seriously? Yeah. Yeah, I did. Sullivan had a soft spot for me, but he wouldn't let that override his own sense of self-preservation. Business came first. Didn't mean I was going to stop, though.

He pulled back and opened the door for me. "Goodnight, Rose."

Chapter 11

The next morning at the diner, while Roxy and I made coffee and refilled salt shakers, Ma ran around putting the final touches on chicken pot pies. Although her bright red lipstick matched her Mrs. Claus sweatshirt, it looked a little wonky—like she applied it without a mirror. Or in the dark.

"I've made twenty pies since last night, girls. Hopefully we'll have a good crowd today." She parked on one of the stools and cradled her cup of coffee. "I didn't realize how tiring this lunch business would be."

"Hasn't Ray been helping?" Roxy asked.

"All he does is moan and gripe about the extra work. It's easier to do it myself."

I'd known Ray five years, and in all that time, I've heard maybe fifty words out of the man. Moaning and griping? Couldn't imagine it. Maybe he just grunted twice as loud?

"I talked to Sullivan last night," I said.

Ma pursed her lips in disapproval. "I don't like that man, and even though he helped you out, and I'll always be grateful, I still don't like him. Don't trust him, neither."

"He's uber hot," Roxy said. "I saw a picture of him. No wonder Rose is all smitten kitten."

I set down the salt and placed my hands on the counter. "I am not smitten. And do you want to know what I found out or what?"

Roxy glanced at Ma and wiggled her eyebrows. "Someone's got it bad," she whispered.

"Fine. Never mind." I went back to pouring salt with my nose in the air.

"Just tell us, toots. I'm not getting any younger over here."

I caved and told them about the hit on Sullivan.

Roxy put her hands on her hips. For some unfathomable reason, a stuffed unicorn the size of a football was sewn onto her blue skirt. "If people are gunning for Sullivan, you'd better steer clear of him."

Ma frowned. "That sounds like good advice, toots."

It probably was. Didn't mean I had to take it, though.

Our early customers started trickling in, so we quit yapping and got to work. Ma found the new kid hiding behind the desk in the office and forced him into the chicken suit.

By our mid-morning slowdown, Ma strode back and forth between the dining room and the kitchen. Ray walked to the counter with my omelet and Roxy's cinnamon roll.

"Ungh. Can't use oven. Driving me nuts," he mumbled. That was practically a soliloquy.

"Just tell her, Ray," I said. "Tell her you don't want to do lunch."

"Ungh." He stalked back to the kitchen.

Roxy's blue eyes grew wide. "I've never seen Ray that pissed. Not even when Ma wanted to put plastic spiders on the fried eggs for Halloween." That hadn't gone over too well with the customers, either.

I was about to take a mouthful of omelet when my phone buzzed. I glanced at the number. "Good morning, Mother. How are you this blessed day?"

"We're having brunch at the club on Saturday. Ten o'clock."

"Good for you. You go, girl." I forked a bite of eggs into my mouth.

"Rosalyn, do not try my patience. I'm still irritated you left my party without saying goodbye. I have not forgotten."

"I don't understand the brunch announcement," I said, after I'd swallowed.

I heard her take a deep breath. "You are coming with us. To brunch. On Saturday. At ten o'clock."

"I have to work." As she should know, since I'd worked every Saturday for oh, the last five freaking years.

"You can miss one day."

"Actually, I can't."

"Fine. Dinner tomorrow night. Seven on the dot. Don't be late."

"But—" I heard a click. After I shoved the phone back in my pocket, I realized I'd been played. Of course she knew I had to work. But she also knew her opening salvo would be rejected. Man, she was good. Still, I had other things to do. Getting Janelle cleared was on the top of my list. Finding out who wanted to kill Sullivan, a close second. Castigation over dinner? Not so much.

"Your mom needs to unclench that ass and live a little," Roxy said. She unwound the cinnamon roll until it was one long strip. "No offense."

"None taken."

After I finished eating, I called Ax.

"Axman. Speak."

"Hey, I have two more peeps for you to look up. Marcus Walker, works at the muffler place on the Boulevard. And some bald guy named Clay. Knows Freddy Libra."

"That's it? Bald and Clay?"

"Yep."

"Well, I accept your challenge, Rose Strickland. And if I dig anything up, I'll bring it over tonight. I got a new movie, *Invaders from Mars*."

"Can't wait. I should be home by five. I'm still looking into things with Janelle." I hung up and got back to work.

Things picked up that afternoon and didn't slow down until after three. My feet ached and my tips weren't much better than they usually were. Mostly because people didn't like to tip on a freebie meal. Those buy one get one specials were bringing people in, but I wasn't sure how much extra money Ma was generating.

After my last customer left, I fell into a chair and buried my head in my arms. Roxy sat across from me and propped her feet up in my lap.

"I'm exhausted," I said.

"Yeah, that lunch crowd is demanding. Some asshole left me fifty cents. That's an insult."

Dillon flapped his chicken feet into the diner. "Look at this." Black singe marks scorched the tips of his yellow feathers. "People threw lit smokes at me. What the hell, man? Who does that?"

I raised my head. "Maybe we should talk to Ma. All of us together. Tell her we think lunch should be off the menu."

Ma burst through the kitchen door, her arms in the air. "Seventy-five lunchers today, girls. That's a new record. And

Dillon, that chicken suit is a big hit. I told you this would work."

Roxy raised one brow. "Yeah, she seems receptive."

Dillon spread his wings and stormed off to change. His feet slapping against the linoleum with every step.

Ma walked stiffly toward us and patted us on the backs. "Good work today. And I have leftover pot pies I can freeze for next week."

Next week? I was hoping she'd give up on this idea long before next week.

Roxy and I slowly rose to our feet and commenced with clean up.

"What are we doing today? Any new suspects?" Roxy emptied the spent coffee grounds from the machine.

"Thought I'd bop on over to the Clip N Curl and talk to someone named Vi. Apparently she and Asshat were close. And then I thought I'd stop over to the muffler shop again and see what the hell Marcus was doing with Crystal last night."

"Yeah, that's an interesting matchup."

When we finished cleaning the diner, Roxy and I stopped by Paco's Tacos for a late lunch. After snarfing down a taco each, we hopped onto Ash Avenue.

There was a waiting line at the Clip N Curl. An elderly woman, two men, one mom holding a squirming toddler with a snotty nose, and one teenager with multiple piercings sat in chairs reading out-of-date celebrity magazines. Well, the toddler didn't. He kept screaming every time his mom set him on the floor to play with his bear.

Roxy and I stood at the reception desk. "But I'm not here to get my hair done," I said. "I'm here to see Vi."

"Hang on one second, hon." The woman behind the desk held up her finger and answered the phone. "Clip N Curl. Sure, we can squeeze you in." She grabbed a pen and flipped through the appointment book.

Tired of waiting, I walked past her and into the salon. Three stylists cut, coiffed and sprayed their clients. I approached a woman with spiky black hair and funky purple glasses. "Sorry to bother you."

She slid a straightener over her customer's long, brown hair. Steam escaped the edges. First she glanced at me, then Roxy. "Love the color, honey. Who does that for you?"

"Thanks." Roxy adjusted her Alice band and smoothed a hand over a blue lock. "Bonita over at The Shag Shack."

The woman nodded. "She did a good job."

"Is Vi working today?" I asked.

She raised a brow and lowered her voice. "She's supposed to be. But she's hiding in the back. Tell her to get her ass out here, would ya? If she thinks I'm giving that little monster a haircut, she's crazier than she looks." She pointed with the straightener toward the back of the room, past three dryer chairs to a curtained doorway.

"Thanks," I said.

She reached out and ran her fingers through my ponytail. "You need a good conditioner, honey."

"I'll keep it in mind." I turned to Roxy and raised my brows.

"My hair's perfectly conditioned," she said smugly.

We walked to the curtain and I pulled it aside to reveal shelves of hair product and a washer and dryer. A blonde in her twenties with glittery gold hair extensions removed brown hand towels from the dryer. She wore a hot pink blouse that showed more cleavage than it covered and her pants were so tight, I wondered how she even got them on.

"Hey, you're not supposed to be back here. It's for employees only." She eyed Roxy's blue mane. "Good color on you. Matches your eyes."

She preened a bit. "Thanks."

"You're Vi?" I asked.

Shaking out a towel, she gazed at me warily. "Yeah. Who're you?"

"She's Jane. I'm Beth," Roxy said.

"We had a few questions about Sheik Johnson." I tucked my hands in my jacket pockets and watched her face. From the tightening of her lips, I'd say just hearing Sheik's name pissed her off.

"What about him?" With jerky movements, she folded a towel.

"He came into some money recently," I said.

"Ha, like I'll ever see any of it."

"He owed you money?" Roxy asked. "How much?"

"That asshole stole my credit card. And the police wouldn't do anything because I'd let him borrow before."

"Did you cancel the card?" I asked.

"Yeah, two weeks after I noticed it was missing. Not only did he give me gonorrhea, he racked up like fifteen hundred dollars on my Visa." She threw the towel on top of the washing machine.

"Are you sure he's the one who gave it to you?" Roxy asked. "The gonorrhea?" she whispered.

"Do I look like a slut to you?" Vi tapped her boob for emphasis. The one with a tattoo that read *Hot Bitch* in Old English script.

"No, not at all," I said. "So you don't know where Sheik got the money?"

"He probably stole it from one of his other girlfriends."

"Do you know who else he was seeing?" Roxy asked.

"I know he saw stripper named Destiny before we met," Vi said. "And I checked his phone once and found a text from some bitch named Crystal." She pursed her bright pink lips. "And there was a whore who works at Huntingford Bank and Trust. Brenda. She's old, like in her forties. She used to text him all the time. Send pictures of herself. When I'm forty, if my tits sag like that, I'll kill myself."

From the front of the salon I heard the little kid scream at the top of his lungs.

"I think that's your next client," I said.

"No way. I'll probably cut off his ear. Not going through that again. Do you know how many capillaries are in the human ear?" She studied me with a critical eye. "You need a trim. Maybe some low lights. Come back and see me."

Never going to happen.

Roxy and I left the salon and climbed into the Honda.

"Think she's a suspect?" Roxy asked.

"Sheik stole her money, gave her an STD, and cheated on her. We should probably add her name."

We stopped at the muffler shop on the way back to the diner. But it turned out our big adventure was uneventful. Marcus didn't show up for work and didn't bother calling in.

I dropped Roxy off by her car in Ma's lot and headed home.

Chapter 12

When I got to my apartment, Axton was waiting for me.

"Sorry I'm late." I stepped over him and unlocked the door. "By the way, Marcus Walker didn't show up for work today."

"Dude, that's always trouble when they don't show up for work." He picked up the pizza and a large brown paper bag and followed me inside.

I dropped my purse and keys on the cherry table in the corner. "I know. Did you find any info on him?" I shrugged out of my coat and hung it next to the door.

"First, we need to address your Christmas issues," he said.

"Ax, I don't have Christmas issues. But I'm beginning to think you might."

He dug into the sack and pulled out an eighteen-inch Christmas tree. "What do you think?"

"Um, it's really pink." But I had to admit, it made me smile.

Ax dumped my purse from the table and set the tree on top. "See? How's that? Get the Christmas blood flowing a little bit?" He pulled out a package of tiny lights.

Despite my recent anti-holiday stance, I moved toward the funky tree. Axton was a sweetie. If he wanted me to participate in a little Christmas, I could do that for him. "All right, let's get this sucker decked."

He grinned. "Now you're talking."

Together we strung the lights over the small tree and hooked mini metallic balls in pink, red, and silver on the boughs. It looked weird. Not traditional. But very fitting in my shabby apartment.

"And now," he said dramatically, "wait until you see what I got for a topper." Watching me, he thrust his hand into the bag and drew out a tiny plastic tiara trimmed in pink marabou.

I started laughing. He placed it on top of the tree and stood back, eyeing his handiwork.

"That looks awesome, dude."

I stood next to him and smiled. "Yeah, it does. Thanks, Ax."

He threw his arm around my neck and gave me a noogie with his free hand. "You're welcome. Christmas kicks ass. Deal with it."

I grabbed plates, the pizza, and paper napkins while Ax snagged two beers from the fridge. "So show me what you found," I said.

"Don't you want to eat first?"

"I'll read while I'm chewing."

He handed me a folder. "Marcus Walker. Got eight arrests under his belt. Not like, a career criminal, but dude's got a temper and isn't picky about offloading stuff that isn't his."

I flipped through it, looked at Marcus' mug shots. A DUI twenty years ago. The charges were reduced to reckless driving and he paid a hefty fine. Two more arrests ten years ago—one for assault, the other public intoxication. Probation on both. He got in an altercation with a girlfriend a year ago, but the charges were later dropped. And he'd been convicted of selling stolen merchandise four separate times. But no details about what he'd sold. Served a one year stint in prison.

"Marcus likes to fight." I took a bite of pizza and continued to read.

"Yeah, but only gets into trouble when he's been drinking." Ax took a very ironic swig of beer. "Now the stolen stuff, that's another story."

"Do we know what he was selling?"

Ax ripped off a large pepperoni from his slice and tossed it in his mouth. "Stolen car parts, mostly. But also a car stereo and a set of rims. But the car parts landed him in prison."

LD had a garage that used stolen parts. Marcus sold stolen car parts. Sounded like a connection to me.

"I'll keep looking for the bald dude," he said.

"Thanks. I think I'll go talk to Marcus tonight. Want to go with me?"

He shot me a look. "Like Robin to your Batman?"

"Yep."

I ate two slices of pizza and Ax polished off the rest. While he ate, I texted Roxy to see if she wanted to go with us. If Marcus wasn't home, we needed to break into the house.

She texted back with a yes, so we stopped to pick her up on the way.

When she opened the car door, Ax held his thumb to his mouth like a microphone. "Playing the role of Batgirl this evening, Roxy Block."

"Whatevs." She climbed into the backseat and I could feel the excitement roll off her. "Need me to pick a lock, huh? You know I've been practicing at home, trying to improve my time."

I twisted around and peered at her. "Don't get too excited, he might be home."

"You need to have a more positive attitude."

I chuckled, even though she wasn't kidding.

"So guess who called and asked me out?" she said.

"Tariq?"

Even in the dark, with nothing but street lights illuminating her face, I could see her grin. "Yep."

"Wait, Janelle's cousin?" Axton turned down the radio and gazed at Roxy in the rearview mirror.

"Someone's got it bad," I said, parroting her words back to her.

"Shut up." She gazed out the window, still smiling.

Five minutes later, Axton pulled across the street from Marcus' bungalow on the southeast side of town. It was dark, no lights on inside. We'd decided that Roxy and I would go up to the house, knock, and if no one answered, we'd slip around back and break in. Axton would keep watch and call us if someone came home.

I was about to get out of the car when Marcus' front door opened and the bald man I'd seen at the strip club stepped out of the house, followed by the weasely, thin guy who'd accompanied him into Freddy's office.

"Duck," I said.

Without asking any questions, Roxy flopped over in the backseat and Axton scrunched down behind the wheel. I hunched over, but popped up a bit to view Baldy's progress.

He swiveled his head and glanced up and down the street as he walked to a dark SUV parked on the curb in front of the house.

"What's going on up there?" Roxy asked.

"Remember that bald guy, Clay, who went into Freddy Libra's office at The Bottom Dollar the other night? Well, he just came out of the house." When the SUV turned around, the headlights hit Axton's car. I waited a few seconds then peeked again. "Coast is clear."

"Did you get a license plate number?" Axton asked.

"Damn. No," I said.

I gave Axton the speedy version of my theory that someone had a hit out on Sullivan. "Could be this Clay guy. Sullivan's face went blank when I mentioned his name."

"I hate to say this," Axton said, "but I wonder if you should call Sullivan for back up."

"If we find anything in the house, I'll call him." I grabbed two penlights and four latex gloves out of my purse, then handed Roxy her share.

"Does Ma know you're swiping these?"

"She'd understand."

As Roxy and I walked toward the house, I scanned the street, tripping over a dirt clod as I checked out the homes either side of Marcus' bungalow. Christmas lights decorated a few eaves and one front yard held an inflatable Santa that swayed back and forth in the breeze. Other than that, no movement.

"You're real graceful," Roxy whispered.

"Shut your pie hole," I said as we approached the front door. I knocked, knowing there'd be no answer, but I needed to be sure.

When no one came to the door, we walked around the side to the tiny back yard.

I shined my light on the door knob as Roxy dug out her Allen wrench. She made quick work of the lock.

What had Baldy and his sidekick been looking for? The money? And where was Marcus? Had he and Crystal gone into hiding? The questions compounded on one another and I still hadn't come up with any answers.

I handed Roxy her flashlight as we stepped into the small galley kitchen. The place was a wreck. Every cabinet door stood open, the contents strewn all over the counters and floor.

"Shit," Roxy said.

"Let's check out the rest of the house."

Picking my way over crap spilled in the kitchen, I tip-toed into the L-shaped living room/dining room combo and swept my penlight over slashed seat cushions, a broken TV, the smashed side table. "Let's go. Either Clay already found what he was looking for or it's not here."

"Whatever 'it' is," Roxy said.

We ran out of the house and through the yard. My eyes flew over the houses and cars along the street as we made our way back to Axton. All was quiet and still.

"Well?" he asked when we climbed in.

"Baldy trashed the place."

"You guys okay?" Axton started the car and glanced over at me.

"Yeah, fine," I said.

Marcus' house was trashed, he hadn't shown up for work, and he drove Crystal to The Bottom Dollar last night. Where was he now?

Baldy had been looking for something. Probably the money. That was the only thing that made sense.

And if Asshat stole the money and the surveillance stuff on Sullivan, then who took all those notes and pictures in the first place? Baldy? His sidekick?

Something didn't feel right. I was off somewhere. I was missing pieces of the puzzle.

Axton reached over and grabbed my hand. "You all right?"

I squeezed his fingers. I loved this guy. He was the brother I never thought I wanted. I turned my head and smiled at him. "I'm good."

He dropped Roxy off at her apartment and she slapped my shoulder. "If you can't sleep tonight, call me." She hopped out of the car and jogged into the building.

Axton propped his elbow on the door. "Still having trouble sleeping, huh?"

"Only sometimes."

"If you want to talk—"

"Ax, I'm fine."

He remained quiet until he pulled up to my apartment. "Let me come inside and check things out."

I leaned over and kissed his scruffy cheek. "I'm a big girl, I can handle myself. See you later."

We both exited the car and he tossed me the keys before sauntering off to Stoner Joe's truck.

When I got to my apartment, I called Janelle and told her about Vi. "Asshat gave her an STD and stole her credit card."

Janelle blew out a breath. "Lucky for me, I quit sleeping with that fool a long time ago. What else is going on?"

I told her about Marcus and Baldy and the trashed house. "I wonder where he's hiding. And how did he and Crystal hook up?"

"She's probably screwing him, too."

"Would Marcus do that to Sheik?" I glanced at my hot pink Christmas tree. "And Sheik was also seeing someone named Brenda who works at Huntingford Bank and Trust. Thought I'd head over there after I get off work tomorrow."

"Good. I'll go with you. Tariq can watch the kids when they get home from school."

Janelle confronting one of Asshat's ex-girlfriends? Not a good idea. "I can probably handle it."

"Forget it. I'm going with you. If she tried to kill Asshat, I'll know it."

"How?" I asked.

"I've seen that look in the mirror a few times."

Roxy popped a piece of gum in her mouth before filling the coffeepot with water. She ripped open a Mylar pack of rich-smelling grounds and poured them into the filter.

"Janelle and I are going to talk to the bank woman. You in?" I asked around a yawn. I'd had a nightmare last night and woke up at two o'clock. I hadn't been able to go back to sleep and as a result, I was gritty-eyed and groggy.

She glared at me, but the effect was spoiled by her black top hat decorated with a mini stuffed bear that wobbled every time she moved her head. "I told you to call me if you couldn't sleep."

"I'm all right," I said as I moved around the diner and pulled up the shades.

Dillon sat at the counter and spun in circles. He wore earbuds and sang falsetto to the music.

Roxy walked by and stuck out her foot, putting a stop to his twirling. She yanked a bud out of his ear. "Get to work."

"Doing what, man?"

"Go to the kitchen and see if Ma needs help," I said.

I think he rolled his eyes, but it was hard to tell through that mop of hair. "Fine." He hopped off the stool and slouched toward the kitchen.

"It's not just me, right?" she asked. "He's annoying?"

"Very," I said. "Now, what about going with Janelle and me?"

"Yeah, but I have to get home early. Tariq and I are going to the movies tonight."

"Don't let him get fresh. Girls who wear bears on their hats shouldn't give away too much on the first date. It's unseemly."

She snorted.

My brain remained in a fog despite three cups of coffee. So when my customers hit the door, I was a little slow in telling them to come back for lunch. Ma pulled me aside twice to remind me.

"Tell them about lunch, toots. Tell them about our chicken soup. That rat bastard Rudy is not going to win, you hear me?"

Yikes, Ma was getting mean. I'd seen her competitive streak a time or two—nearly lost my hand in a game of spoons—but this was getting ridiculous.

By eleven, we had another large lunch crowd. And like the two previous days, my tips were dismal.

I got texts from my sister and Sullivan, but I didn't have time to answer either one until after three, when my last customer left.

I pulled out my phone to call Jacks when Janelle walked in. "Hey, girl." She glanced at Roxy and her top hat. "Tariq said he asked you out? What are you going to wear?"

I headed to the office to make my call. The new kid was asleep on the floor behind the desk, so I nudged his rear with the toe of my tennis shoe. "Go help Ma."

He gave me a look of disgust and stood, stretching his skinny arms above his head. "All you guys do is ride my ass. Jeez." He shuffled out the door.

I parked myself on the desk and called Jacks.

"Hey," she said, "how's the car thing coming along? I talked to Allen and if you need a loan or anything—"

"No, I'm using Ax's car for now. I'll be fine."

"I want to remind you about dinner tonight. Don't be late or Mom will have a cow."

"Jacks, I'm not going to dinner. I'm too busy with this Janelle thing."

She tried for several minutes to talk me into it, but I held firm. I knew she wanted me to play nice with Mom. Christmas would be even colder if my mom decided to freeze me out.

"I'm sorry, sis. Not tonight."

I think she was a little ticked off I didn't fall into line.

My next call was to Sullivan.

Chapter 13

"Have you found the money?" Sullivan asked in lieu of greeting.

"Nope. Any word on who put out the hit?"

Predictable pause. "If you find anything, call me immediately."

"You could always ask instead of demand. And it's a two-way street, you know. If you hear anything about Asshat, let me know."

He hung up without saying goodbye.

I stared at the phone in irritation. He really was a jerk sometimes.

I walked back into the dining room and helped Roxy finish cleaning up while Janelle played with her phone.

When we were through, Roxy grabbed her fuzzy bear head purse and her long Victorian coat from beneath the counter. "Okay, losers, let's go find Asshat's cougar."

"You guys go ahead," I said. "I'll tell Ma we're leaving."

I walked through the kitchen door, heard the roar of the running industrial dishwasher, and found Ma and Ray standing toe to toe. Of course, Ray dwarfed her by almost two feet.

"We need more chicken and this was my goddamn kitchen long before you got here. Your father and I started this business, don't forget."

"Need room to bake the rolls," Ray rumbled.

This was an explosion waiting to go boom. Every day Ma bitched at Ray about trivial perceived mistakes—too much cinnamon in the rolls, not enough salt in the ham—and Ray always, *always*, let that shit slide. The fact he was speaking in words and not grunts was monumental.

I wedged my way between them. "Listen, you two." I tried to shove Ray back with my arm, but he was like a mountain. "We're not going to get anywhere unless we can compromise." I shoved at Ray again and this time he took a step back, but the low-browed scowl didn't disappear.

"Hate this lunch thing," he said.

"Well, that's too damn bad because we're doing lunch," Ma said. She tugged on her sweatshirt and adjusted her specs. "I'm going to crush Rudy's Roundup, and you're either with me or against me."

Ray made a series of unhappy, guttural sounds.

"Ma, is there any way you could cook the chicken the night before and warm it up?" I asked.

She crossed her arms, casting her eyes to the side, and shrugged. "Maybe."

"And Ray, Jorge could get here two hours earlier and help with the cinnamon rolls and biscuits. I know he could use the extra money."

Jorge stuck his head between the vertical plastic strips that blocked the entrance to the cooler. "That's true. Could always use more cash."

"Ungh," Ray said with a nod.

"See? We can all get along here." Crap, I was starting to sound like my sister, Jacks—the poster girl of diplomacy. "We're okay?"

Ma shrugged.

Ray lifted a shoulder.

Jorge exited the cooler with a grin.

The new kid was AWOL.

I left the kitchen and moved through the dining room. This lunch thing was putting us all on edge.

I shrugged into my coat and left the diner. The temperature had dropped and the sky was overcast. At least the weatherman wasn't calling for snow. Yet.

I climbed into the backseat of Janelle's PT cruiser. "There's trouble brewing. Ray was using human words."

Roxy turned to look at me. "Lunch is bullshit. I'm so over it, I could yark."

Word.

Huntingford Bank and Trust had two locations—one in the swanky part of town and one next to the mall. We decided to hit the swanky one first.

"Okay," I said as we exited the car. "I think one of us should do the talking."

Roxy smacked her gum. "And I suppose it's going to be you?"

Janelle put her hands on her ample hips. "Yeah, why does it get to be you?"

I eyed them both. "Because it's your ex-husband and you're too emotionally involved, and you," I pointed at Roxy, "look like the Mad Freaking Hatter."

"I have a certain style. Don't hate, hater."

God help me. I strode into the building and let them follow. The teller line was a short one. When I got to the window, Roxy and Janelle flanked me, but kept silent.

A balding man with glasses and a brown tie fluttered his eyes at us. "Um, may I help you?"

"I need to talk to Brenda."

"There's no one here by that name. Sorry."

That had been très anti-climactic.

We trudged back to the car and drove across town to the second location. "You going to forbid us to talk again?" Janelle asked.

"She's worried we might embarrass her," Roxy said.

I leaned forward in my seat. "Trust me, I quit being embarrassed by the both of you a long time ago."

This Huntingford Bank and Trust was located in a small building next to the mall, which was a snarling tangle of Christmas traffic. Which reminded me I needed to do some shopping, but not only was I short on time, I was very low on cash.

We entered the bank and the line was much longer here. I scoped out the tellers and decided to stick with the one who looked closest to Vi's description of Brenda. A white woman in her forties, well put together with a bob of brown hair, seemed to fit the bill.

Roxy smacked her gum and fiddled with her phone, and Janelle made a grocery list as we waited.

When we finally got to the front of the line, the woman smiled pleasantly. "May I help you?"

I glanced at her name tag. Brenda. Bingo.

"We need to talk to you about Sheik Johnson."

The smile faltered. "I'm...I don't. I'm working right now."

I glanced at the people in line behind me and then faced Brenda once more. "It's really important."

"Like vital," Roxy said.

Brenda swallowed. "Yes, all right. I get off in forty-five minutes. I'll meet you at the mall. The west entrance." Her eyes darted around nervously. "You have to go now. I don't want to get into trouble."

Once we left the building, Roxy heaved a dramatic sigh. "I'm supposed to get ready for my date with Tariq."

"And I've got kids to feed. Tariq will let them eat chips and cookies and they won't be hungry for dinner. Damn."

Instead of driving, since the traffic was insane, we hot-footed it over to the mall.

The place was packed tighter than Santa's suit after the holidays. Decorations filled store windows, and white cotton snow mounds and plastic signs pointed the way to the North Pole village. The line of kids and parents stopped at the foot of the food court where Roxy practically ran for a smoothie.

"Try this. Mango berry. Full of antioxidants."

"No thanks, I'll take your word for it."

"I need to bring Sherise out here. Let her get a picture with Santa," Janelle said. "Last year she got kicked out for biting him on the nose."

"Maybe she's mellowed," I said.

Janelle led us to Macy's where she picked out a long-sleeved polo from the sale rack. "What do you think, Roxy. Will Tariq like the stripes?"

Roxy handed her smoothie to me and took the shirt. "I think he'd look better in red."

"Red's not on sale," Janelle said. "I'm getting blue."

A harried saleswoman approached us. "No food or drink in the store. Get that out of here." She pointed at the smoothie.

"That's my cue," I said. "You better hurry, Janelle, so we have time to meet Brenda." I left the store and stood next to the railing, watching the kids take turns on Santa's lap. That always seemed a little pervy to me, hopping up on some old guy's lap and asking for gifts.

Janelle and Rox came out a few minutes later and we headed toward the west entrance.

I half-expected Brenda to be a no-show, but she arrived on time and sat down on a bench next to a cell phone cover kiosk. The three of us crowded around her.

"What's this about Sheik?" she asked.

I sat next to her and tried to put her at ease. "Why don't you tell us how you met?"

"I was at a bachelorette party. One of the girls at the bank was getting married and we all went to a club one night. Not my usual sort of place."

I smiled encouragingly. "And Sheik was there?"

She nodded. "He's so handsome and charming."

Janelle rolled her eyes. "Right."

I shot her a look. "So what happened?"

Brenda shrugged. "It was nice, having someone that good looking want me. Say hot, nasty things to me."

Whoa, Brenda was over-sharing. "I think I under-stand," I said.

She closed her pale blue eyes and took a deep breath. "The things that man could do with his tongue."

"We get it," Roxy said.

I snuck a glance at Janelle. She'd crossed her arms and pursed her lips.

But Brenda was on a roll. "You forget how much you miss having a man touch every part of your naked body."

"Brenda," I said her name sharply.

She opened her eyes. "Yes?"

"How long have the two of you been dating?" I asked.

"We'd see each other a couple of times a week. Things were great. Very…passionate."

"The two of you fucked like rabbits," Janelle said. "It was all real magical. Move on."

"Then he wanted to borrow money," Brenda said. "One of his kids needed surgery and Sheik lost his job."

"Oh, hells no," Janelle all but yelled.

Roxy elbowed her in the arm. "Shhh. Go on."

Brenda looked startled.

Janelle wasn't going to be able to keep her yap shut, so I went with the truth. "Janelle was married to Sheik and his kids are just fine."

"Oh," Brenda said. "Well, that's good, I suppose."

"So Sheik took money from you?" I asked.

"Six thousand and some change."

"You're not alone," Janelle said. "That's what he does best—he takes money from women."

Brenda raised an eyebrow. "I wouldn't say that's what he does best. He had this one move where he'd twist his—"

"Whoa, please," I said. "No more sex talk, I beg of you. Back to the money. Sheik recently came into some. Did he mention anything about that?"

"No. I actually haven't seen him in a few weeks." She shifted on the bench. "Right after I loaned him the money, he quit calling. I still miss him. I know now he was using me, but in a way, I was using him, too. He awakened a sexual side in me I never knew I had."

"I don't know how to say this, Brenda, but Sheik may have given you...," I winced, trying to find a delicate way to say the words.

"Gonorrhea," Roxy said.

Brenda nodded. "He did. And I wound up giving it to my husband."

"Oh, shit," Roxy said. "You're married? You don't wear a ring."

"Well, my little affair with Sheik put an end to it." She glanced down at her naked finger.

I touched her sleeve. "Sheik's in a coma. Someone attacked him. Do you know of anyone who would want to hurt him?"

She paled. "Just my husband."

After a little prodding, Brenda gave us her husband's name and place of business. And I added him to my growing list of suspects.

Janelle drove us back to the diner. She had to run home and feed the kids and Roxy had a hot date. I had no plans at all, so I swung by Crystal's condo, but she wasn't home.

I should have packed it in for the night, but I was feeling too restless to sit around the apartment, so after I grabbed a sandwich, I called Ax. "Hey, are you busy?"

"Hang on." I heard video game sounds in the background. "There, I'm paused. Never too busy for you. What's up?"

"I thought I'd head over to The Bottom Dollar. Want to go with?"

"Duh. Wait, I actually get to see the strippers, right?"

"I'm counting on it."

I picked him up ten minutes later and he came out of the house with his roommate, Stoner Joe. They clambered into the car, Ax sitting shotgun and Joe in the back.

Tall with long, greasy hair and a purple tuque permanently attached to his head, Joe never met a pot brownie or a bong load he didn't love. Don't get me wrong, Ax liked to spark up, too, but he could function. Had a job, friends, a life. Stoner Joe was just a stoner.

"Rosarita," Joe said, slapping my shoulder. "How's it hanging?" He made the whole car smell skunky.

I glanced at Ax. "Really? Did you have to babysit tonight or something?"

"Joe wanted to come."

"Like, literally." Joe breathed a wheezy laugh from the backseat. "Loves me some strippers, man. Titty power, you know?"

I rolled my eyes. "Okay, you guys act like you don't know me when you go in. Try and talk to the strippers. I want to know who Crystal's sugar daddy is. Ask them who's paying her bills, okay?"

"Dude, I've got bills." Joe leaned forward and stuck his head between Ax and me. "Gonna stuff some g-strings, get a lapper." He slapped the air with his hand. "Whssh. Yeah."

I sighed.

"Don't worry, Rose. I promise I'll talk to every stripper I see," Ax said.

Why did I think this was a good idea?

When we pulled up to The Bottom Dollar, almost every spot in the lot was full. I'd been here so often over the last few days, I was starting to feel like a frequent flyer.

Instead of walking in the front door, I motioned to Ax that I was going the other way. He nodded and waved.

I stumbled around the building. Sure enough, the smell of smoke tinged the night air and grew stronger the closer I got to the far side of the club.

The side door was propped open with a brick and light from the hallway cut through the dark. Three ladies stood in coats, puffing away, their smoke mixing with their frosty breath as they exhaled. Two blondes, one brunette.

"Hey," I said, with a friendly smile.

"Who're you?" one of the blondes asked.

"Wondered if I could ask you a few questions about Crystal Waters?"

The brunette's eyes narrowed as she inhaled. She held the cigarette aloft as she angled her mouth to blow smoke in the opposite direction. "Jess said you've been coming around, asking about Crystal."

"Yeah, is Jess working tonight?"

"No," said one blonde. "She's on a takeout. Should be back by midnight."

"A takeout?" I asked.

Blonde Number Two, as distinguished by her hot pink eyelids and matching nails, offered me a cigarette, but I declined. "Takeout is an off-site job, like a bachelor party."

I was learning all sorts of interesting, useless information. "Do you know the name of Crystal's sugar daddy?"

"No, she just called him Daddy," Blonde Number One said.

"Did you guys ever see him?"

The brunette shook her head. "Nope. He paid her bills, took her on trips, said she was going to quit dancing pretty soon. Stupid ho."

"What do you mean?" I asked.

"Guys always say that," said Number Two. "They're going to take you away from this life, buy you a house, marry you. It's all bullshit. Either they're trying to live some kind of rescue fantasy or they're trying to get a blow job."

Number One nodded. "Truth."

"Crystal never lets anything slip? What about her friends, does she tell them anything?"

Blonde Number One took a drag. "What friends? No one likes her. She's a stone cold bitch. Stole girls' regulars, stole their boyfriends, and offered extras, which made us all look like whores."

"What about any other boyfriends she might have?"

"Other than Sheik?" The brunette took a long drag. "She stole Diane's boyfriend right out from under her nose."

"That wasn't her nose, and they were engaged. Have a kid together and everything," Number One said. "Crystal dated him off and on for a year. Said bitchy stuff to Diane as often as she could. Just mean shit."

"Who's Diane?" I burrowed into my jacket.

"Diane Myer. You got a card or something I can give her? You'll get an earful about Crystal."

I dug out my little notebook and scribbled my number and fake name. "Here you go." I handed it off to Number One. "What can you tell me about Clay?"

The camaraderie we had going abruptly ended. "Nothing," said the brunette.

"He's scares the shit out of me," said Number Two. "And he makes Freddy give us a quota for drinks and dances, then takes forty-five percent."

"Shut up," the brunette said.

"What about the little skinny guy?" I asked.

"Stuart Weiner?" asked Number Two.

The brunette stubbed her cigarette out with the toe of her monster heel. I could tell she didn't like the way the conversation was going, so I directed my words at Number Two. The chatty one. "What's Clay's last name?"

"That's enough," said Number One. "We'll give Diane your number."

Both the blondes stamped out their smokes and all three of them stepped inside the building, kicking the brick away to shut the door and leave me out in the cold.

I wasn't much further clue-wise now than I had been. All I knew was that Crystal was some piece of work and the ladies were afraid of Clay. And the skinny guy's name was Stuart Weiner.

I texted Ax that I was ready to go and made my way to the front of the building. When I was done, I tucked the phone in my coat pocket and sniffed as I turned the corner. The frigid air was making my nose run.

I glanced up and saw Clay walk out of the club, his skinny little friend, Stuart, right behind him. Clay looked up, and when he saw me, he said something to his minion and pointed in my direction.

Oh crap.

Chapter 14

Either Clay remembered seeing me outside Freddy Libra's office the other night, or Freddy was a big fat tattletale and blabbed that I was asking about Crystal. Whatever, I must have tripped Clay's wire. Why else would he send Stuart the Weiner Weasel after me?

I started backing away, then turned and ran through the parking lot, using the cars as a shield. I ducked down behind a sedan and peeked over the trunk to watch Stuart slowly troll through the lot, turning his head left and right, like he had all freaking night to find me.

I crouched back down and tried to figure out what to do. But my phone started playing the *Star Wars* theme song—Axton's ringtone. Crap.

Despite the traffic zooming along the street twenty yards away and the muted dance music coming from the club, it still seemed really loud. I reached into my pocket and turned it off.

I poked my head up a bit. He stood only four feet away, right in front of the car where I hid. Damn. I slowly crouch walked to the next car, keeping my ears peeled for footsteps.

I kept creeping further away from the club, car by car. But when I got to the fourth car, I stumbled and set off a goddamn alarm. The loud blasts hurt my ears. I prairie dogged over the hood to locate Stuart and he saw me.

I took off running, looking over my shoulder, watching in horror as he gained on me. I darted in between cars and finally hit the center of the lot and pumped my legs as hard as I could. Why did this keep happening—people chasing me in parking lots? It was starting to piss me off.

I faced forward and continued to run, but skidded to a stop when a black SUV braked in front of me. The passenger door flew open and Sullivan sat behind the wheel.

"Get in."

I stared at him. Where the hell had he come from?

"Get in the fucking car, Rose."

I snapped out of it and ran the three feet to the car, jumped in, and slammed the door. Sullivan peeled out of the lot with squealing tires and sharp turns that made my stomach lurch.

Once we got on the street and he'd put some distance between us and the club, I glanced over at him. He was several degrees of pissed. With a clenched jaw and narrowed eyes, he stared straight ahead, refusing to look at me.

"Thanks," I said.

He didn't respond.

"Where are we going?"

Still nothing. And this wasn't our usual Mexican standoff, this was the silent treatment. But I'd been raised by Barbara Strickland, I could withstand *days* of silent treatment.

I pulled out my phone and texted Ax that he should drive his car home and I'd call him later.

"Can we stop and pick up a burger or something? I'm starving."

He did look at me then, his head slowly rotating to glare at me. Even in the dark, I could see a muscle twitch near his eye. Then he focused on the road once again.

I wondered if he'd been following me. I also wondered where Henry, his trusty sidekick-slash-bodyguard was tonight. But if I asked him right now, he'd just freeze me out. And I wouldn't give him the satisfaction.

Sullivan drove through the seamier part of town to a large brick building in the middle of an abandoned industrial neighborhood. He touched a button on his keychain and a door slid open. After he pulled the SUV inside, the door slid shut behind us.

"What is this place?" I unbuckled my seatbelt and peered through the windshield. The space was huge with brick walls and concrete floors. An old factory. "What do you do here?"

He turned off the ignition, then reached over and hauled me onto his lap.

I gasped and grabbed his lapels in response. His orange and sandalwood scent filled my senses. I looked up into his eyes and they were as dark as I'd ever seen them. And he was still mad.

He cupped my head and kissed me hard on the mouth. His tongue stroked mine. It wasn't a sweet, romantic kiss. No, this kiss was aggressive and punishing. He poured all of his anger into it, into me.

And I loved every freaking second of it.

I tunneled my fingers through his soft hair and tried to kiss him back, but he was too damn domineering, wouldn't let me reciprocate. So I just closed my eyes and enjoyed the ride.

When he finally came up for air, he thrust me back in my seat and slammed out of the car.

I did the same and scurried to catch up to him. He walked through the large room, toward the back and down a narrow hallway where he opened a door. Inside, Henry sat behind a bank of monitors that showed the perimeter of the building from various angles.

He frowned at me. "What's she doing here?"

"See anything?"

"No." Henry turned his gaze back to the monitors.

Sullivan shoved me back into the hallway. He strode further along the darkened corridor to a room on the right.

He flipped a switch and light flooded the cavernous space. It was my apartment times three, and all it contained was a metal desk, a laptop, and a sofa angled in one corner.

Sullivan moved behind the desk, typed on the keyboard, ignoring me. Did he plan on keeping me prisoner here? Well that wasn't going to happen. I had things to do, people to question, lunch to serve.

"So what's the plan?" I asked.

He still ignored me.

I hoisted my purse higher on my shoulder and walked out of the room. This was a crappy neighborhood, but Ax would come and get me. No worries.

I pulled out my phone and began a text, when he plucked the phone from my fingers.

I pivoted and glared at Sullivan. "Give it back." I glanced from his face to his clothes. He wore a smooth black sweater and dark jeans.

"No." He shoved the phone in his front pocket.

"You can give it back or I can take it back."

If he thought I wouldn't fish my hand in there and retrieve it, he was in for a big surprise.

I probably was, too.

"Now that might be interesting." He was still pissed, but there was a little twinkle in his eye. He was laughing at me. I hated it when he did that.

"I need to get out of here. Now, I can walk, but this is a very bad neighborhood and I know you don't want me to do that. I can call Ax to come and pick me up, but then he'd know the whereabouts of your secret bat cave. Or you could drive me home."

He crossed his arms. "Option four: I keep you here and out of my way."

I wasn't that wild about option four, but I wouldn't put it past him. I thrust my hands in my coat pockets and stared at him.

He stared back.

Oh good Lord, this could have gone on all night, so to expedite things, I gave in first. "Sullivan, cut the bullshit and tell me what's going on. Why were you at the strip club tonight? Were you following me? And why is Henry all black ops in that room instead of hauling your ass around town, like he always does? Who's been following you and taking notes? Where did the money come from? And where are all your other henchmen?"

"Henchmen?"

"Yes, henchmen. Where are they?"

He shifted his stance, his eyes hardened. "I cut everyone loose except for Henry."

"Why?" My brain began churning. Why would Sullivan get rid of his muscle? Someone was watching his every move. Someone who worked for him? "Did they turn on you? Is the hit an inside job? How do you know you can trust Henry? I never liked him."

"You're a pain in the ass." He sighed. "Come back in the office and we'll talk." Without waiting to see if I followed, he walked away.

Of course I trailed him. He still had my phone after all. I parked on the nubby green sofa and crossed my legs. "So, talk."

He sat down next to me, hunched forward, his hands dangling between his knees. "I wasn't following you. I came to the club for other reasons and saw you flying through the parking lot being chased by Stuart."

"Stuart Weiner?"

He raised a brow at me. "You've been very busy."

"Yes, and I'm not going to stop until the prosecutor drops the charges on Janelle." And until Sullivan was safe. But I didn't want to cop to that one. At least not out loud.

I studied his tension-filled face and bloodshot eyes. "When was the last time you slept?"

He laughed. "Don't remember."

"Tell me about Clay," I said.

He lounged back against the sofa as he rubbed his eyes. "Not much to tell."

"Why is he always at the strip club?"

I was cold now. I buttoned my too thin coat and pulled on my one glove, shoving my bare hand under my arm.

"He owns it. And he likes to keep a finger in every pie."

"I thought Freddy Libra owned it," I said.

"Freddy's a shill."

"The strippers are afraid of Clay. They won't talk about him."

He raised a brow at me. "That's because Clay Davidson is a ruthless motherfucker."

"You're not exactly a Sunday school teacher." I glanced over at him. Up close and personal, I could see the whiskers on his face. I fought against reaching out and rubbing my un-gloved palm against the roughness.

"He'd pimp his mother on a street corner if he thought she could make money."

That was pretty ruthless. And now Clay had seen me twice. Sent Stuart after me. That was a little frightening. "Maybe we should work together," I said. "Pool our re-sources? Share information?"

"We have separate agendas. And what resources do you have?" He shook his head. "Besides, you're a distraction I don't need."

I wasn't sure if I felt flattered or insulted. "You know Asshat's involved in all this. He had pictures of you, your itinerary. And what about Crystal? She's been looking for the money, too. Maybe she knows who's behind the hit?"

He stood. "I don't think so."

"Fine. I'll continue on my own." Dismissing him, I reached into my purse and pulled out my little notebook. I scribbled in the new info about Clay Davidson and Stuart Weiner.

Sullivan peered over the book. "Is that your crib sheet?"

"I have a hard time keeping track of all the players oth-erwise." I snapped it shut and stuck it back in my purse.

He looked amused. "Tell me who the players are in your little drama."

Now that just pissed *me* off. "It's not a little drama, jackass, it's Janelle's life." I hopped up from the sofa and planted myself in front of him. "If I don't find out who bashed Asshat, she's going to jail for years. I think Asshat was attacked because of the money. The money that leads back to you and the surveillance stuff I found at his house."

He sighed. "All right then, tell me everything new."

I went over Muffler Shop Marcus, Vi, the hairdresser from hell, and Bank Teller Brenda. "Brenda's husband is a possibility of course, but this doesn't feel like a jealous husband thing to me. The missing money keeps rearing its head. I think whoever hit Asshat was after it."

He stared through me. "And you say this Marcus is missing, too?"

"Well, he didn't turn up for work yesterday."

"Maybe he and Crystal took the money and are in it together. You said he gave her a ride from the strip club."

"Maybe." I tapped my chin and paced in front of the sofa. "Why would someone put a hit on you? Who did you piss off?"

He shrugged. "I have a successful business. If I'm out of the way, it's up for grabs."

His business? Illegal endeavors was more like it. Sullivan was a criminal. Period. Of course he would be a target for other criminals who wanted to move up the food chain. I forgot sometimes who he was, what he did. "What were you doing tonight at The Bottom Dollar?" I stepped toward him. "It's Clay, isn't it? Clay wants you dead. Clay wants your business."

Sullivan just stared at me.

I placed a hand on his chest. "My God, you're so stubborn."

He covered my hand with his own, stroked my wrist.

"Boss."

We jerked apart and turned our heads toward Henry, who stood in the doorway. "Just heard on the police scanner, the cigar bar is on fire."

Chapter 15

Sullivan swiftly pulled his phone out of his pocket, realized it was my phone and thrust it at me. I took it and slipped it in my coat pocket while he called someone. "What's happening?" he asked. "Do you know how it started?" His eyes narrowed as he listened. "I'll be right there." He hung up. "I've got to go. Henry, stay here, keep watch." He stormed out of the room and down the hallway. I had to run to keep up with him.

"I'm coming with you," I said.

"I think I should go with you, too, boss. This sounds like a way to draw you out." Henry followed us.

"I agree," I said. "Let Henry drive."

Sullivan stopped and I ran into his shoulder blade. I rubbed my nose and took two steps back.

"Fine," Sullivan said.

"Let me grab my stuff," Henry said.

I wondered if by stuff he meant guns and illegal weapons. I kind of hoped so. Made me feel safer.

I climbed into the backseat of the SUV and Sullivan took shotgun. Henry trotted toward us a moment later, pulling his coat over his brawny shoulders. I caught a glimpse of a holstered gun strapped to his side. He slid behind the wheel and when the factory door slid up, he backed out of the building.

Henry shifted out of reverse when I heard a deafening crash. For a second, I tried to figure out what had happened. Then I realized a bullet had ripped through the cargo door window and whizzed past my ear.

Sullivan threw himself into the backseat, tossing me down until I lay across the floor. He covered me with his body. "Get us out of here," he yelled.

Henry peeled out, balls to the wall. I heard two more pings.

Oh my God. Someone was shooting at us. My brain finally caught up to the reality of the situation. Took it long enough.

We raced through the streets, twisting, turning, with the wind whipping loudly around us through the shattered window. I felt nauseous and scared. My cheeks were cold, but the rest of me, covered in Sullivan, was warm. He placed his hand protectively on the top of my head, his other hand on my hip.

Eventually, he eased off me just a bit, his knee wedged between my thighs. "Are they still behind us?" he yelled up at Henry.

"Don't see 'em."

"Keep driving, make sure."

He moved away from me and the cold hit, making me shiver. He sat on the bench seat, poking his head up, looking out of the busted back window.

Then he faced forward, keeping his head low. I crawled up to join him, but he placed a hand on my shoulder. "Stay down," he yelled above the howling wind.

I sat on the floor but leaned my back against the door. What a crazy freaking night. I glanced at my phone and read the message from Ax. He and Stoner Joe were home, but hadn't discovered anything about Crystal from the other dancers.

After half an hour of circling the city, we finally stopped on a dark, deserted road. When Henry pulled over to the shoulder and the wind died down, quiet descended over the car. I blew out a breath, could see it fog in front of my face.

"What now?" Henry asked Sullivan.

"We need to get to one of the safe houses," he said.

"How do you know they haven't all been compromised?" I asked. I stretched my legs and climbed up onto the seat next to Sullivan. I ran a hand through my cycloned mane, trying to brush out all the tangles.

"I don't." He rubbed his forehead.

"There's no place safe, boss. She's right, we have to assume they're all a target."

"I know a place," I said, "but you're not going to like it."

"It's not much, but I've got some sleeping bags you can pitch down here. You'll have to use the bathroom upstairs," Axton said.

I glanced around the dated rumpus room. Red and white shuffleboard tiles covered each end of the long narrow floor. The walls were patterned in green and white checkered wallpaper that gave me eyestrain, and two burnt orange lamps hung on chains in opposite corners.

Sullivan nodded. "I appreciate it. But you can't tell anyone we're here."

Stoner Joe stroked a braided string on his purple tuque. He pointed at Henry. "Dude, you look familiar. Did I see you in an episode of Law and Order?"

I rolled my eyes. Poor Joe's brain was fried. I didn't think he was all that smart to begin with, but add in years of pot usage and he's were down to a handful of functioning cells.

"Ax, why don't you take Henry upstairs and show him the facilities?"

Axton glanced from Sullivan to me. "Right. Come on, Joe." I was surprised Ax didn't whistle and pat his leg, like he was calling a dog.

Joe shuffled after Ax and Henry. Once I heard the door shut, I gazed up at Sullivan.

"What's going to happen now?"

"Don't worry, I'll figure something out." He hesitated. "I'm sorry I put you in danger tonight."

Sullivan feeling guilty. That was a new one. And I realized he wasn't going to help me find Asshat's assailant. We weren't going to team up like Superman and Batman to stave off the forces of evil—oh my God, I was starting to think like Axton. I rubbed my temples.

I was on my own in the Asshat investigation. Sullivan had his own problems, but his new threat added to my worries. It was important to me that he was alive and well and involved in various criminal enterprises. Well, I wished he would get out of his various criminal enterprises and go legit. I cared about him.

Damn it, when did that happen?

I realized I'd been staring at him like he was an alien pod person from one of Axton's movies, so I looked away. "I'll bring sheets and towels tomorrow."

He pulled out his wallet and handed me a wad of cash. "Take this. Bring some food, too."

"You know, I think I'll start calling you the Bossy Jackass again," I said, tucking the bills into my pocket. That's what I called him before I discovered his name. Apparently it still fit.

"Do you want me to beg?"

I scoffed. "Yes, I'd love it. But I'll settle for a please."

He glared at me instead.

"Fine, I'll be by tomorrow evening." I moved to climb the stairs, but his hand snagged mine, pulled me back.

"Thank you."

I didn't linger. I was afraid I might hop on him and ride him like one of the strippers at The Bottom Dollar.

I jogged upstairs to confer with Ax in the dining alcove and looked around the house for the first time. Green garland, two decorated trees—with dueling themes of *Star Trek* and *Star Wars*—and mistletoe abounded. There was even a miniature snow-covered village set up on the dining room table with *X-men* figurines mingling amongst the villagers.

"Ax, it looks like Christmas threw up in here."

He shoved his hands into the pockets of his faded jeans and grinned. "I like it. It's the season of yuletide and cheer and all that. You need to give in, Rose." He unpocketed one hand and poked my shoulder. "I know you like, harbor the spirit of the season somewhere."

I couldn't even begin to think about the season and presents and cheer. I had too many problems. "Nobody can know that Sullivan's staying here. He's not trusting his own people at this point."

Ax nodded and stroked a patch of facial hair. "You got it. What else do you need?"

"Clay Davidson and Stuart Weiner."

I waited until he finished laughing. "Yes, I said Weiner. That's Baldy and Weasel to you. Anyway, Stuart chased me through the parking lot of the strip club tonight. That's where Sullivan picked me up."

"I'm on it," he said, still grinning.

"I'm going to get some supplies and bring them over tomorrow. You have to keep Stoner Joe in the house. He's like a geyser, you never know when he's going to spew out information."

"Yeah," he said, "I'll make up a batch of brownies and dole them out, judicious like. Just make sure you bring over lots of chips tomorrow. And Funions. He loves those."

I touched his shoulder. "Ax, I know you might have some bad feelings about Sullivan and you have every right—"

"Rose," he grabbed my hand and patted it. "He helped you, man. I'm not harshing on the dude."

Axton Fuller Graystone had the purest heart of anyone I'd ever known.

The next morning, I filled Roxy in on the excitement of the previous night. Except the kiss. I wanted to keep it to myself.

My tale was a long one and she had oodles of questions. We continued to talk as we got ready to open for business. "You can't tell anyone about Sullivan, Rox. I mean no one."

She shoved a second piece of gum into her mouth. "I got it. But shit, someone shot at you?"

"Say it a little louder next time. I don't think they heard you over in Kansas." I didn't want Ma to get wind of what went down. She'd only worry and she had enough on her plate. Namely chicken. She remained in the kitchen, stirring some chicken concoction over the stove as if it were witches' brew.

Roxy glanced over her shoulder to make sure we were alone. "You get so dramatic when it involves Sullivan."

"Not the point," I said. "You have to be discreet. Also, I texted Janelle last night after I got home. We're going to put some pressure on Sheik's brother, LD, see if he's heard from Marcus."

She grabbed the napkin holders on the counter and shoved two in my direction. I automatically began filling them.

"Why the personal visit?" she asked.

"He probably won't talk to us over the phone. Janelle threatened to rip his balls off the last time we saw him. We're going to his garage this time."

She made a face as she attempted to stuff more napkins than the holder could handle, causing one side to bulge. "What makes you think he'll talk to you in person?"

"I'm not sure he will, but we have to try. I stopped by Crystal's last night, but she wasn't home. And other than Bank Teller Brenda's husband, which is number two on my list of places to visit, LD's the only angle I can work right now."

She sighed dramatically. "All right, I'll come with you. You never know when you might need a little backup."

I gazed at the flounces, bows, and ruffles on her red and white dress. She looked like a five-year-old on her way to a birthday party, not ball-busting backup. But I wasn't picky and I knew how scrappy she could be.

"It's a date. Speaking of dates, how was yours with Tariq?"

"He's kind of awesome."

"Is he a good kisser?"

"None of your beeswax."

"That good, huh?"

Before we opened, I went to the office and roused Dillon from his slumber behind the desk. "Get to work, kid, before I sic Roxy on you."

Grumbling, he stood and ambled to the dining room. "This job is stressing me out."

As soon as I flipped the open sign, Roxy and I hustled. At eight, in the middle of a rush on eggnog French toast, a very tall man in his sixties with a potbelly and skinny legs thundered into the diner. With his thick mane of silver hair, coupled with his brown suede coat and western shirt, he had the look of a used car salesman.

Rudy Jorgenson—Ma's nemesis. The theme song from *The Good, The Bad, and The Ugly* ran through my head.

He pointed at me. "I want to talk to Ma."

Customers stopped eating and stared at him. There was an anxiety to the silence. We all held our collective breaths. In the corner, Roxy, her blue eyes as wide and round as marbles, stopped chomping her gum.

I kept my gaze trained on him, but kicked the kitchen door open with the heel my foot. "Ma," I called over my shoulder, "trouble's done come to town." I stepped aside so the swinging door wouldn't hit me in the ass as Ma walked out of the kitchen.

When she saw him, she placed her hand on one hip and sneered. "Well, well, well. Look who's here. Come to take your medicine like a man, Rudy?"

He took two steps forward and Ma mirrored him, until they stood a foot apart.

"You're trying to horn in on my lunch business." He nodded at me. "That little gal was handing out flyers in my parking lot."

I slowly stepped from behind the counter so I could be on hand in case violence broke out. Not that I thought Rudy couldn't fend for himself, but I didn't think he'd fight back against a seventy-nine-year-old woman.

Ma smirked. "You bet she did. And she's going to do it again."

The hell I was.

He bared his clenched teeth. "You're going to tick me off, Ma. And I don't think you're ready for the fallout."

"Get the little girl a tissue, toots. I think he's going to cry," Ma said.

Rudy pushed back the edges of his coat and placed his hands on his hips. "Don't push me."

"I'm going to push you right out of business. You're nothing but a snake, trying to steal away my breakfast customers. That was a mistake, sonny."

"Your chicken special was a mistake, old woman."

She squinted her eyes at the insult, causing her wrinkles to deepen. "You thought you could go against Ma Ferguson? You fool. I'm going to hang your ass out to dry. I own breakfast in this town."

Oh dear. I made a move to step between them. "I think there's enough room in this town for Ma's and Rudy's breakfast. There's no need for name calling."

She fixed her slightly mad eyes on me. "You going against me, toots?"

I backed away. "No, not at all."

Rudy turned his back on Ma. "Listen up everyone, it's buy one get one free on unlimited pancakes at Rudy's Roundup Restaurant." He whipped around and speared Ma with his glance. "And we have fruit toppings."

She gasped. "Well, it's buy one lunch special get *two* free here at Ma's Diner. And no one can touch my chicken specials. Certainly not someone who squirts ketchup on noodles and calls it spaghetti."

Rudy turned purple. "Choke on my dust, woman." And he stormed out of the diner, leaving the cold air swirling around our feet.

Ma glanced over at me. "Saddle up, toots. I have a feeling lunch is going to be hopping." Then she marched into the kitchen.

My gaze found Roxy's. She rolled her eyes and resumed chomping.

Chapter 16

We usually hit a lull at ten, but business was brisk this morning. Jorge helped us bus since Dillon was on chicken suit duty. At ten-thirty, Dane Harker walked in. Incredibly handsome, he looked like a fish out of water with his Burberry coat and expensive suit. He ran a hand over his short, dark hair as he wiped his feet on the mat. He stepped up to the counter where I'd just served a plate of eggs to an old timer.

"Can we talk?" he asked in a low voice.

"Sure, give me a sec." I topped off Bill's coffee cup with a smile before leading Dane into the office.

I stuck my hands in my back pockets. "Sorry I don't have a lot of time, we're crazy busy. Do you have news about Janelle's case?"

"No, sorry. I just wanted to let you know Penn's Cigar Bar caught fire last night. There's talk of arson."

I tried to look surprised. "Was anyone hurt?"

"No, fortunately. But since Sullivan owns it, I thought you'd like a heads up."

"Thanks."

"Are you still in contact with him?" he asked.

I shrugged. "He called to check on me."

His light blue eyes searched mine. "The police want to question him. He hasn't been seen for a couple of days. His employees don't know where he is. It looks suspicious."

Not only did Sullivan have someone after him, now the police wanted him, too. "How do you know all this?"

"There was a breakfast fundraiser this morning. The police chief, Martin Mathers, was the guest speaker. There was lots of talk about the fire. Anyway, I just thought you'd want to know."

"What about Janelle's situation? There are other suspects in Sheik's attack. Lots of suspects. He had ex-girlfriends with jealous husbands. He owed money to everyone."

He reached out and squeezed my shoulder. "I don't want to see her go to jail for something she didn't do, either. Shoot me a list of your suspects. And please, be careful?"

I thought it was a little lame I had to do his legwork for him, but if it helped Janelle, it was worth it.

Throughout the day, Roxy, Jorge, and I worked at a furious pace until our new closing time. By three o'clock, I was hungry, achy, and bitchy. Roxy was worse.

"I hate this. Do you know how much I made in tips today? Less than yesterday and I worked twice as hard." She grabbed a rag and wiped down the counter.

I stuffed sugar and artificial sweetener packets into white caddies at each table. "I know."

Dillon flapped into the diner. "I'm exhausted, man."

"Yes, I'm sure flashing your chicken butt and flipping people off was very draining," I said.

Roxy snort laughed.

Before we left, I yelled at Ma and the boys through the kitchen door. "See you tomorrow."

Ray glanced up at me, his brow so furrowed I couldn't see his eyes. Jorge threw me a tired wave. Ma sat on a tall stool next to a stainless steel countertop, with her chin resting on her palm and said nothing. This lunch thing was wearing her out. But she was hardheaded and wouldn't give in until she was ready.

Roxy and I hopped in the car and sped over to Janelle's. The kids were already home from school, but Sondra was there to babysit. Damon looked a lot better, but was quiet—an unusual state for him. Sherise and Sondra's boys were glued to the TV.

In Janelle's car, I sank into the front seat and Roxy slid in the back. She slipped on a pair of heart-shaped sunglasses and stared out the window.

"How are you holding up, Janelle?" I asked.

"Eh. Asshat's still in a coma. They're not sure if he's going to come out of it. I wished his ass dead too many times to count, but now that he's almost there, I feel bad."

"It's not your fault," I said. "And we're going to find out who did this." I gave her the rundown on the strip club scuttlebutt from the night before. Minus anything pertaining to Sullivan.

"So no news on Chicken Licker?"

"Nope, not yet. I stopped by her place, but no answer."

"Maybe we should head over to her house after we see LD," Janelle said.

I glanced at Roxy in the backseat and raised my brows. "Not sure if that's a good idea, Janelle. You and Chicken Licker in the same room?"

Roxy leaned forward. "We don't want you to get arrested. Again."

As we drove downtown, I tried to fit all the pieces into the puzzle. Crystal, Marcus, Clay, Stuart. These were my key players. I didn't think Vi or Brenda had anything to do with bashing Asshat. I still wanted to eliminate Brenda's husband as a suspect, and they all had motive, but I was convinced it had to do with the missing money. And Sullivan.

As we sat in early rush hour traffic, my phone rang. "Hello."

"Is this Jane?" asked a female voice I didn't recognize. One that sounded like it had smoked a pack a day since the first grade.

"Yes, who's this?"

"This is Diane Myer. Tracy gave me your number, said you were interested in information on Crystal Waters."

After a second, I put it together. Diane was the stripper with the kid, the one who lost a fiancé to Crystal. "Hey, Diane. I was wondering if I could meet up with you, buy you a cup of coffee?"

"Sure, I work tonight, but maybe we could meet around one tomorrow? How about McDonald's so my kid can play while we talk?"

I hung up and looked at Janelle. "Another woman whose man fell victim to Crystal's open door vagina policy. I have to meet her at one o'clock tomorrow."

Roxy popped her head between us. "How you going to do that? I can't serve lunch by myself."

I batted my eyelashes at Janelle. "Pretty please?"

"Shit, I don't know how to wait tables."

Roxy laughed. "If Rose can do it, anybody can."

I slapped the top of her head before she slid back in her seat. "I shouldn't be gone that long."

"I'll try. It's the least I can do," Janelle said.

We exited the freeway and drove through the downtown business district toward LD's garage. Buildings with colorfully graffitied initials and cars that could double as tanks lined the streets. Groups of kids in their teens, some in coats, some wearing nothing but baggy jeans and hoodies, huddled together on street corners. Then out of nowhere, suddenly Janelle stomped on the brake, causing me to slam forward and my seatbelt to seize up.

"What the hell?" Roxy asked.

Janelle poked her driver's side window with a yellow fingernail. "That bitch. See that hot pink Camaro?"

I looked where Janelle pointed half way up a side street. "It's hard to miss. Looks like Barbie's dream car."

"That's Chicken Licker's car." She wrenched the wheel to the right and rolled slowly toward the Camaro.

The car sat in front of a three-story brick building. The windows had been busted out and boarded up, the front door chained with a padlock.

"What's she doing down here?" I asked.

"Think she's squatting somewhere?" Roxy asked, peering up at the abandoned building.

Throwing her car into park, Janelle yanked her keys from the ignition. She got out and slammed the door behind her.

Roxy and I jumped out, too.

"Don't do anything stupid," I said.

Janelle slowly circled the car. When she got to the driver's side, she leaned down and peered through the window, angling her head to get a good look at the interior.

"Anything in the car?" Roxy asked.

"Empty Red Bull cans and cigarette cartons," Janelle said. Then she held up her key and gouged it into the door.

"Janelle, stop. This is a bad idea," I said.

"I know she hit Asshat. And now I'm taking the fall."

I glanced around but saw no signs of life. At least there were no witnesses. The afternoon light waned and a blast of freezing wind whipped up trash and debris, and left me chilled to the bone.

Janelle continued her trip around the car, leaving deep grooves in the hot pink paint. The sound of metal scraping against metal made my teeth hurt.

Why would Crystal leave her Camaro in the middle of this abandoned neighborhood? It was obviously her baby. She even had pink rims to match the car. Something was wrong.

Roxy pulled a screwdriver out of her bag. "Let's see what's in the trunk. Maybe she's got the money stashed in here." She stuck the end of the screwdriver into the trunk lock and wiggled it around until the lid popped open. "Fuck," she whispered.

A sense of dread washed over me. I slowly walked toward her and glanced into the trunk.

Crystal Waters, aka Chicken Licker, was dead.

Chapter 17

The trunk light cast a gray pallor onto Crystal's artificially tanned skin. Her long dark hair, matted with blood, fanned out behind her.

I felt sick and lightheaded. I heard Janelle and Roxy talking, but I couldn't stop staring at Crystal. Their voices seemed far away as if I were underwater. I swayed a bit. I'd seen this before. My psycho stalker. His head was bashed in like that. I'd been the one to do it.

Janelle reached out her gloved hand and shut the trunk lid. "We got to get out of here."

I still didn't move. Poor Crystal.

"Rose, let's go," Roxy tugged on my sleeve, but I stood like a wobbly statue. My knees trembled, yet I didn't move from my spot on the pavement.

Janelle grabbed my other arm and they dragged me to the car. None of us said anything on the ride home. I felt shocky, nauseous.

Finally, as we neared Janelle's street, Roxy broke the silence. "What now?" Her voice was barely a whisper.

"We didn't see anything. Nothin'," Janelle said. "Like it never happened."

"You going to tell Sullivan?" Roxy asked me. She leaned forward and said to Janelle, "He's hiding in Axton's basement."

Something snapped inside me. "What the hell part of discreet don't you get?" I lashed out, not recognizing my own voice. I pressed my fingers over my eyes and took a deep breath. "Sorry, Roxy. Sorry."

"It's okay."

But it wasn't. This was my issue, not hers. She shouldn't have told Janelle, but I didn't have to snap like a bitch because of it. I was still dealing with the fallout from what had happened over six weeks ago, and seeing Crystal's lifeless body dredged it all up again. The blood. So much blood.

Janelle shot me a glance. "What's Sullivan doing hiding out with Ax?"

"Someone hired a hit on Sullivan. For his safety, no one can know where he is," I said.

"Hey, that man got my ass out of jail. My lips are sealed. You got that?" She stared at Roxy in the rearview mirror.

"Got it. Jeez, I knew Janelle would be a locked box. It's not like I'm going to go around shouting it from the rooftops."

I tried to think, but all I could see was Crystal's unblinking eyes. Dead eyes.

When Janelle pulled into her driveway, she sat in the dark, gripping the steering wheel. None of us made a move to get out of the car.

After a minute, she glanced at me. "I can't go to prison. They're going to try and nail Chicken Licker's death on me, too. I need to take my kids and get out of here. Go to Mexico or something."

I shoved down the churning mass of guilt and pain and shock I felt, to concentrate on Janelle and her more immediate problems. "I'm doing everything I can to find out who did this. I talked to Dane today. I'm going to give him a list of suspects. If you run now, you'll look guilty. Please don't do anything rash." I pictured an armed manhunt, hovering helicopters, Janelle's mug shot plastered all over the news.

Tears filled her eyes and she nodded. "I'll hold on for now. But I'm not making any promises."

I shifted in my seat. "I'll go talk to that dancer tomorrow afternoon, then after I get off work, I'll look for Marcus. The last time you guys saw Crystal alive, she was with him."

"I can't believe Marcus would do something like that," Janelle said.

"He might if he thought he could keep all the money for himself," Roxy said.

I patted Janelle's hand. "Come to the diner at twelve tomorrow and I'll walk you through the lunch service. You'll be fine."

Roxy and I climbed out of Janelle's Cruiser and into Ax's Honda.

"I agree with Janelle," she said. "Her kids need her. If she has to flee to Mexico, I say we help her."

Frowning, I shook my head. "What if she gets caught? She's not a criminal mastermind."

"Sullivan is. He could help." I backed out of the drive and sped off toward Apple Tree Boulevard.

"No, Sullivan has his own problems. The hit, remember?"

I pulled into Walmart and together we shopped for what one man, one giant, one stoner, and one Axton might like to eat. Basically a lot of red meat and munchies.

I was on autopilot as I grabbed blankets, pillows, sheets, towels and toiletries. Flashes of Crystal shot through my brain. I could tell Roxy was freaked out, too. She remained silent as we moved through the aisles. Christmas merchandise, Santa figurines, and bright shiny decorations seemed inappropriate after what we'd just seen.

When Roxy and I got to Axton's house, we found him in the middle of a video game. Stoner Joe sat zoned out next to him on the corduroy couch, staring at the wall, his eyes glassy.

Roxy sat down next to Ax and I walked with the groceries into the kitchen. I was shocked to see Henry standing over the stove, wearing an apron that looked like a *Star Trek Next Generation* uniform. After flipping four grilled cheese sandwiches, he glanced up.

I set the bags on the kitchen table. "Where is he?"

"Downstairs. He's taking care of business so he may not want to be disturbed."

I walked closer and leaned against the counter next to him. "Who do you think turned on Sullivan? Had to be one of your fellow employees."

He lifted a shoulder. "Could be one of the bartenders or wait staff. One of the card dealers or croupiers."

"Basically anyone in the organization, then?" That didn't narrow anything down. "What's your gut say?"

"Don't know. But when I find out, that person will no longer be a problem." His gaze once more settled on his grilled cheese sandwiches. Henry was a very scary guy.

"Why doesn't he get out of town until he figures it out?" I'd been in such a panic the other night, I hadn't thought about the ramifications of bringing Sullivan to Axton's house. I hoped I hadn't put Axton and Stoner Joe in the line of fire.

"He doesn't cut and run. We'll find out who's behind this. And we'll take care of it."

Note to self: Never get on Henry's bad side.

Digging into the grocery sack, I pulled out a bag of Funions and returned to the living room. "Heads up, Joe." I threw the bag at him, but it bounced off his tuque and landed on the floor. He made no move to retrieve it. Those brownies must have packed quite a punch.

I headed down the stairs where Sullivan paced back and forth from one end of the shuffleboard court to the other, his cell attached to his ear. "Close it down. No games until you hear from me. I don't give a fuck. Close it down." He hit the end button and glared at me. "Did you get everything?"

I dug into my jeans pocket and pulled out the receipt and his one hundred dollar bill I didn't use.

He waved his hand, distracted. "Keep it."

Sounded fair, so I stuck it back in my pocket. "I have some bad news."

He sighed. "Is there any other kind?"

"Crystal Waters is dead."

Silence. "How do you know this?"

I swallowed and placed a shaky hand to my forehead. "Her body was stuffed into the trunk of her car outside an abandoned building downtown."

"How do you know this, Rose? Was it on the news?"

"No, Roxy popped the trunk and we found her."

"How did she die?" he asked, softly.

I hugged myself, rubbed my arm with one hand. "Bashed on the head." I felt cold and clammy at the same time. "Her hair was covered in blood." The red and white numbers on the floor became a little blurry.

"Are you okay?" He stepped closer and ran his hand down the length of my back.

I spun and swatted at his arm. "What kind of lame ass question is that? Of course I'm not okay. I saw a woman who'd been beaten to death. Why would I be okay about that?"

He stared at me, his gold eyes intense and focused.

"Would you be okay?" I asked. "Would it even bother you?"

He didn't respond. Not even a twitch.

"I'm not like you, Sullivan. I'm not a fucking robot. I can't see something like that and not…" Tears filled my eyes. I cleared my throat. "It's not okay for her to be dead."

His gaze never wavered.

Flushing under his scrutiny, I lowered my eyes, unable to meet his gaze. A sob escaped me. Then another.

He pulled me to him and cradled me in his arms.

I hadn't cried in over six weeks. Not one tear. Now it felt like I would never stop.

Sullivan stroked my hair, slid his hand up and down my back in a soothing rhythm. He was silent and comforting.

Eventually, I got myself under control and pushed out of his arms. With the back of my hands, I wiped my face.

"You have to come to terms with this, Rose."

I walked to the hanging orange lamp and brushed my finger over the glass globe. It was hot to the touch. "How do you come to terms with killing someone? Do you just wake up one day and it's over? You never think about it again?"

"You're alive. He's dead. And there's nothing you can do to change it."

I faced him. "I decided my life was more valuable than his. Why do I get to make that decision? I'm not God."

"He got what he deserved."

"And what about Crystal? She was a horrible person. Did she get what she deserved?"

"No."

"So where do you draw the line, Sullivan? Who gets to live and who has to die? Is it that easy for you?"

His eyes became shuttered. "It should never be easy. If it is, you're in trouble. But stop feeling guilty you saved yourself. You did what you had to do. Now get the fuck over it."

I scrubbed a hand over my cheek. He was right. My psycho stalker would have killed me and I fought to live. But hearing Sullivan's version of tough love wasn't pleasant. "You are such an asshole," I whispered.

We didn't talk for several minutes. Then, with his back to the wall, Sullivan slid to the floor, balancing his arms on his upraised knees.

I walked over and crouched down next to him.

"Have you talked to LD?" he asked.

"No. We were sidetracked by finding Crystal."

"I assume you didn't bother the police with what you found."

"No. That's the last thing Janelle needs. Speaking of the police, they want to question you about the fire. Your absence has been noticed."

"Where did you hear this?" he asked.

"Dane stopped by the diner to let me know."

"I'm sure he did." He glanced over at me. "I'll bet he couldn't wait to tell you. He still wants you."

I rolled my eyes. "I'm not discussing this with you."

"Do you know LD's address?"

I raised my brows and nodded.

"Then let's go talk to him."

"Are you insane?" I asked.

He gave a tired chuckle. "Maybe. Why?" The stress lines near his gold eyes fanned out like rays.

"You can't go wandering around. You have a hit out on you. You've suspended all your business, someone is double crossing you, and now the police want you, too. You have to stay here. Besides, I don't want you leading anyone back to Axton."

He shook his head. "I need to find out who betrayed me. Asshat had the money and LD's his brother. It's worth following up. And I'll be careful with Axton. You have my word."

I stopped glaring at him and stared at the dizzying green and white wallpaper. "Okay." I understood his position. If someone was gunning for me, I wouldn't want to hide in a rumpus room straight out of *The Brady Bunch*. I'd want to find the bad guy and put an end to it.

Standing, I held out my hand. He grabbed onto it and pulled himself up. There was a little spark where we touched.

He looked into my eyes a moment and jerked me into him, until my breasts brushed his chest. "If you hadn't killed him, I would have. And I'd have made him suffer."

Chapter 18

The temperature had dropped down to the thirties. My nose, ungloved fingers, and toes were freezing, despite the fact I'd maxed up the heater. I pulled the car into LD's apartment parking lot and was about to shut off the ignition when I saw movement out of the corner of my eye. "Look." I pointed to the front row of cars next to the building. Through the yellow glow of the parking lights, we watched Marcus walk inside. "Now we can question them at the same time."

Sullivan grabbed my arm. "Hang on. Let's wait a few minutes."

"Why?"

"I'd like to see if they go somewhere. And what are you going to ask them anyway, 'Which one of you killed Crystal?' Just give it a few minutes."

"What if they sit up in that apartment and watch TV all night?"

"Then we go up in an hour."

I shoved the key back in the ignition and let the car idle. "One hour."

"You need to learn the art of patience." He settled into the seat and leaned his head back. With his hands resting on his thighs, his long legs stretched out as far as the tight space would allow, he seemed perfectly at ease.

"Have you started emulating Michael Jackson?" he asked.

"What?"

He pointed at my hand. "The one glove. Trying to bring that back?"

"Funny. I lost it."

He resumed his watch on the building and I spent my time updating my list of possible suspects.

Little Donnell, Asshat's brother.

Marcus Walker, Asshat's friend. Together with LD, they were mixed up in some kind of stolen car parts ring.

Brenda, the bank teller. Asshat gigolo'd her, stole her money, and gave her gonorrhea.

Brenda's husband. Ended the marriage, maybe it wasn't enough (considering he also received the gift of gonorrhea), beat Asshat in a jealous rage?

Vi, the hairdresser. Also gave her gonorrhea, stole her credit card and left her with a hefty debt.

Diane, the stripper with the kid. Crystal stole her boyfriend, but how did Asshat and the money figure in?

Clay Davidson and Stuart Weiner, strip club owner and his sidekick. Not sure how they connected, either, but Asshat was flashing cash at their club right before his attack. Maybe Asshat stole Clay's money?

I re-read my short list, then carefully drew a line through the name at the very top of the list: Crystal, aka Chicken Licker, and sent the whole thing over to Dane.

Still no sign of LD or Marcus, so I played an online word game with Roxy in which I kicked her ass. Henry had made her a grilled cheese sandwich, and she had gotten a ride home from Ax.

After finding Crystal's body, I still didn't have an appetite. And all this sitting around left me too much time to think.

At close to an hour, I was ready to march up to LD's apartment and demand some answers. But just when I thought I couldn't sit there another minute, LD and Marcus emerged from the building and climbed into a dark Explorer with LD behind the steering wheel. "There they are."

Sullivan didn't say 'I told you so' but I could feel it.

I kept my headlights off until we hit the street and I tailed them down the Boulevard, trying to keep two cars between us at all times. It was harder than it looked, keeping an eye on LD's truck and the bustling holiday traffic.

I turned down the heat and shifted in my seat.

"You're doing well," Sullivan said. "Just stay with them, don't let them get too far ahead."

LD drove to the muffler shop, which was closed up for the night. Following them into the small lot was impossible if I wanted to remain undetected, so I pulled into a bar two doors down and parked facing them, then cut my lights.

"What do you think they're doing? They haven't gone inside."

"Look." Sullivan pointed and I saw a figure get out of the SUV and head around the side of the building. A minute later, the tow truck pulled out of the lot. The Explorer and tow truck took off in separate directions.

"Who do we follow?" I asked.

"We know where LD lives," he said. "Follow the tow truck."

"Try to keep an eye on him." I couldn't watch for the tow truck and merge into traffic at the same time. After waiting forever, I saw an opening and gunned it, pulling out on the street, and narrowly missed getting reamed by a minivan. But no sooner did I drive a few feet, that I got stuck at a red light. Damn.

"Don't worry, we'll catch up." Sullivan ran his hand down the length of my ponytail and tugged. I glanced over at him and he smiled. Boy, he looked good when he did that.

The light turned green and I sped through the intersection, wove around slower moving cars, and finally caught sight of the tow truck. At least I hoped it was the same one. I eased up on the gas and kept him in my line of vision, but once again put a few cars between us.

"I don't see LD's truck so I assume this is Marcus driving," I said.

"That's my guess. And if this doesn't lead to anything, we can always go back to LD's apartment and you ask him anything you want."

That made me feel marginally better. I liked having a backup plan.

The tow truck led us to the mall, which was even more crowded than it had been yesterday afternoon. Multicolored lights outlined the perimeter of the building and the light poles. I stayed two aisles over as Sullivan navigated the truck's position.

"He's turning left," he said.

I turned left and rolled through the lot, watching for hustling pedestrians and cars backing out of their spots.

"He's stopped."

So I did, too, and put the car into park.

Sullivan tapped the window. "Right there."

I unbuckled my belt and leaned toward him. My breast brushed against his arm and our cheeks almost touched. Being this close to him, I had to force myself to focus.

The tow truck backed up to a midsized sedan. Marcus hopped out and quickly hooked the car to the truck, jumped back in the cab, and sped off.

I glanced up at Sullivan. "What the hell just happened?"

"Marcus stole a car."

"Are we sure?" Even in the dark, I could feel his eyes on me.

"Only one way to find out. Let's head to LD's garage."

"Shouldn't we call the police?"

"No," Sullivan said.

I settled back into the driver's seat and re-buckled. "The same thing happened to my car. How is that owner going to feel, coming out of the mall only to find their car missing? And, of course, the police won't give a shit."

"Neither do I. We have more pressing matters."

I really hated it when he was right.

I slowly made my way out of the mall traffic and hit the highway, taking the exit for LD's garage.

I parked across the street. Five minutes later, the tow truck backed up to the garage and honked the horn. The bay door slid up and I saw LD outlined against the bright light.

Marcus slowly backed the car into the garage and LD released it from the truck. Marcus drove to the front of the building before walking into the garage. When LD slammed down the bay door, the street was dark once again.

"Janelle was right, Marcus is shady. So what now? We leave?"

"Let's wait a while longer. See what happens, where they go."

I crossed my arms and hunkered down. Even with the car running, it was still cold. "That's what Officer Hard Ass thinks happened to my car. Older cars get chopped for parts. It's so sleazy."

"There are better ways to make a living."

"You don't get to judge here. Your hands aren't exactly clean in the criminal department."

He slid his arm along the top of my seat, his fingers idly stroked my hair. "I don't force anyone to play. People want to gamble, I provide a service."

"It's that easy, huh? You don't take into consideration their families or the fact they could lose everything? That it might ruin them?"

"If they don't care about their families or their reputations, why should I?"

How could I argue with that? "Why did you go the criminal route anyway?" He was a smart, talented guy. Why not have a legit business instead of all the illegal crap?

He leaned toward me, his lips almost touching my ear. "Are you hoping to reform me?" His deep voice caused goose bumps to rise across the surface of my chilled skin.

Honestly, the thought never occurred to me. I knew I didn't have that kind of power over anyone, especially him. I turned my head and our lips were inches apart. "If I was going to reform anyone, I'd start with myself. And maybe get Ax off the doobs."

"What would you change about yourself?"

I studied his shadowed face, but in the dim glow of the streetlight, I couldn't read his mood. My breathing became shallow with him so close, our lips within kissing distance. I itched to touch him and gave into the temptation by rubbing the back of my fingers over his stubble-covered chin. "My indecisive career goals. I can't figure out what the hell I'm going to do with my life and I'm not getting any younger."

He laughed and leaned his forehead against mine. "Yes, you're ancient."

I moved my fingers from his chin, across the hollow plane of his cheek, and plunged them into his silky hair. "It's not funny." Touching him could get addictive.

"Come work for me." His thumb danced along my jawline.

I pulled back a bit. "Doing what, running illegal card games? I don't think so."

"I could always use an assistant. Or you could manage one of my properties. I have some legal angles."

I let go of his hair and put my hand back in my lap. "Thanks, but no thanks."

"Your call." He gave me a chaste kiss on the forehead before returning to his side of the car. "What do you want out of life?"

That was the million dollar question. "I'm not sure. I only seem to know what I don't want."

"That's a start," he said. "And you'll figure it out."

"What makes you so sure?"

"Because you're Rose Strickland, that's why."

Well, he had me there. Feeling restless and full of pent up energy, I shifted in my seat and watched the garage. Two minutes later, an SUV pulled up to the building.

"Someone's here." I shut off the ignition and sat up straight.

The garage door lifted and I got a good view of the chopped car. It was now a metal shell of its former self. The tires were gone, the doors were missing, even the hood had been taken off. "I didn't realize they could break it down so fast."

"Doesn't take long to get the parts they need."

Stuart Weiner emerged from the SUV. I'd know that slick-haired weasel anywhere. He approached LD and Marcus.

LD wiped his hands on a rag, pulled a white envelope out of his back pocket, and handed it to Stuart.

Stuart opened the envelope, appeared to check the contents, then climbed back into the SUV and sped away.

"A pay off?"

LD walked back into the garage and came out with two beers, handing one off to Marcus. The men drank and lit up cigarettes while Sullivan and I watched.

Fifteen minutes later, they'd finished the beer, but stood outside the garage talking when a flatbed truck approached. It backed up to the auto bay where LD and Marcus winched the car remains, hoisted some chains, and it drove off into the night. Then LD hopped into his Explorer, Marcus climbed into the tow truck, and they left as well.

"So LD's paying off Clay?" I asked. "Do you think Clay is the real owner of the garage, like he is with the strip club?"

"Seems like a safe bet." Sullivan pulled out his phone and said a few terse words.

I put the car in gear and headed for the highway.

"Before we go back to Axton's, I need to make a stop."

I glanced away from the road. "Where?"

"The police station."

Chapter 19

"Are you serious?"

"Very."

He didn't elaborate and I knew if I asked all the questions swirling around my head, he'd just ignore me, so I said nothing and drove to the police station.

"Pull around back."

I did as he instructed, but couldn't keep my mouth shut any longer. "What the hell, Sullivan? Are you going to ask for police protection?"

He hit the unlock button and the back door opened. A young, dark-haired man in a police uniform climbed in, slamming the door behind him.

"Mike Goedecker, Rose Strickland."

I turned in my seat. "Hey, I know you." This was the cop I'd talked to the day my car was taken.

He pointed at me and smiled. "Right, the stolen car. How's that going?"

"I think it's gone for good."

"Stolen cars are pretty common around here," he said. "But I know a guy who can get you a good deal if you're in the market."

"Goedecker, cut the bullshit," Sullivan said. He didn't turn around in his seat, he simply angled his head toward the back. "What did you find out?"

"You were right. Someone used an accelerant on Penn's. Your name's being floated around. Detective in charge wants to question you. Best keep your head down. Also, your guy, Marcus Walker, is a regular at the pawn shops in town. Has a record for unloading stolen merchandise. Anything from jewelry to tennis rackets to clothes."

"Good, stay on top of it. Also keep an eye on Donnell Johnson. Owns a chop shop off of Oak."

"Will do."

Mike was gone as quickly as he entered.

I twisted in my seat and stared at Sullivan. "You have your own informant on the police force? How much does something like that cost? I am so jealous right now."

He laughed before capturing my face in his hands and kissing me hard on the mouth. It left my lips tingling and my heart pounding.

"What was that for?"

"A consolation prize for not having an informant."

Consider me consoled.

The next morning, diner business was steady. By eleven, the lunch line had a waiting time of twenty minutes. Janelle pushed through the standing room only crowd at noon.

"What the hell's going on, Rose?" she asked, glancing at the mob of people.

"What?" I asked over the loud chatter. I filled two glasses with Coke, one with water and wound my way through the throng to the table in the far corner. Janelle followed.

"What's with all the people standing around?" she asked, raising her voice.

I set the glasses down and grabbed the order pad from my apron pocket. "Ma's doing lunch specials. Buy one, get two free."

"That's what we want," said the water man.

I jotted it down and smiled. "Be right back." I jerked my head at Janelle, so she'd follow me behind the counter. "Three lunch specials," I yelled at the pass thru window.

I stopped and took a second to fill Janelle in on the process and the prices. Then I let her shadow me for thirty minutes before I felt comfortable enough to leave her alone. "You'll be fine. Ask Roxy if you have any questions."

Roxy blew by us in a blur of black and white tartan. She slammed three specials on a tray. "So help me, if I get stiffed on a tip again, I am ripping someone's head off."

Janelle elbowed me in the ribs. "Remind me not to piss her off."

I handed her my pad and pen. "Good luck."

"I'm not sure I want to do this," she said. "Those people waiting to eat are getting their dicks in a knot." She nodded to the front door where two future customers glared at existing customers.

One of the men grabbed Roxy's sleeve as she passed. "Can't you hurry these people along? Those two are just sitting there, drinking coffee." He gestured toward Bob and Bob, two geezers who ate here every morning.

Roxy snapped her gum. "You don't like it? Get out. Go to Rudy's and choke on it."

They seemed shocked by her rudeness, then spun around and squeezed their way through the crowd and out the door.

I patted Janelle's arm. "I'll be back as soon as I can. Just try and hold it together."

I grabbed my purse and slipped into the kitchen. Ma attempted to haul a big tray of chicken and noodles out of the oven. I grabbed the hot pads from her and took it out myself, setting it on the counter. She must be a hell of a lot stronger than she looked, because that tray was heavy.

"Thanks, toots. My arms are getting sore."

"Where's Dillon?"

"He's not out front bussing tables?"

I didn't bother to bitch about the new kid. No time. "I left Janelle out there with Roxy. You might check on her once in a while. I'll be back as soon as I can."

She sighed. "All right, but hurry. They customers are getting restless. We're going to put that Rudy out of business." She didn't have any enthusiasm as she said it. She'd pushed the sleeves of her reindeer sweatshirt up past her wrinkly elbows and her normally spiky hair lay limp against her head.

I didn't know who would crack first, her or Rudy.

I left the diner and hopped into Axton's car, making it to McDonald's with five minutes to spare. Sick of chicken, I ordered a burger and fries from the dollar menu and walked to the play area.

Saturday afternoon and it was crammed with screaming kids bouncing in the balls and scrambling through the tunnels. Every table was in use—babies, diaper bags, and half-eaten food covered the tops.

But at one table near the tunnels, a thin woman with large breasts and highlighted hair wore a pink track suit.

"Diane?" I asked.

Without makeup, she was pretty. I'd bet when she put on her g-string and false eyelashes, she raked in the cash. When she stood, her zipped jacket rose to show a taut, tanned stomach. "You're Jane?"

"Nice to meet you." I held out my hand and we shook. Her acrylic nails were alternately tipped with red and green glitter. Very ho ho ho.

I placed my sack of food on the table and sat down. "Thanks for meeting with me."

"The girls said you were looking for dirt on Crystal." She pointed at the ball area. "Josh loves to bounce around in that thing. He actually takes a nap when we get home."

I watched a toddler with light brown hair pick up a ball and hurl it at a little girl in diapers. When it hit her in nose, she howled. "Yeah, he seems like a sweetie. What can you tell me about Crystal?" I dug into my sack and grabbed the fries, offering one to Diane. She declined and watched me nibble them, one by one.

"Crystal's a man-snatching whore. That's basically all you need to know."

"Yeah, I got that much, but I was hoping to get a little more. Do you know who she was dating?"

Diane raised one perfectly groomed brow. "Besides my fiancé, you mean?"

I nodded. "What's his name?"

"Brent Crandall." She sighed and reached into her Louis Vuitton bag. "Look, I'm not proud of this, okay, but when Brent left me for Crystal, I went a little…" she circled her temple with one finger. "I followed Crystal and took pictures of her. I thought if Brent could see what a slut she was, he'd come back to me." She pulled an envelope full of photographs from her purse and handed them to me.

I flipped through a stack of about fifty pics. One thing was apparent. Diane was a horrible photographer. Most of them were out of focus and the rest were headless.

I glanced up. "Do you know who all these men are?"

Diane shrugged. "Yeah, I made it my business to know. There were three of them. Some big wig cop, a body-builder at the gym, and another dude named Sheik."

"Hang on." I shoved a fry in my mouth then dug through my purse for my notebook and pen. I jotted Brent's name to my long list.

"Now, you said something about a big wig cop?

"Yeah, Martin Mathers."

Wicka, wicka, what? I leaned toward her. "Martin Mathers? Are you sure?"

"Yeah. He's like the head police guy."

He wasn't *like* the head police guy. He was *the* freaking head police guy. "How sure are you?"

"Really sure. They met at The Huntingford Motor Lodge every Wednesday. Three o'clock every week. He was in and out by four. But they were so stupid, they would stand outside the motel room door and make out." She reached for the photos and shuffled through them. "Here. It's kind of blurry. But Crystal's in her underwear and he's just standing there, playing grab ass for all the world to see."

I glanced at a photo. I supposed that blur could be a man and a smaller figure might be a woman. One thing was clear, it was time for Diane to invest in a better camera.

"They even used the same room every time. Number six."

I glanced at the photo again. So the police chief was Crystal's sugar daddy. And he was in debt to Sullivan. I wasn't sure what this meant to Janelle's case. Maybe nothing. I tried to pull myself together so I could ask a few coherent questions.

"What can you tell me about Martin?" I dropped the sack of fries on the table.

"He's an older guy, married. Bet his wife wouldn't want to see those pictures."

Fortunately for Mrs. Mathers, there wasn't much to see. I, however, could use a smoking gun right about now.

Diane turned her head and watched the ball area, then yelled at her kid. "Josh, quit throwing balls at that little girl."

I peered over my shoulder and watched him completely ignore his mother and continue to pelt the other kids, making some scream and some retaliate.

"Did you follow him anywhere else?"

"Just back to City Hall. That's how I know who he is. He parked in the spot reserved for the police chief."

"Tell me about Sheik." I probably knew more than she did, but it never hurt to ask.

"He used to come to the club after he and Crystal started seeing each other. And I do mean come. You catch my drift?"

Yeah, I got it. And it was gross. But I already knew Crystal gave extras.

"Crystal dumped my ex, Brent, when she started dating Sheik. Brent was devastated. I tried to tell him that's what she's like, but he wouldn't listen to me."

"Devastated how?"

She hesitated and I leaned forward. "I won't tell a soul."

"At the time, it ate me up with jealousy. Seeing how much he loved her. Brent's a liquor sales rep, so he comes to the club at least twice a week. It was disgusting, watching them together." She stared out the window, but I had a feeling she wasn't looking at the cars in the drive thru lane. "Having to drop Josh off at Brent's while Crystal was there, smiling, waving, playing with my kid." She snapped out of it. Glancing at me, she shrugged. "After Crystal broke it off with him, he got all pathetic."

"What do you mean?"

"He sent her flowers, candy, gave her hundreds of dollars in tips. Parked in her zone every Tuesday morning like clockwork. He went from boyfriend to customer. Three hours he spends getting all worked up while she humps him. But she wouldn't give him a happy ending, like she does for practically every other guy. And she laughed about it."

"That must have been really hard for you, seeing the father of your son acting like that with Crystal?"

"Yeah, you could say that. And she used to torture me with it. Made fun of me. Told me he was unsatisfied with my performance, that he loved her and he never loved me."

"I'm sorry, Diane."

She nodded and glanced at the kids playing. "Josh, play nice," she called.

"How long did this go on?" I asked.

"Until about two weeks ago. One Tuesday, he just didn't come in."

"Do you know what happened?"

"Maybe he came to his senses. We never talked about it."

"So who was the bodybuilder Crystal was seeing?"

"Kyle Amsted. He works at Fit and Flex." She flipped through the photos once again. "Here. Freddy gives all the girls a membership to the gym. Crystal and Kyle were going hot and heavy, always laughing and talking as she worked out."

I glanced at the photo, couldn't make out any details, but I dutifully wrote down Kyle's name. Not quite a suspect, yet, but Brent Crandall certainly might be. Another jealous ex.

"So whatever happened between you and Brent?"

She shrugged. "Even after I showed Brent these pics, he accused me of making it up, just to get him back. She was such a horrible bitch."

"Was?"

She blinked, her focus shifting from her son to me. "What?"

"You said was. She *was* such a horrible bitch."

"You know what I mean. She doesn't work at The Bottom Dollar anymore. Even Freddy got tired of her bullshit."

"Why exactly was she fired?"

"She made a scene when Sheik came in tossing a ton of money around." She grinned. "He picked me to go to the VIP room. I worked him up that night until he begged. And Crystal threw a shit fit. It was awesome."

"And Freddy threw her out," I said.

"Yeah. Then Freddy pulled Sheik into his office and the party was over."

I paused, a French fry half way to my mouth. "Freddy Libra asked Sheik to come into his office?"

"Yeah, that's what I just said."

"How long was Sheik in there?"

She played with the straw stuck in her large cup. "I don't know. I got busy with other customers."

"Was Clay there that night?"

"Um, yeah, I think so. Clay's there most nights. Stuart likes to get a dance from a different girl every night. And he never tips."

I felt her pain. "I heard Crystal went into The Bottom Dollar a few days ago and talked to Freddy." I studied her reaction carefully.

"Probably wanted to get back on the roster. But she's not there now, is she?" Hmm, no incriminating expression, no blurted confessions. Damn.

A young woman approached the table and addressed Diane. "Excuse me, but you need to discipline your son. He's throwing balls at the other kids and that's not acceptable."

Diane's face hardened as she stood. "Are you telling me how to raise my kid?" She wagged her sparkly-tipped finger at the woman. "I *know* you didn't just say I'm a bad mother."

I shoved the photos into my purse and grabbed my burger. I needed out of there before fists started to fly instead of plastic balls. "Thanks, Diane. I'll call you."

I made my way back to the diner. I'd only been gone an hour, but I was scared to see what had happened in my absence. I hoped the place was still standing.

Chapter 20

When I walked into the kitchen, Ray and Jorge rushed around furiously, getting out food, ladling chicken and noodles. Ray raised his head and spied me by the door.

"Get out there. It's gone nuts." Ray using full sentences? He'd passed stressed and was in full panic mode.

I hastily tied on an apron as I stepped through the swinging door into the dining room. There were now twice as many people as before I left. And no Janelle or Ma.

Roxy trotted up to me. "Good, you're back. Take over your tables, but I get the tips." She grabbed the coffeepot.

I jumped in and started serving customers. Dillon was actually bussing tables and wiping them down. Better than being stuck in a chicken suit, I supposed. Eventually, I noticed people traipsing in and out of the office.

I pulled Roxy aside. "What's going on? Who's back there?"

"Duh, Janelle." She grabbed four plates from the pass thru and whisked them off to the table near the window.

Ignoring my customers, I stomped down the hallway and barged into the office. Janelle stood against the wall and smiled, her arm thrown around a woman with short hair.

Ma held a phone in her hand and with her chin raised, she snapped a picture. "Oh, that turned out nice." She handed the phone to the woman.

"Thanks. Good luck on the trial."

I stepped in front of the metal shelves to let the woman pass. "What the hell is going on in here?"

Ma peered at me through her trifocals. "Glad you're here, toots. Roxy could use some help." She leaned her head out the door. "Next," she yelled down the hall.

A man in his twenties stepped into the room and handed his phone to Ma. "Just push this button." He stood next to Janelle and smiled.

"Say 'she's innocent.'" Ma clicked the camera and looked at the screen. She clicked a button and frowned. "Let's try that one more time."

I walked over and yanked the phone from her hand. "What is going on?"

Ma jerked the phone back. "Now the screen thing is off. How do I get back to the camera?"

He took the phone, pushed a few buttons, and handed it back.

"One more time, kids. 'She's innocent.'"

They repeated the phrase. Ma checked the screen and nodded with satisfaction. "Looks good."

He pulled a twenty from his pocket and gave it to Janelle, which she tucked into her ginormous bra. "Hope things turn out for you."

"Thanks, baby," Janelle said.

"Have you lost it?" I asked. "You're taking pictures with customers? You know that's going to wind up on the internet. Someone's probably already posted it."

"Hey, I'm getting twenty bucks a pop. I need to feed my kids and that lawyer you hired ain't cheap."

"Plus, we've doubled our customers," Ma said.

"This isn't going to make you look innocent, Janelle. This is going to make you look callous, like you don't care that Asshat's in the hospital."

She pointed a yellow nail at me. "Listen, I got laid off at the Quickie Mart after my arrest. I need to make some bank."

"This is not the way to go about it."

"You're interfering with free enterprise, toots. Move it along and send the next sucker in."

I finished my shift and handed the tips off to Roxy, which only further irritated me. Once the crowd cleared out, it was after four. Roxy counted her money while I flipped the closed sign.

"Did you know Janelle was having her picture taken with the customers?"

"Yeah, so?"

I threw my hands up in the air. "Am I the only one who has a problem with this?" My phone vibrated and I pulled it out of my pocket as I walked behind the counter. Dane. Oh, perfect.

"Hello?"

"Her picture's gone viral. What the hell is she doing?"

I leaned on the counter to relieve the pain in my feet. "I know it's not the smartest move—"

"Smart? It could tank our whole case."

I perked up. "You actually have a case? You've been investigating other suspects?"

"I just got your list and I'm going through it. But this little stunt sure as hell isn't going to help her."

"I don't control her, Dane. And I've another suspect to add to the list. Diane's boyfriend, Brent Crandall."

"Keep her out of trouble, would you?" he asked and hung up.

I flipped through my messages and read a text from my sister, Jacks, reminding me that tonight was Scotty's school Christmas pageant. I wouldn't miss his performance for anything. As an elf, he was very proud of his curly-toed shoes and pointy ears. Axton was coming, too. He and I were both alumni of the Academy, Huntingford's most prestigious private elementary school.

"I'm exhausted," Roxy said, falling into a chair. "Did you find out anything new from that stripper?"

"You won't believe," I said.

Janelle sat at the counter and stuck her hand down her shirt, retrieving wads of cash. "Give us the news, girl."

I began cleaning the diner and told them about Crystal's sugar daddy, Martin Mathers, and Brent, her humiliated ex who still wanted her back. "Diane hated Crystal, too. For good reason, but still."

"Eight hundred-twenty dollars," Janelle said. She slapped the bills on the counter. "Not bad for an afternoon. Bet those strippers don't even make that much."

"I still say this is going to end badly." The words had barely left my mouth when a short man in his forties with a military haircut strode through the door. Officer Andre Thomas followed close behind.

"Janelle Johnson?" The shorter man held up a silver badge he wore on a chain around his neck. It clashed with his rust-colored tie. "I'm Detective Bradley. I'd like you to come down to the station and answer a few questions."

Janelle's eyes widened. She was on the verge of running, I could tell by the way she focused on the front door.

I laid my hand on hers. "It's all right, I'll come with you and I'll call Dane." I kept my hand on Janelle's and addressed Officer Hard Ass. "What's this about?"

The detective did the talking. "We just need to ask Ms. Johnson a few questions."

Roxy sidled up to the men. "What about? She has a right to know."

Detective Bradley quickly scanned Roxy and dismissed her. "Ms. Johnson, Crystal Waters was found murdered. We'd like to talk to you about that. Your friend can follow along, if she chooses. But you're not under arrest at this time."

Janelle swallowed. She opened her mouth to speak, but I squeezed her fingers hard.

"She's not going anywhere until she speaks to her attorney." I finally released her hand and dug my phone out of my pocket. Of course I couldn't reach Dane, so I left him a message.

Officer Hard Ass watched me closely, with his cold, hazel eyes. Then he took Janelle's arm. "Please come with us, ma'am." By this time, it was obvious she was in shock.

"I'll call Sondra and we'll be right behind you," I said. "Don't say a word without Dane." I glanced over at Roxy. She clutched the rag tightly as she watched Janelle get escorted from the diner and stuffed into the back of the police cruiser.

"Is that legal? Can they do this? She's not under arrest," she said.

"I don't know. Do you want to go to the station with me?"

Roxy's face paled and looked ghostly against her bright blue hair. "Yeah. Of course."

"Give me a sec and I'll let Ma know what's going on." I walked to the kitchen and explained the situation.

Ma gasped and covered her mouth with one hand. "Oh my Lord. It was the pictures, wasn't it? I got her in trouble?"

I patted her arm. "I don't think so. Can you please keep calling Dane?" I programmed his number into her phone.

The dishwasher was running and Jorge banged pots and pans around, so I slipped into the pantry to call Sondra. She was understandably upset, but promised to take care of the kids until Janelle got home. If she got home.

As Roxy drove, I kept trying to reach Dane until his voicemail was full.

At the police station, in the little room across from the front desk, Roxy and I walked, too nervous to sit still. I kept texting Dane as I made circuit after circuit around the room.

Finally, after two hours, Janelle walked toward us. Her eyes were red and puffy from crying. When we tried to ask her about what had happened, she shook her head and waved us off. "I just want my kids."

"Roxy, why don't you drive Janelle to her car and follow her home." I dug out the wad of cash Janelle had left at the diner and added the extra hundred dollar bill from Sullivan. "I'll call you later."

I watched them drive off and texted Axton to come and pick me up. As I waited by the glass front door, I shivered from the cold air that seeped through the edges. Blue and white lights brightly outlined the gazebo across the street, but they didn't make me feel the holiday spirit. Janelle hadn't put Asshat in a coma and she sure as hell hadn't killed Crystal. But if we didn't find out who did, she was going to go to jail for both.

Deep in my thoughts, I nearly leapt off the ground when a hand touched my shoulder. I twirled around and found Officer Hard Ass giving me the hairy eyeball.

"You didn't leave with your friend?" he asked.

"You know, with detecting skills like that, I can't believe you're still in a uniform."

He hitched his fingers in his belt and rocked up on his heels. With broad shoulders and chiseled features, he'd be handsome if he weren't such a joyless human being.

"Some of the dancers who worked with Miss Waters said a woman matching your description has been asking a lot of questions. You wouldn't happen to know anything about that, would you?"

"Nope."

His gaze flickered over my face. "If I find out you had any part in this murder, I'll personally see to it you spend the rest of your life in jail."

Did that threat scare the crap out of me? Um, yes, but I wasn't about to let this guy sense my fear. "If you want to find this murderer, maybe you should be looking a little closer to home." Police chief, Martin Mathers, had just as much of a motive as anyone, the way I figured it. Maybe Crystal threatened to go to his wife. Plus, he was a crooked law man.

He frowned, pulling his lips against his teeth. "What does that mean?"

A honk sounded on the street in front of the station. I glanced out the door and saw Stoner Joe's small tan truck. I didn't bother to answer, but strode outside and down the steps.

"Thanks, Ax," I said after climbing in. "Oh my God." I held a hand over my nose. The whole cab smelled of skunk weed.

"Yeah, Joe likes to toke up while he drives. Which is why I hide his keys. Are you coming back to my place after the program? Henry made a killer stew and baked a cake for dessert."

"That just seems wrong somehow, Henry baking. And speaking of Stoner Joe, he looked pretty out of it when I came by the other day."

"Pot brownies do that to him. He's in like, a semi-stupor. But he's blinking again."

"I'll go back to the house with you. I need to talk to Sullivan. But first I want to stop by Brent Crandall's house."

"Who's Brent Crandall?" He pulled into the Academy and circled the lot for a parking space. Spots filled up fast. Parents and grands wanted a good seat to watch their little darlings.

"Diane Myer's ex-fiancé."

"Who's Diane Myer?"

We finally parked on the street. Hunched in my jacket and sporting my one glove, I walked next to Axton for three blocks. On the way, I told him about my lunch with Diane, the stripper with the sparkly nails and her burning hatred for Crystal, Janelle's latest run in with the police, and the Crystal's sad death. So much had happened in the last two days.

"That's brutal, man. Poor Crystal."

"I know. So what about you?" I asked. "How are you getting along with Sullivan and Henry as roommates?"

"Sullivan spends all his time on the phone and Henry cooks. Today he made me a turkey sandwich on homemade bread with this killer avocado sauce. And he's sent me to the store twice for more supplies."

Ax and I walked into the crowded auditorium. The public and parochial schools in town had cafeteria-cum-gymnasiums. The Academy boasted a state of the art auditorium with plush seats decorated with brass plaques inscribed with a donor's name on each. My parents' names covered twenty-five chairs. It was a status thing.

We snagged two seats in the back at the center of the row. I hated having to squeeze by people, waving my butt in their faces. But it was better than standing. And after working extra hours this week, my feet were sore.

I studied the program the usher had handed me. "Do you remember being in these pageants when we were kids, Ax?"

"Yeah, I was always the Christmas tree," he said. "I loved that gig."

I tasked Ax with getting the address for Brent Crandall and he went to work on his phone while I craned my neck to find Jacks and my parents. I had no luck, so I let my mind wander over Asshat and Crystal.

I'd been assuming this whole time Asshat was bashed over the head because of the money. But what about Crystal? She was looking for the money, but did she find it? Was that why she was killed? And by Asshat's attacker? Pretty coincidental to not be the same assailant.

But there were other reasons for each of them to be attacked. Sheik owed everyone money. And he'd been doling out STDs like the mall elves handed out candy canes. Lots of pissed off exes and their partners. Brent Crandall and Bank Teller Brenda's husband, for starters.

Crystal had her own enemies as well. Diane hated her. Hell, all the dancers hated her. Plus, she'd made a fool of Brent. He'd gone from boyfriend to customer, from lover to a guy she wouldn't get off. That had to sting.

She was with Marcus the night she'd been asking Freddy Libra about the money. Presumably the money Sheik had been tossing around. Why was she asking Freddy about it in the first place? And is that why Clay and Stuart were searching Marcus' house?

"Hey, did you get any info on Clay and Stuart?" I asked.

"Nope, too busy at work today. Servers down again," Ax said, not looking up. Then he nudged my arm. "Got Brent Crandall's address. After we talk to him I've got to get some of that cake. Henry called it Better Than Sex cake. We'll see, my friend."

I was still chuckling as the lights lowered and the school administrator stepped onto the stage. Mr. Frunk had been here since the beginning of time. And yes, his name was the constant source of juvenile amusement.

He gave his welcoming spiel to the crowd and then the curtains swished open. The elves carried brightly wrapped presents and twirled around the Christmas tree. Scotty leaped and danced his little heart out. I could see the gap where his two upper teeth should be. My God, he was the cutest thing ever.

Sometimes I wondered if I'd made the right choice, dropping out of real college and dating guys in garage bands. I could be Mrs. Upstanding Huntingford by now, with a starter condo near the country club. Maybe get a puppy, and in a couple of years, have a Scotty of my own.

The Scotty part sounded pretty sweet, but the rest of it was snooze worthy. I didn't want a condo or a country club membership or a socially acceptable husband. But what did I want? I couldn't see myself as a career woman, phone glued to my ear, or a stay-at-home, organizing play dates. So where did I fit in?

I needed to get my act together, that was undeniable. But how? Doing what?

I couldn't come up with any answers, so I sat back and enjoyed the program. Santa and the elves delivered presents to all the good boys and girls across the globe, as represented by kids dressed in stereotypical and racially questionable costumes. And then some little kid came out and spouted off about the season of giving.

When the lights came up, I noticed Axton wiping his eyes. "Were you crying?" I whispered.

He sniffed. "No. I have serious allergies."

"Since when?"

"Back off, Rose. That crap about the season of giving was touching. You're a scrooge, dude."

I rolled my eyes as we made our way to the cafeteria. Cookies and punch time. I could use the sugar. I hadn't had anything to eat since that burger from McDonald's.

As Ax and I stood along one wall, I called Janelle. Tariq answered the phone.

"Hey man, she's out. We gave her a shot of whiskey and she's been snoring ever since. Roxy's still here, though."

"How are the kids?" I asked. "They need anything?"

"Nah, man, we're cool."

As I tucked the phone back in my pocket, I spied my family near the cookies. "I'm going to congratulate Scotty."

"I'm going to find the Christmas tree kid. He did a pretty good job. But maybe I can give him pointers for next year."

"Meet you back here in fifteen." I strode past parents who looked like they'd come from work—suits and dresses with the occasional mom in a bulky Christmas sweater. I, on the other hand, was still dressed in the same wrinkled t-shirt and jeans that I'd been wearing all day.

I stopped in front of my family. "Great program."

My mother eyeballed me from head to toe. "Rosalyn, why can't you ever make an effort?"

Scotty threw his arms around my legs. He had red circles painted on his cheeks and black eyelashes penciled around his eyelids.

"Hey Sport, you were the best elf ever." I knelt down and held up my hand for a high five.

He grinned and slapped my palm. He had a fruit punch stain around his lips. Sweat matted his blond hair beneath his pointed red and white elf hat. "Did you see my dance, Aunt Rose?"

"Yeah I did. You rocked it."

"Why were you late?" Jacks asked. She looked very beautiful in a red sheath dress.

"Long story."

"Have a cookie, Rose." Allen handed me a gingerbread man wrapped in a green napkin.

"Thanks." I ate his foot and broke off a piece for Scotty. "You want a leg?"

He giggled and stuffed it in his mouth. Then a kid with a beret and a black and white striped shirt ran up and tagged him and Scotty was off and running.

"Good to see you, Rosalyn." My dad bent down and kissed my cheek. "How are things at the diner?"

I threw my mom a look. "You mean the small family firm where I work in public relations?"

Jacks poked me in the back. "Don't provoke," she whispered in my ear.

"Things at the diner are great, Dad. We're open for lunch now."

"How thrilling." My mother stood straight, her spine rigid, her coat draped over her crossed arms. "I assume you're taking more classes next semester?"

"Yes, Mom." I didn't want to talk about my education with her. It was a sore subject. That and every other topic I could think of.

The men started talking golf and shut us out.

"What classes are you taking?" Jacks asked. My sister, so well-meaning and yet so clueless.

"Um, criminal justice—"

"Planning on an exciting career as a prison guard?" my mom asked.

"Well, there is that anal cavity search everyone keeps raving about," I said.

Jacks pinched my arm. Hard. "Mom thought we should have Christmas Eve luncheon at the club this year, Rose. Doesn't that sound fun?" she asked through clenched teeth.

"Darn, I'm working. You know, since we're serving lunch and all." For the first time, I was actually glad Ma had the crazy lunch idea.

"Surely that woman doesn't expect you to work on Christmas Eve. That's Dickensian." Only Barbara Strickland could use the word Dickensian and not sound ridiculous.

"Well, she lets us have an extra piece of coal, so it all balances out. Look, I've got to run, but I'll call you later," I said to Jacks.

"But we haven't seen you all night. And I promised Scotty we'd all go out for ice cream."

"Her family is never a priority, Jacqueline. You should know that by now."

"That's not true, Mom. I'll explain later, I promise." I touched Jack's shoulder as I passed and went looking for Ax. God, my mother exhausted me.

I found Axton near the window in a deep discussion with a kid who looked about ten-years-old, dressed in green sweats.

"You have to be one with the tree, you know?" Ax said. "You have to feel it in here." He pounded his chest. "What's Christmas without a tree, man? You *are* the holiday, little dude."

The boy nodded. "I feel you."

"Ax, you ready to go?"

We wove our way through the crowd and stepped out into the cold. The half-moon hung low in the starry sky. The businesses along the street had painted their windows with Christmas themes—Santa, trees, holly. Hanging holiday banners flapped in the breeze. Ax was right, I was a scrooge, but I couldn't muster up any enthusiasm for Christmas. I hadn't bought one present. Hadn't eaten one candy cane. All this drama with Janelle and Sullivan dwarfed the holiday. What was the point if Janelle spent the rest of her life in jail or Sullivan was hiding from a hit man?

Chapter 21

"You ready to talk to Brent?" I asked.

"You bet."

We climbed into Joe's truck and my phone vibrated. "Yeah?"

"Are you coming over tonight?" Sullivan asked.

The words sent goose bumps up my spine and heated my cheeks. I knew he didn't mean it that way, like we were spending the night together, but his smooth voice asking me to come over made me wish otherwise.

"Yeah. Right now Ax and I are going to talk to a suspect."

Annoyingly long pause. "Be safe."

Ax took his eyes off the road for a second to watch me. "Sullivan? You know, for a bad guy, he's pretty okay. In fact, I'm cool with having him around. You know, in case you guys start hooking up or whatever."

I didn't want to talk about hooking up with Sullivan. It was too complicated. I flipped on the radio. *Jingle Bells* filled the car and Axton forced me to sing along until we pulled up to Brent's house—a nice, brick, middle-sized ranch with a three car garage.

"Being a liquor sales rep must pay pretty well."

"Nah, he inherited this place from his grandma."

"You got that from your phone before the pageant?"

He shrugged. "I'm just that good, man."

A light burned in the window and a big ass truck with an extended cab sat in the driveway. Nine forty-five was late to be dropping in unannounced, but tough.

I knocked on the door and felt someone stare out at me. Then the carved door opened, but the screen door stood between Brent and us.

"Who are you?" he asked.

He was very handsome. Tall, muscular, blond hair with all-American good looks, but he wasn't the man from the photo on Crystal's bedside table. Who was that guy?

"Brent Crandall? I'm Jane Smith and this is…" I glanced at Ax.

"Bruce Wayne. Nice to meet you."

Really, Ax? Batman? I refrained from a serious eye roll.

"I was wondering if we could talk to you about Crystal Waters?" I asked.

His eyes flickered between the two of us. "What is this about?"

Okay, hard part time. "I assume you heard about Crystal?"

He audibly swallowed. "Yeah."

"We're looking into her death," I said.

"Why?"

"We work freelance for an insurance company," Axton said. "Just want to make sure Crystal didn't take her own life. And, there's a double indemnity clause on her policy if she was murdered."

Wow, call me impressed. I couldn't believe he pulled that out of his ass. And he sounded so sincere.

"Crystal would never kill herself," Brent said. "She loved life. Loved dancing. Well, the attention, really. She was kind of an exhibitionist. Besides, she was found in the trunk of her car. The police said she was…" He paused and shook his head. "They said she had been hit. Shouldn't it be obvious she didn't commit suicide?"

"I know it doesn't make sense, but the insurance company has to be very thorough," I said.

He held open the screen door. "Come in."

He led us to a living room that hadn't seen an update since Grandma passed. Gold-leafed mirrors and floral wallpaper. He nodded at a seafoam green sofa. "Have a seat."

"I'm sorry about Crystal," I said.

"Yeah, the police called me this afternoon. A shock. We didn't date anymore, but I still loved her, you know?"

What was it about Crystal that had men falling for her? Besides her obvious physical attributes, of course. By all accounts, Crystal had been a mean girl. Maybe men didn't care about pretty on the inside.

"What can you tell me about Sheik Johnson?" I asked.

Brent's face changed from grief to hard-edged anger. "She broke up with me for that fucking loser a year and seven months ago."

He was still counting the months. Bad sign. I pulled out my little notebook and pen. "Tell me about her. Did Crystal have any girlfriends?"

He looked a little dazed by the change in topic. "She was straight. She might have danced with other girls, but she preferred men."

"No, I mean friends who were girls. Pals?"

"Um, not really. Other girls were jealous of her."

"She was very beautiful," I agreed.

"I know." He rubbed his cheek with a palm and rose. "Wait here, I want to show you something." He left the room and headed to the back of the house.

I turned to sneer at Ax. "Bruce Wayne?" I whispered.

He shrugged. "It's the only thing that came to mind. Jane Smith isn't exactly original."

Brent came back and handed me two photos. In one, he stood with his arm around a stunning Crystal. They were at the beach. Her body was toned, tanned, and stacked like a brick outhouse in a tiny silver bikini. She wore expensive oversized shades and diamond hoop earrings. Brent was obviously very proud of her.

Ax leaned closer to get a peek. "The two of you look very much in love," he said.

Brent sniffed. "We were until she dumped me for that asshole. I gave her everything she wanted. I told her to give up the dancing, that I'd take care of her, but she wouldn't do it. I could live with that. But when she left..." He widened his eyes to prevent the tears from falling and he sank back down in a chair.

"We heard Crystal was pretty brutal to you after you guys broke up. That you became a regular."

His cheeks infused with color. "Who'd you hear that from? Look, it's the only way Crystal would talk to me. She wouldn't take my calls, wouldn't see me. What was I supposed to do?"

"What about family?" I asked. "Did she have any relatives she was close to?"

Brent shook his head. "She wouldn't talk about her family. She left home when she was seventeen."

I flipped a page in my notebook. "What about your relationship with your former fiancé, Diane Myer? I know she was upset when Crystal taunted her at the club."

"What does my relationship with Diane have to do with Crystal's death?"

"Just background information, sir," I said. "Now, about Diane?" I looked him in the eye and tried to keep my expression neutral. I fully expected him to realize we were lying through our teeth and call the police. But he just continued.

"Diane and I were never engaged," he said. "We dated for six months and she wound up pregnant. Diane wanted a relationship, but I wanted to keep it casual. I take care of Josh, see him twice a month, but I never loved Diane."

Somebody give this guy a father of the year award. Still, he was a better dad than Asshat had been.

"And you met Crystal at the club?" I asked.

"Yeah, The Bottom Dollar is in my territory. I'm a liquor sales rep. Vodka. All flavors." That explained Crystal's bizarre vodka collection.

"I go into the club two or three times a week. Crystal and I started talking one day. She said I was a good listener."

"And you didn't think it would bother Diane that you were dating one of her fellow dancers?" I asked.

"I didn't really think about it." This guy's lack of sensitivity was astonishing to me. The mother of his child had to see him come into her workplace and flirt with his new girlfriend. That sounded very painful. And another good reason to keep Diane as a suspect. But what was her motive for bashing Asshat?

"After you and Crystal broke up, how often did you see her at the club? When you worked, I mean."

He blew out a breath. "Two, three times a week. And she ignored me. Like I was nothing." His eyes lost focus as he gazed at the green carpet. "I had to watch her with other men. Grinding on them. Shaking her tits in their face." His voice took on an angry edge. "And she just fucking ignored me. That's why I became her regular."

Not only wasn't he over Crystal, he was still bitter about their break up. But was he angry enough to kill her?

"Well, thank you for your time." I stood and held out the photos.

He took a deep breath and came back from the dark place in his head. "You can keep those, if you want. I have duplicates. Do you have a card or something?"

I patted my jacket and made a show of looking in my purse. "Damn, I must be out of them." On my trusty pad of paper, I wrote down my number and handed it over. "Call me if you think of anything else."

"When will I know about the insurance money? I'm the beneficiary, right?"

"We're not at liberty to say," Axton said and gave Brent a broad wink. "But you'll be the first to know our findings."

Back in the truck, I angled myself to face him. "We look nothing like insurance inspectors. I can't believe he bought that."

"People always want to think they've fallen into money. It's just like, human nature."

"So what about Brent? He could have hit Asshat and killed Crystal. He had motive." I buckled my seat belt and faced forward. "Jealousy."

"Yeah, that had to kill him, seeing her naked with other dudes. I think I might dig a little deeper into Crystal's past. Why wouldn't she talk about her family? And why did she leave home as a teenager?"

"Maybe her parents kicked her out. It happens." I was living proof of that.

"Maybe, but something smells off," he said.

"Before we get your Better Than Sex fix, one more stop?"

He dropped his head to the steering wheel and groaned. "Where?"

"Huntingford Motor Lodge, room six."

"What are we expecting to find?"

I slid my fingers over the old school metal key. "Probably nothing. I just wanted to have a look around. This is where Crystal and Martin Mathers spent at least an hour together every week." I slid the key into the door and flipped on the light.

It was every bit as tacky as I imagined. Ugly blue carpet, a polyester bedspread in stale hues of gray, a floating laminate desk.

"Okay, now what?" Axton shut the door and moved into the room. "Surely they clean this place at least once a week, right?"

"Maybe. Maybe not." I walked to the bed and threw back the bedspread. "Help me lift up the mattress."

Together, Ax and I hoisted the mattress and I checked underneath. Nothing. We let it fall back in place.

"I'll get the bathroom, you check under the bed?"

"Yep," he said.

I checked behind the shower curtain, lifted the lid on the toilet tank. This was a waste of time and twenty-six bucks.

"Hey Rose, bring me the roll of toilet paper."

I stuck my head out of the bathroom. "We are not stealing the toilet paper."

"Just toss it here. Do you still have a flashlight from the other night?"

"Yeah." I popped off the half-roll of paper and tossed it at Ax. "What are you doing?"

"Remember I told you that I've been checking for porn violators at work?"

"Ax, is there something you need to tell me?"

He scoffed. "Anyway, the philosophy prof digs these sites with amateur, hidden camera crap. Girls in bathrooms, dressing rooms. It's creepy. So I checked with some of my techie friends on how to tell if there's a camera in the room, because now I'm all, like, paranoid."

I dug out my flashlight and handed it over. "How often does that happen, people using a hidden camera?"

"More often than you think." He shut off the light switch and slowly panned the flashlight over the room. "Dude. You have to see this."

"I can't see anything."

"Don't move." He pointed the light at my face.

I held up a hand to shield my eyes. Then he was next to me, shoving the flashlight into my hand.

"Hold the toilet paper roll up to your eye."

I felt like an idiot, but I complied. "Now what?"

He spun me in the opposite direction. "Flash the light up there." He guided my hand.

"The smoke detector?"

He moved the light around, flashing it at different angles. "Do you see the light reflect back at you?"

I moved the light in a circle, beaming it on the detector. There was a little spot that seemed brighter. "Oh my God. I think I did."

"I did, too," he said.

He moved away from me and hit the light switch. "Now, let's check it out." He grabbed a chair from the floating desk and pulled it over to the smoke detector. He climbed up, pried the detector from the wall, and peered at the back. "Yep."

"Let's see." I grabbed the detector while he jumped down.

The camera was a small black square and attached to a circuit board. Bigger than a postage stamp, but not by much.

A knock sounded at the door. "Open up, please. This is management."

I glanced at Ax. "Shit."

Ax ripped out the camera and shoved it in his pocket. "Play it cool. Just maintain."

I rolled my eyes. "I'll be fine." I took the smoke detector and opened the door.

A man in a maroon vest and navy slacks with a severely receding hairline stood before me. "The computer alerted us to an error with the smoke detector. Is there a problem here?"

I thrust it at him. "Yeah, check the battery. It kept beeping every ten seconds. Totally blew the mood for this one." I wagged a finger at Ax.

"Yeah, thanks a lot, dude."

We shoved past him and walked at a normal pace toward Stoner Joe's truck. The manager watched as we drove out of the lot.

"So they have old fashioned keys, but updated computers?" I asked.

"Maybe it's a law. The detectors have to be monitored or something."

"Crystal and Martin Mathers had room six every week. Never deviated. So was he taping her? Or was she taping him?"

"Maybe a third party was taping them both," Ax said.

Chapter 22

We pulled up to Axton's house and he practically sprinted inside, convinced Joe had scarfed up all the Better Than Sex cake. I followed at a more sedate pace.

When I entered the living room, Sullivan waited for me in the dining alcove. "How'd it go?"

"Oh my God." Axton walked out of the kitchen with a slab of cake on a plate and a full mouth. "This is literally almost better than sex, Rose. You have to try this."

I glanced at Sullivan and saw a glimmer of amusement in his eyes. "Let's go downstairs and talk." He gestured for me to lead the way to the basement.

"Take a piece of cake with you," Axton called after us.

"I found out lots of interesting things today," I said.

Sullivan sat on a folding chair and crossed his legs. "Do tell."

I walked to a Chewbacca sleeping bag and collapsed on top of it. It smelled like citrus and sandalwood. I wrapped my arms around the pillow and gazed at Sullivan. "Your boy, Martin Mathers, was Crystal's sugar daddy. And Ax and I just checked out their love nest, better known as the Huntingford Motor Lodge. Always room six, which just so happened to contain a hidden camera in the smoke detector. What do you think about that?"

"You're sure about this? That it was Martin Mathers?"

I yawned. "As sure as I can be. He sleeps with strippers, he gambles. How can you trust someone like that?"

"Who says I trust him?"

"I thought you owned his ass. What with his gambling debt and all."

"Let me tell you about men like Martin Mathers. They play all sides. You can never trust a dirty cop. Not unless you have a lot of information that could ruin him. And even then, if a cop's on the take, you have to be on your guard."

"Do you? Have a lot of information that could ruin him?"

He raised a brow. A Sullivanism for 'duh, of course I do.'

"Well, someone recorded his little trysts with Crystal. That wasn't you, was it?"

"No. So what else did you find out today?" he asked.

"Crystal's ex, Brent Crandall, is one angry jilted lover. Diane, his ex and Crystal's fellow stripper, hated her guts. And the police know that Crystal is dead. They took Janelle in for questioning and released her two hours later."

"You did have a busy day," he said.

I rose on my elbow and watched him. "I've been thinking about your situation. Why would Clay go to all that trouble to put a hit on you? Why wouldn't he just have Stuart do the deed? Why outsource when he already has Stuart on the payroll?"

He stroked his chin with his thumb. "I've thought about that. Maybe Clay wanted someone down the chain so it couldn't be linked back to him. Or maybe he wanted Stuart's hands clean for some reason."

"No, Stuart is hired muscle, just like Henry."

"Henry's more than just muscle," he said.

"Do you two have a bromance I should know about?" I flopped my head back on the pillow. "I keep thinking about Crystal's ex, Brent. He went from boyfriend status to customer. That had to suck. Crystal dumped Brent for Sheik. Brent could have attacked Sheik in jealous fit and then when Crystal wouldn't take him back, he killed her."

"Jealousy's a powerful motivator. So where's the missing money in this scenario?"

"Crime of opportunity. Brent took it because it was there. But if Clay isn't behind the hit, who is? Just how many enemies do you have?"

He narrowed his eyes in thought. That was troublesome. Did he have so many enemies he needed to stop and think about it?

"Did you ever do something stupid over a girl?" I asked.

His expression changed and a grin spread across his face, causing little creases to appear around his mouth. "What do you think?" he asked.

"I think you probably ruined your rival's life and crushed his soul."

"That sounds about right."

"So, what did this girl look like?" I don't remember his answer, because I zonked out.

When I awoke, I was sore, stiff, and starving. I blinked at the sleeping face two feet away from me.

Henry was a drooler.

I sat up and arched my back as I glanced around the basement. No Sullivan.

A horrible stench rose from Henry's sleeping bag. The fart of death.

I scrambled up the stairs, readjusting my ponytail as I climbed. I walked through the kitchen door and the bracing scent of brewed coffee hit me in the face. I need a cup or six.

I glanced at the wall clock—five-twenty. I still had time to get to work.

Sullivan walked into the kitchen, dressed in the clothes he wore the night before. He looked good in the morning. The beginnings of a beard covered the planes of his face and his longish hair was in disarray.

"Good morning." He walked toward me and reaching out, brushed my upper cheek.

"Sorry I stole your sleeping bag."

"You were tired. I did all right on the couch," he said.

"But you stuck me next to Henry. He's smelly and he slobbers like a dog."

"I'm sure he'll be thrilled to hear that."

"Is Ax up?" I asked. "I need to bum a ride to work. I left his Honda at the diner yesterday and never went back for it."

"I'll take you. Want to run home and change first?"

Is this what a morning after would be like? Tender caresses and driving me home? No, in my fantasies there were way more sexy parts. Plus, I wore fancy lingerie and my hair looked fabulous.

"Yeah, that'd be great." I used the bathroom and when I came out, Sullivan handed me a travel mug of coffee. I would have kissed him if—A) we had that kind of relationship and B) I didn't have morning breath. So I said thanks and let it go at that.

Instead of heading outside to Stoner Joe's truck, Sullivan used the connecting door from the kitchen to the garage. I grabbed my purse and followed.

A black Mercedes with tinted windows sat where the SUV with the shattered back window used to be.

"When did you get this?" I climbed into the passenger seat. The interior smelled delicious. A combination of new car, leather, and Sullivan.

"Yesterday."

As we drove, I dug out my notebook and made a few notes from last night. "Feel like calling Martin Mathers today and questioning him about Crystal?"

"Absolutely not. And you're not going to either." He shot me a warning look that I could see, even in the dark. "He may be a crook, but he's still the chief of police."

He pulled into my apartment lot. Expecting Sullivan to wait in the car, I was surprised when he cut the engine and followed me inside. I hoped I didn't leave any unmentionables lying around. I peeked in the door before entering. No bras or panties visible, thank goodness.

Sullivan made himself at home on my futon while I took a speedy shower and threw on some jeans and a sweatshirt. For vanity's sake, I even put on a little makeup and lip gloss.

When I emerged from the steamy bathroom, Sullivan eyed me from head to toe. He also held my phone in one hand, wiggling it between his thumb and forefinger. "Roxy just called. Wondered why you were late. Your mother left a bitchy voicemail, said you were rude last night. Dane left a message and said he's looking into the list of suspects you sent. How sweet."

"Give me that." I made a grab for the phone, but Sullivan held it out of reach. I extended my arm further, lost my footing, and wound up sprawled across his lap. We stared at each other for one long moment before I hastily climbed off him and tugged down the hem of my shirt. "Give me the damn phone." I held out my hand, palm up.

He continued to gaze at me, his eyes turning to a darker, burnished gold before he dropped it in my hand. I grabbed my jacket and didn't look at him again as I walked out the door.

We didn't speak on the ride to the diner. But when he parked at the back door, he placed a hand on my arm. "I'll be busy today. If you find out anything new, call Henry."

"Do you really think you should be driving around in broad daylight? You're a target. And not just to the hit man, but with the police."

He narrowed his eyes. "I can't stay cooped up in that house one more day."

I understood his predicament and would have felt the same way, still I worried. "Be safe," I said.

"You, too."

I hopped out of the car and strode in through the kitchen.

Ray stood at the counter rolling out biscuits. He hadn't shaved. His shaggy mane was a tangled mess beneath his hairnet and his black t-shirt was inside out.

Jorge brushed glaze on cinnamon rolls. "Hey Rose. Ray and Ma were up all night roasting chickens." No wonder Ray looked exhausted.

I grabbed an apron and tied it as I walked into the dining room. Ma sat at the counter. With her eyes closed and her chin propped on her crossed arms, she snorted softly. Once again, no Dillon.

I gazed past her to Roxy, who made the shushing gesture. "She's worn out." She waved me over to the window.

I kept an eye on Ma as I walked from behind the counter. "How long has she been like that?"

"Half an hour. I didn't have the heart to wake her." Then she smacked my arm. "You had sex with Sullivan and didn't tell me? WTF, Rose?"

"I didn't have sex with him," I kept my voice low.

"Then why did he answer your phone this morning?" she hissed.

"Because he's an intrusive ass. And what about you and Tariq?"

Her cheeks turned red, clashing with her blue hair. "Not yet."

I raised a brow. "Oh, really?"

"Fine, not technically."

I wasn't sure what that meant, but before I could question her further, Ma suddenly popped up. "What?" She whipped her head around and spied us. "What happened?"

"You took a snooze, Ma," I said.

She sniffed and rubbed her tired eyes beneath her frames. "I don't have time to snooze. I've got chicken and rice to get in the oven." She slid off her stool and slowly made her way to the kitchen.

"I'm worried about her," Roxy said.

"Me, too. She's not going to be able to keep up this crazy pace."

Roxy smacked her gum. "She won't listen to us. Rudy's going to have to call off this breakfast crap first."

After I rousted Dillon from the office, Roxy and I plucked the chairs from the tables. By the time we flipped the open sign, customers were lined up.

We busted our humps serving breakfast and lunch, and by the end of my shift, I was tired and hungry. I didn't even have time for my breakfast omelet.

Jorge stepped out of the kitchen, tossed a dish towel over his shoulder. "Hey girls, I'm worried about Ma and this lunch thing. She was up all night and I don't know how much longer she can keep up the pace."

"I know," I said. "I'm worried, too."

"She reminds me of my abuela," he said. "Loud and feisty. She needs to slow down."

"But she's so stubborn, and Rudy is such an ass, I don't see either one of them giving in," Roxy said. She plopped down on a chair and pulled her tips out of her pocket. "I don't know how much longer I can do this. I'm going to have to pick up a second job or Ma's going to have to quit giving away food."

Jorge patted her shoulder on his way to the kitchen.

I whipped out my phone and glanced at my messages. One from my mother, one from Janelle, one from Jacks. I called Janelle first.

"Rose, it's not good news. Dane says they might arrest me for Chicken Licker's murder any second. But I'm not guilty and I'm not taking a damn plea. I think I might head out of state tonight."

"Janelle, no. Please don't do anything rash. After work I was going to question Brenda's husband, Dave. Then I was going to hit some pawn shops, see if Marcus has been around."

"Why the pawn shops?" she asked.

"Marcus steals cars, chops them. I think whatever he finds in the cars, he takes to pawn shops."

Frankly, I was desperate, but I didn't want to tell her that. My theory was if Marcus had pawned something he stole, it might be enough to get him arrested, and then maybe the cops would start looking at someone besides Janelle for Crystal's murder. After all, he was with her a couple days before she died. It was a pretty crappy theory, but it was all I had.

"I'm going with you, Rose," Janelle said. "This is my life, and I can't leave everything to you."

"Please, just stay home with the kids."

"No, I have to do something," she said. "I can't sit around this house. I'm going crazy." She and Sullivan had something in common.

Then she began sobbing. Janelle was the toughest person I knew. To hear her cry like that ripped at me.

"We're going to find who did this, okay? I'll pick you up after I get off work."

I hung up and found Roxy staring at me. "Things aren't looking good for her, are they?"

I shook my head. "No."

Next, I called Jacks.

"Hey, wanted to remind you about the cookie exchange Tuesday night," she said.

Crap. Every year, my sister and her friends got together, drank too much eggnog, bitched about their overworked doctor husbands, and tried to out-Martha each other in the cookie department. Me? I stopped at the Walmart bakery and bought thirteen dozen sugar cookies.

"Jacks, with all that's going on right now with Janelle, I'm not sure I can make it."

"Oh." There was a lot of judgment and hurt in that little word.

"It's not that I don't want to be there—"

"No, I get it. It's a stupid party. You've got more important things to do. Don't worry about it." Her pitch rose with each word.

"I'll be there."

"It's fine. I'll talk to you later." She hung up.

"Shit."

"What's wrong?" Roxy asked.

"Christmas sucks," I said. "And I have to go to the cookie exchange party."

She curled her lip. "Gross."

I decided not to return my mother's call. Between my sister and Janelle, I couldn't add Barbara's drama to the mix. Not today.

Roxy and I scrambled to clean the diner and headed out at four. Before I left, I grabbed the yellow pages from under the counter. I needed the addresses for the pawn shops in town.

We climbed into the Honda and I let it heat up. The day was cold and overcast. So far we'd only had the occasional flurry, but I had a feeling the real stuff was on the way.

"Before we go to Janelle's, I need to swing by Rudy's," I said.

Roxy raised a brow. "What's your plan? Going to have a shootout?"

"I'm hoping for a cease fire."

I drove to Rudy's and pulled around the back of the strip mall. I hopped out of the car, Roxy hot on my heels.

"I hope this is a good idea," she said.

Me, too. I knocked on what I assumed was the kitchen door.

A skinny guy in his late twenties opened it. "Who are you?"

"Let me talk to one of your waitresses. I'm from Ma's diner and I come in peace." I held up Spock fingers. *Thanks, Ax.*

"Hang on." He shut the door in my face.

A moment later, it opened again and a red-haired woman with bright orange lipstick stepped outside. She wore a blue Rudy's uniform with a flared skirt and fringe on the sleeves. Thank God Ma let us wear what we wanted. Roxy would be stifled in a dress like this.

"Who are you?" she asked. Her gaze trailed over Roxy's purple dress and the layers of lacy petticoats.

"I'm Rose, this is Roxy. We work at Ma's Diner."

"I'm Sarah. What can I do for you?" She hiked a thumb over her shoulder. "I've got a full house, so make it quick."

"Do you like this breakfast situation?"

She sighed. "No. I've got a kid in grade school and I have to drop him off at my mom's at five-thirty every morning. I'm thinking about looking for a new job."

"How's breakfast going? You guys breaking even?"

She scoffed. "Are you joking? Rudy's giving it away like the town whore. Free pancakes—which are cheap enough—but when people eat stacks and stacks of 'em, it adds up. And the fruit toppings are expensive, especially the blueberries."

I nodded. "Yeah, likewise with lunch. I suggest we pool our staff and have a little sit down with Ma and Rudy. You think if she backs off of lunch, he'll give up breakfast?"

She looked skeptical. "I don't know. He's a stubborn bastard."

"Yeah, Ma, too."

"Let me feel him out and I'll call you." We exchanged numbers and I climbed into the car.

"Think it will work?" Roxy asked.

"Hope so. Lunch is wearing Ma out."

She patted my head. "You're such a little peacemaker."

Chapter 23

Dave Hutchens worked at Watley's, an upscale grocery store on the ritzy side of town. I never shopped here. Too expensive. Muzak played over the sound system—an upbeat version of *O Little Town of Bethlehem.*

Roxy hummed along as she, Janelle, and I cut through the bakery aisle to the meat department. I took in all the artisan breads. Smelled heavenly.

The end caps were filled with Christmas baking supplies which reminded me that I needed to buy some sugar cookies. If I waited until the last minute, I'd be stuck taking off brand Oreos. Then Jacks would really be pissed.

We stopped at the meat counter where two burly men in bloody smocks and latex gloves helped customers. I grabbed a number tab from the top of the counter. Lucky thirteen.

"Who the hell can afford to shop here?" Janelle asked. "Look at that turkey. It's all organic and skinny and shit. Looks more like a chicken than a turkey. Costs three times as much as a butterball."

Roxy groaned. "Please don't mention chicken. I can't take it."

We had a five minute wait, and when a man with frizzy hair and a mustache called our number, all three of us stepped forward.

"We're looking for Dave Hutchens," I said.

"He's in the back. Can I help you with something?"

"Nah, we need to talk to Dave. It's important," Janelle said.

The man went behind the glass and spoke to one of the two men using cleavers to hack away at a hunk of beef. He put down his cleaver and wiped his bloodied hands on his apron.

He frowned as he approached us. "What can I do for you?"

Dave Hutchins was pleasant looking. Late forties, had most of his salt-and-pepper hair. Nothing to get worked up over, but not bad. No wonder Brenda fell for Sheik and his seductive moves.

"We'd like to speak to you in private, if we could," I said. "It's about Brenda."

The frown deepened, causing lines to form across his forehead. "What about Brenda? Is she all right?"

I glanced around at the customers waiting for service. The girls and I were quickly getting hemmed in by all the grocery carts. "We need some privacy."

"Come on." He moved around the counter and led us through the store, through the employees only door, toward the loading dock. The doors were closed, but it was still cold.

He pulled a cigarette from his pocket and lit up. "Not supposed to do this here, but what the hell, right?"

Roxy closed her eyes and took in a lungful of secondhand smoke. "Mmmm."

I nudged her arm. "Focus." Then I turned to Dave. "Mr. Hutchins, we're looking into the attack on Sheik Johnson."

He frowned again. "That asshole slept with my wife." He threw down the smoke and twisted his shoe over it. "What is this about? I thought you had a message from Brenda."

Janelle and I exchanged glances. "Not exactly," she said. "Sheik's my ex-husband."

Dave laughed without humor. "You have my sympathy."

"I guess you must have been pretty angry when you found out not only did Brenda have an affair with Sheik, but she gave him money, too."

He shifted from slightly tense to a defensive posture, stood straighter, hands fisted at his sides. "What the hell? What money?"

Whoops. "Brenda loaned Sheik money. I guess you didn't know."

He gazed a stack of wood pallets. "You're telling me that everything we worked for, all the years of saving to retire a little early, and she just gives that fucker money?"

"Must have sucked. Knowing Brenda gave her lover money and in return he gave her the clap," Roxy said.

I elbowed her in the side.

"What?" she asked. "It's all true."

Dave's color became mottled. "Brenda and I have been married twenty years. Twenty goddamned years. And she pisses it all away. Says she's in love with this new guy." He turned to Janelle. "Your husband."

"Ex," she said.

Dave didn't let her correction stop him. "Said she's going to leave me for him." He pointed a thumb at his chest. "What about me? Am I disposable? She's tired of me, so she can just throw me away?"

Dave's anger was palpable. I took an involuntary step backward.

"Where were you last Saturday night?" I asked.

"Around one a.m.," Janelle said.

He was breathing heavily, a bulging vein in his neck fluttered. "I don't have to tell you shit. Get out of here. All of you. And the next time you see Brenda, tell her I'm not giving her a dime. And I'm taking the boat." He stomped off, kicking out a stack of cardboard boxes, sending them crashing to the concrete floor.

"Wow, I thought Brent Crandall had anger issues."

"Wait, who's that again?" Janelle asked.

As we walked back to the car, I reminded her about Brent and gave them the lowdown on how angry he was at losing Crystal. I also told them about the hidden camera, secret tryst, police chief connection to Crystal.

"What a mess. Asshat and Chicken Licker deserved each other," Janelle said. "But finding her dead, it's stuck with me, you know?"

Roxy nodded. "Me, too. I dreamed about it last night."

I didn't want to talk about it, so I changed the subject. "Dave Hutchins was certainly angry enough to hit Asshat. His wife was having an affair and the whole STD scenario, but what would his motive be for killing Crystal?"

Roxy and Janelle both shrugged.

Yeah, my thoughts exactly. I mentally crossed him off my suspect list.

In the car, I grabbed the yellow pages and handed them to Janelle. "Let's start hitting the pawn shops," I said. I wasn't sure how late they stayed open, and it was already five o'clock.

Turns out, some pawn shops stayed open until midnight. Since I'd never been in one, at first I found myself spellbound by the disparate and bizarre array of items. Rifles lined the wall next to guitars. Tools were stocked side by side with well-worn cowboy boots. All types of jewelry—real and fake, sparkled in glass cases.

At the fifth shop, Janelle and I wandered around and looked at the handguns in a locked cabinet—who knew they made pink revolvers—while Roxy stared at the moose head mounted to the wall.

By now I had my story down pat. The four other places knew Marcus, but claimed not to have seen him in weeks. Hopefully we'd hit pay dirt soon. I was tired, my feet hurt, and I was starving.

I walked to the front counter where a bald man wearing a leather vest watched my approach. He was covered in tats. Even his bald head had a large spider web inked on the dome.

"What can I do for you?" he asked. He laced the words with a healthy dose of innuendo and leaned his arms on the counter.

Janelle propped her hip on the case next to me. He glanced up at her, but his eyes quickly settled back on mine.

"I'm in a bit of a bind."

"Tell Jay all about it, sweetheart," he said.

I placed my hands on the counter. "My friend, Marcus Walker, pawned something for me, but I lost my ticket."

He shook his bald web head. "That's a damn shame, honey. Wish I could help you out."

I leaned closer. "You could give me some peace of mind. If I just knew my item was safe, I'd sleep a whole lot better. Just until I find the ticket."

His gaze strayed from my eyes, to my flat chest and back again. "I'm not supposed to do that. It's against policy."

"I'll never tell," I whispered.

"Sorry, honey."

I pushed off the counter and left the shop. Janelle and Roxy followed.

"I can't believe you girl," Janelle said. "Flirting with a man like that. You really do love me, don't you?"

Roxy caught up to me and bumped her hip into mine. "Wait until Sullivan finds out he's got some stiff competition."

"I think you've got the stiff part right," Janelle said. "I thought baldy was going start humping her leg right there in front of us."

I lightly slapped her arm. "Don't be disgusting."

After I dropped the girls off and before heading home, I stopped at Axton's.

"You're just in time for Henry's pot roast," he said. "I've already eaten and you are in for a treat."

I walked into the house and took a deep breath. Normally Ax's house smells of eau de pot, but since Henry had taken up residence, it smelled like a home.

Ax led me into the kitchen where Henry stood, his meaty hands shoved into reindeer oven mitts. "I was saving this for Sullivan, but he's late." He took a foil-covered plate from the oven and pealed back the layer of aluminum.

Steam wafted up from the plate and my stomach growled. "This smells delicious, Henry."

He handed me a knife and fork and set a napkin-lined basket of biscuits in front of me. "I made honey butter." He went to the fridge and grabbed a plastic container and placed that on the table, too.

I smiled up at him. "You don't want to bake thirteen dozen cookies for my sister's cookie exchange, do you?"

He frowned and sat next to me. "When do you need them?"

I cut a piece of roast. "I was just kidding. I wouldn't ask you to do that."

"It's just that I have this chocolate espresso cookie recipe I've been wanting to try."

"Only if you want to. It's Tuesday night."

"I need to start a list." He rose from the table and left the kitchen.

Ax plopped down across from me.

"Where's Sullivan?" I asked. I forked the food in so fast, it burned my mouth.

"Out doing Sullivan like stuff, I guess. Called and said if you showed up, to wait for him. Oh, I found out some crap on our crew."

He hopped up from the table and came back a few seconds later with brightly colored folders. "Each player has a different color." He handed me the yellow folder. "Clay is Colonel Mustard."

I set down my fork, and flipped through the pages. Clay had a record from the eighties—burglary, assault. No shock there. But according to his stats, no arrests since.

"Okay, who's Professor Plum?"

"Stuart Weiner. That, by the by, is the *least* pimp ass name ever," he said.

"I concur." I flipped through his stats. "Mmm, Stuart's done hard time. Manslaughter, assault with bodily harm." I glanced up from Stuart's mug shot. "Didn't Marcus do a stint in prison?"

Ax flipped through the green folder. "Mr. Green, aka Marcus Walker, served thirteen months of a two-year stint from June twenty-oh-one to July twenty-oh-two. Leavenworth." He glanced up at me. "Good memory."

"Stuart was there at the same time. Coincidence?"

Ax shrugged. "Possibly. Stuart spent a total of fourteen years in the hoosegow. Probably did time with a lot of people.

"And the only thing I found on Brent Crandall was a charge of vandalism on Crystal's car. Apparently, they got in a big fight and he busted the headlights on her Camaro."

I finished gobbling my roast and slathered honey butter on a still warm biscuit.

Ax rubbed his hands together. "Guess what Henry made for dessert? Chocolate pie. From scratch. I'm going to be sad when that dude leaves."

I leaned back in my chair. "Wish I'd left room. I'm stuffed. Tell Sullivan I couldn't stay. I'm heading to Fit and Flex before they close. See if I can find Crystal's boyfriend, Kyle. Diane said they were hot and heavy during workouts."

"Will do. I'd go with, but I promised Joe I'd make some more brownies tonight," Ax said.

I washed my dishes and left them drying in the rack by the sink. In the living room, Henry sat next to Stoner Joe on the sofa, watching a *Law and Order* repeat. The blinking Yoda Christmas lights edged around the window caught my eye. When Ax said he loved Christmas, he wasn't kidding.

"Thanks for dinner, Henry, it was great."

He twisted around. "Did you get a piece of pie?"

"Next time," I said.

I glanced at Stoner Joe who was practically catatonic. I poked him in the arm and he didn't respond.

"Ax," I called.

He stepped into the room as he unwrapped a stick of butter. "Yeah?"

"Take it easy with the brownies. I'm not sure Joe's brain can handle much more."

"Will do, Rosie."

Chapter 24

Fit and Flex had its own freestanding building next to the library. The large, foggy plate glass window was trimmed in silver garland and as I peered inside, I didn't see any flabby people working out. Truth in advertising.

Nautilus equipment filled the middle of the room. Treadmills and ellipticals lined the walls. The mingling smells of sweat and pine-scented air freshener weren't pleasant.

I walked to the desk situated between the locker rooms, where a tanned guy with overdeveloped muscles smiled at me. "Hey there. I'm Zeke, how can I help you?"

"I'm looking for Kyle."

He peered around the room. "Did you have an appointment?"

"No, I just wanted to chat with him for a sec."

"Well, we've got a special holiday discount. We'll get you into shape for the New Year. New Year, new you."

"Maybe next year, next me."

He shrugged, running his glance over me with a look of disappointment. Thanks to my mother, I was immune to that look.

"Kyle's probably working out. Walk around, you'll find

him." Since I didn't know what Kyle looked like, that might be a problem.

I weaved my way through the equipment, caught admiring glances from two guys on the treadmills. Suck on that, Zeke.

I finally spied a man in his late twenties with spiked blond hair performing butterfly presses. Thick muscles layered his arms and legs and fat veins trailed across his skin like highway lines on a road map. The guy from Crystal's framed picture.

"Kyle?" I asked. He looked like he was in the zone—eyes closed, jaw clenched, lips pressed into a thin line. When he opened his eyes, bright blue irises stood out in contrast to his tanned face.

"Yeah," he said, continuing to bring his arms together, blocking his face from view every other second.

"I need to talk to you about Crystal Waters."

He stopped. "Who are you?"

I offered my hand. "I'm Jane."

He grasped it for a brief shake. "What's this about?"

I swiveled my head and took in the men and women watching us. "Can we talk somewhere private?"

He grabbed a white hand towel and rubbed his face with it. "Sure." He led the way through the machines, toward the back of the building to a small office. He gestured at the sofa while he grabbed a Gatorade from the small fridge in the corner, twisted off the cap, and took a long pull on the neon blue liquid. He wiped his mouth with the back of his hand. "How do you know Crys?"

"I was hoping you could tell me the same thing. I know the two of you were a couple."

Laughing, he shifted his eyes to the floor, his shoulders shaking. "Crys and I aren't together. I'm gay. She and I...we're complicated. But what does this have to do with you?"

It dawned on me that this guy was talking about Crystal in the present tense. He didn't know she was dead. Had the police not gotten around to questioning him yet? And how the hell was I supposed to break the news?

I took a deep breath and looked at his Adam's apple, unable to meet his gaze. "Kyle, I don't know how to tell you this." I swallowed and forced my eyes to his. "Crystal's dead."

He laughed again. "What?" His gaze darted over my face. "What?" he asked, soberly this time.

"The police found her body. She was murdered."

He slammed the bottle on the desk. "What are you talking about? Crys isn't dead. I talked to her two days ago."

I stood. Guilt and sympathy flooded me. "I'm so sorry." I turned to go, but he caught me by the arm and drew me back. I winced at his tight grip.

"No, you're going to tell me what happened. Crystal's dead? How? Why? Why didn't the police call me?"

I pulled away and he let me go.

"The police came by to question my friend, Janelle Johnson, about Crystal. Apparently, they found Crystal's body, but I'm not sure about any of the particulars." *Liar.* I could have reported her death Friday, but I didn't. Now that I saw the pain in this man's eyes, I felt terrible.

"Can you tell me about the men she was dating?"

"Janelle Johnson?" he asked, shaking his head. "Sheik's ex-wife?" He seemed in shock. I wasn't sure what to do for him.

I took his arm. "Why don't you sit down?" He let me lead him to the sofa.

"I can't believe it. Dead? Are you sure? Did that Janelle have something to do with it? Did she kill Crys?" He looked up at me, anger coloring his features, turning his tanned cheeks deep red.

"No, I swear to you she didn't. I want to find out why Crystal was killed. I want to know who she was dating and why she was asking Freddy Libra about money the other night."

He blinked up at me. "You know about the money?"

I nodded. "I know Sheik had a bunch of cash he was tossing around and after he was bashed on the head, the money went missing."

He swallowed. "I know where it is."

Now it was my turn for shock. "What?"

He nodded. "Crystal gave me a bag full of it, found it in the trunk of one of those cars Sheik has on his lawn. She told me to hide it. She said Sheik had stolen it." The cars, of course. They were so broken down, it never occurred to me Asshat might have hidden the money in one of them.

It hit me then—if Roxy and I had found the money, would we have ended up dead in the trunk of a car? I shivered at the thought.

"Kyle, you have to turn that money over to the police. First Sheik was bashed in the head and now Crystal's dead. Whoever wants that money isn't afraid to kill for it."

"I promised I wouldn't give it to anyone but her. I'm not sure what she would want me to do."

"Who did Sheik steal the money from?"

"I don't know. She wouldn't say."

I parked myself in front of him, crossing my legs. "All right, let's start at the beginning. How did you know Crystal?" I reached into my purse and pulled out my notebook.

"Her name wasn't really Crystal Waters. She was my sister, well, half-sister. We shared a dad. He was a bastard. I didn't know about Crys until two years ago, when she showed up and said we were related."

"What was her real name?"

"Tammy Amsted. She changed it to something she thought was peaceful." Tears filled his blue eyes. "Now she's dead."

"I'm so sorry."

"Yeah. Me, too." He wiped at his eyes. "Okay, what else do you want to know?"

"Who was she dating?"

"Crys needed men's attention, you know? I didn't blame her for that. It was how she was raised. Her mother was a drug addict and our dad, well, like I said, he was a bastard. He beat the crap out of me and my mom until he left. But Crys...he did more than that to her."

"She was seeing Martin Mathers?"

I didn't want to throw his name out there. Like saying Voldemort or something, but I needed to know everything Kyle knew.

"Yeah. I warned her about that. Police chief, married. But she claimed he loved her. He paid her bills, gave her presents, took her on vacation to California last year. But she was also dating Sheik. She actually loved that asshole."

"What about Brent Crandall?"

"That guy's crazy. He was so jealous of her, pressured her to stop dancing. He even followed me around for a while.

Threatened me. Told me to stay away from Crystal or he'd cut my dick off. She broke up with him over that."

That put a different spin on things. I'd almost felt sorry for Brent. "Was he abusive to her?" I was just thinking out loud, trying to reason this out.

Kyle thrust his fingers through his short, blond spikes. "Not physically. Like I said, the guy's crazy. He would check her phone, follow her around, constantly question her about the other guys she was dating, dancing for. He was possessive and it scared her. Bashed in her car lights one night when she was over at my place. She didn't want to call the police, but I insisted. Do you think he killed her?"

I shrugged. "I don't think anything right now. Do you know Clay Davidson? Crystal wasn't sleeping with him, was she?"

He shook his head. "Not exactly. She thought he was a creep, but he owns the club, so she always kept him happy, if you know what I mean."

"Extras?"

"Yeah. He expects the girls to have these stupid quotas. That's how Crys justified what she did. Said she made her quotas that way. But our dad fucked her up. I didn't judge."

"What about Freddy Libra?"

"She thought Freddy was a joke. He's not the real owner, you know. Well, he is on paper, but Clay is the man behind the curtain."

"What else do you know about Clay?"

Kyle leaned back and blew out a breath. "Nothing."

"And Stuart Weiner?" I asked.

"Crys mentioned him a couple times. He works for Clay or something?"

"What about Marcus Walker?" I asked.

"I met him with Sheik once." He ran a hand over his mouth. "I told her to get help, you know. Like see a shrink, go to school. She was smart, but she didn't always act like it."

I scribbled off my phone number. "If you think of anything else, call me. And I'm so sorry about your sister, Kyle."

"She wasn't a bad person. She was just messed up. Who isn't?"

I stood and slung my purse over my shoulder. "Where are you hiding the money? You don't have to tell me, in fact, I'm not sure I want to know, but it's safe, right?"

"It's locked away, that's all I'll tell you."

I left him with his grief.

Fat snowflakes fluttered in the cold night air and stuck to the ground. I let Axton's hatchback heat up as I shivered in the front seat. My one cheap glove offered little protection against the freezing steering wheel.

I ran over the pertinent events in my head, leaving out Vi, the hairdresser, Bank Teller Brenda, and her angry husband, Dave. Sheik stole the money, possibly the hit money to kill Sullivan.

He was indiscreet, tossed it around at the strip club that Clay owned. Crystal knew he stole it and she wanted her share.

The next day, Janelle confronts Sheik, and after she leaves, he gets slammed over the head. Sheik's brother, LD, gets roughed up. Probably because of the missing cash.

Crystal comes to the club and asks Freddy about the money and leaves with Marcus. Next, she winds up dead, and the only one still around to tell me anything was Marcus. Why was he with Crystal that night?

And what about Clay? If he was behind the plan to kill Sullivan, how could we get him to leave Sullivan alone?

The snow started coming faster and I flipped up the speed on the wipers. They pushed at the accumulating snow, carving out a space on the windshields, both front and back. It was piling up quickly and I wanted to get home and get warm. Make a cup of instant cocoa—the kind with the tiny, hardened marshmallows—maybe call Sullivan, bounce some of these ideas off him.

Carefully and slowly, I pulled out of the parking lot and took the outer road toward home. It was hard not to stare at the snow as it swirled toward me, like some real life snow globe. The street was a narrow two-lane affair that curved down a steep hill next to a tree-filled embankment where the branches turned white with snow.

The road was deserted except for the bright lights that filled my rearview mirror. Must have been a truck or an SUV because the lights sat up high. I flipped the mirror down to give my eyes some relief, but this jerk didn't let up.

What the hell was he doing? The weather conditions were getting worse and instead of easing off, he was right on top of me. I had nowhere to go and needed to brake going into the curve. But he stayed with me, didn't slow down.

When he bumped into me, my heart lodged somewhere in my throat. My stomach took a nose dive and my hands shook as I gripped the wheel and pumped the brake.

He bumped me again, harder this time, causing me to slide toward the embankment. Scared out of my wits and desperate to stay on the road, I spun the wheel, overcorrecting myself and slid sideways into the other lane. Fortunately, it was clear.

But the truck behind me was playing bumper cars for real. It rammed into me again, from the side this time. Hard. My whole body jerked to the right, straining against the tightened seat belt. My neck wobbled back and forth as I held fast to the steering wheel.

It pushed at me again, as if I were a hockey puck on the ice. Still in the oncoming lane, I panicked as a car headed up the curve, coming straight for me. I accelerated, tried to get out of the way, wound up sliding toward the car.

I pumped the brakes again and fishtailed. The oncoming car ran into the driver's side back panel, forcing the car to spin out at an angle and with enough impact that I slammed the left side of my forehead into the window. Hard.

After I finally stopped, I touched my head with a shaking hand and gasped in pain.

Axton's car was still running, both headlights shone through the night, highlighting the snow. Maybe Axton's car wasn't completely totaled.

I jumped when a man knocked on the car window.

"Are you okay?" Tall and balding with hipster glasses, he pointed to my head. "You've got a goose egg forming. You probably need to go to the hospital, just in case."

Cold air filled the interior of the car. "I'm fine. I just hope I didn't bust the car. It's my friend's. Mine was stolen." I realized I was babbling, so I closed my mouth. "Did you see a truck? That truck tried to run me off the road?"

He glanced over his shoulder at the now empty street. "Yeah, kind of. I wasn't paying much attention as it drove off. I was more worried about you."

"What did it look like?"

"Dark. Sorry, I didn't think to get a license plate or anything. Sure I can't take you to the hospital?"

"No, thanks. Hopefully the car's in good enough shape to get me home."

"Do you want me to call you an ambulance? You might have a concussion."

I couldn't afford an ambulance. "I'll be fine."

We quickly exchanged insurance info. I assumed I was at fault for being in his lane, but right then, I didn't care.

I rolled up the window and got back on the road. I said a prayer of thanks that Axton's car still worked. It took me forty-five minutes and I drove about ten miles an hour, but I managed to make it home.

By the time I got to my apartment, my head was killing me. I called Ax and gave him the bad car news.

"Jeez, I don't care about the car. Let me take you to the hospital."

"I'm fine, it's just a bruise. I'm so sorry, Ax."

After I hung up, I went to the bathroom to assess the damage. Damn, I looked like a mutant. A large, purple, misshapen lump protruded over my left eyebrow. Perfect.

I stripped and threw on sweats, popped two generic Tylenol, and curled up on the futon. Leaving the lights on, I drifted off. An hour later, a knock at my door woke me up.

Chapter 25

Feeling disoriented, my head still pounding, I checked the peephole before I opened the door to Sullivan.

"Are you all right?" he asked.

"Yeah, just a bruise, I think."

As he stepped into the apartment, the snowflakes covering his dark hair quickly dissolved and left damp spots. Keeping his eyes on me, he shrugged out of his coat and hung it beside the door. "Let's go to the bathroom where I can get a good look."

"I'm fine, really."

He ignored my protests and nudged me into the bathroom where he examined my forehead. "Did you put ice on this?"

"No."

"You could have a concussion." He looked into my eyes, not in a romantic way, but in an are-your-pupils-dilated kind of way.

He stalked out of the bathroom into the kitchenette, and opened the freezer. "Where's your ice?"

"I don't have an ice machine." I curled back up on the futon and pulled a throw over my legs.

He turned and glared at me. "You really are a pain in the ass."

"I didn't ask you to come over here."

"No, you never ask for yourself. For Janelle, for Axton, yes. But never for yourself. You're an idiot. You should have called 911 and had an ambulance take you to the hospital."

I sighed. "Do you know what it's like to be poor? I'm not about to start racking up hospital bills. They would have told me to go home and put a bag of ice on it, which I can't do because I don't have any freaking ice."

Leaning against my kitchen counter, he crossed his arms and glared at me. "Unlike you, I was poor most of my life. But your father is a goddamned doctor. You could have called him."

"It never occurred to me, okay?" All this yelling was making my head pound harder.

He stalked toward me, stopping when he got to the futon. He leaned over and thrust his face toward mine. "There's a difference between pride and stupidity. You crossed the line."

"Someone ran me off the road. On purpose."

He reared back, surprise registering on his handsome face.

I shrugged. And it hurt. "A big dark truck ran me off the road. LD has one, Brent Crandall, Crystal's psycho ex-boyfriend, has one. Plus, Stuart Weiner drives a black SUV. Take your pick."

"Shit." He lifted my feet and sank down on the futon, then rearranged my legs to drape over his.

He pulled out his phone and called someone. I never thought I'd be able to sleep with half my body lying on top of

Thomas Sullivan. But it didn't take ten minutes before I was out for the count.

When I awoke the next morning, bright sunlight shone through the window and I was alone. I glanced at the clock. Shit.

I grabbed my cell and called Ma's. "Ray, sorry I'm late."

"Heard about the accident. Stay home." He hung up.

It was after eight. I couldn't remember the last time I slept this late.

I went to the bathroom, and when I washed my hands, I gazed at myself in the mirror. A large knot jutted from my forehead. Black and purple seeped downward, giving me a partial black eye. Fan-freaking-tastic.

I needed to go into work. It wouldn't be pretty, and my customers might lose their appetites, but I wasn't seriously injured, thank God. I just had a bump.

I took two more pain relievers and a quick shower while the coffee brewed. As busy as we'd been at the diner, I needed to get caffeinated before going in. I poured myself a cup and doctored it. I stood at the counter, blowing at the surface when someone knocked.

I opened the door to Officer Mike Goedecker, who looked very official in his uniform and police jacket with the faux fur collar.

"Come on in. You want some coffee or something?"

"No thanks, I'm good. Sullivan called last night, said you had an accident? You okay? That's quite a lump there."

I puttered to the kitchen. "Some asshole ran me off the road."

He shrugged and his nylon jacket made a scratchy noise. "The conditions were terrible. We had over thirty accidents reported in a four-hour time frame. Where were you coming from?"

"Fit and Flex."

Mike grimaced. "Maybe during the next snowstorm, you can curb your urge to work out?"

"Crystal Waters' brother, Kyle, works there. He didn't know she was dead."

"God, that's awful." A v-shape crease wrinkled his brows. "Did you see what kind of car hit you? Model, make?"

"Big dark truck. It was deliberate. Someone rammed into me several times and tried to push me down the embankment."

"The roads were so slick, I'm not sure anyone would have the control to purposefully run you off the road."

I closed my eyes and replayed the events. Someone had deliberately rammed into me. They didn't back off, they tried to plow me over.

I opened my eyes. "Someone ran me off that road."

He looked doubtful. "Without a make or any description, there's not a lot we can do."

"Is there any news about Crystal Waters' death?" I asked. "Any clues as to who killed her?"

He glanced at the floor. "Janelle Johnson seems to be the only suspect. Crystal died by blunt force trauma to the back of the head. Sheik was hit the same way. If I find out anything else, you want me to give Sullivan a call?"

"Yeah, please. Thanks."

"Sure, and maybe have a doc look at that?" He gestured toward my head. "It looks painful."

I finished my coffee and made it to work close to nine. Every table was full. Even Dillon was getting out orders.

I wasn't at my speediest, service wise. But most of the customers felt sorry for me and my battered state and gave me a nice tip. Maybe I should sport a black eye and a head wound more often.

I was even slower during lunch—chicken pot pie again. But there weren't as many customers, so that was good.

During a lull, Roxy cornered me. "Why didn't you call me after the accident?"

"I just wanted to sleep. I was fine, really. If it had been serious, I totally would have called."

She smacked her gum and narrowed her eyes. "So Sullivan stayed with you all night?"

I shrugged. "I don't know. He was on the futon when I fell asleep and he was gone this morning."

She poked a finger at me. "Next time, call me."

I held my hands up in surrender. "I promise."

After we closed, Roxy and Ma insisted I go home and rest. Or as Ma put it, "You look like a shit pile, toots. Get the hell out of here."

As I climbed into Axton's bangled up car, Sullivan called.

"How's the head?"

"Fine. Ugly. Mike Goedecker stopped by and you shouldn't have turned off my alarm."

"Sue me. I'll call you later." He hung up before I could interrogate him about what was going on with the hit.

A half hour after I got home, Henry arrived with a few groceries. And by a few, I mean he bought out the whole damn store.

"How am I supposed to use all this food before it expires?" I asked.

He unpacked lettuce, tomatoes, cucumbers, radishes, steak, chicken, apples, and bananas. Who ate radishes voluntarily? And he slung a ten pound bag of ice in the freezer.

"Boss said stock you up. So I did. "

After he left, Ax called.

"How are you?"

"Sore. Headachy. Your car is banged up."

"Insurance will take care of it. No big."

"I want to pay the deductible."

"We'll haggle later."

"Hey, I found out Crystal's real name last night. Tammy Amsted." I spelled it for him. "Her half-brother is Kyle Amsted. He's not her boyfriend after all. And Martin Mathers took her to California last year."

"I'll get on it. Get some rest," he said. "And call me if you need anything."

I managed to fall asleep and felt better when I awoke.

Janelle came over later in the evening and brought lasagna. I ate a little bit of it and washed down more pain pills. It took the edge off, but it still felt like someone sat inside my skull, beating my forehead with a hammer.

"You think this was because of Asshat and Chicken Licker?" Janelle asked. She removed her coat and arranged herself on the futon.

"Yeah. What else could it be?"

I closed my eyes and tried to remember something important. It was on the tip of my brain, but I couldn't quite remember. "Go on home to the kids. Have you heard from the police?"

"No, thank God. And no offense, Rose, but that Dane is working my last nerve. He hasn't come up with anything new, hasn't had time to talk to more suspects. He keeps telling me to be patient, but I have two children to take care of. I need this cleared up."

The next morning at work, I was pumped full of NSAIDS and feeling better. As I scampered around the diner, getting the place ready for customers, I got a call from Sarah, my alter ego from Rudy's Roundup Restaurant.

"I can't take anymore," she said. "Yesterday one of our fry cooks called in sick and the place was a madhouse. The customers were hostile, Rudy's been a pain in the neck to work for. I've had it. What's your plan?"

I didn't have an actual plan, per se. More of a vague notion these two diner dynasties should cut us some slack.

"How about we get Ma and Rudy to sit down and talk this out?" I asked.

"Rudy won't go to Ma's. He said he'd never step foot in there again. Called it enemy territory."

Oh, brother. "Fine. I'll have Ma there this afternoon at four."

I hung up to find Roxy with a skeptical puss on her face.

"How do you plan to do that? She won't willingly go to Rudy's."

"She will if we lie about it. Or if we have Ray hogtie her and stick her in the trunk."

She shrugged. "Whichever way works for me."

Later in the morning, while Ma used the ladies room, I filled Ray in on my idea of getting Ma and Rudy together in one room. His brows lifted slightly, he rumbled something, and nodded. I took that as permission to do whatever was necessary to broker peace.

Lunch wasn't as crowded. The meds I had taken were wearing off, so I was happy we weren't slammed.

As I served a customer in the far corner, I saw something yellow streak by the window.

I leaned over to get a better view and saw Dillon in his chicken suit, running down the sidewalk, being chased by a man in a trucker cap.

I set the coffeepot on the table. "I'll be right back," I said and strode out of the diner.

Dillon flapped his wings and as he glanced back at the man chasing him, he got tripped up in his chicken feet and fell to the ground.

I jogged toward them. "What the hell's going on?"

"Get this guy away from me," Dillon said. He tried to stand, but wound up rolling from side to side, unable to gain any purchase.

"I just wanted his phone number," the man said. He held his hand out to Dillon to help him to his feet. "I've got a thing for chickens."

"Huh?" I asked.

"Not real chickens. Stuffed chickens. And I'm not ashamed," he said.

"Oh my God," Dillon screamed in a high pitched voice, sounding like a thirteen-year-old boy whose nads hadn't dropped. "Get the hell away from me, man." He slapped his wings at the man's hand.

"It's just a fetish," the man said. "Like people have with feet or pregnant women. It's completely harmless."

"No means no, mister. Even for chickens," I said.

"I just really get off on chickens, you know." He walked back to the street where he'd illegally parked.

I grabbed Dillon by a wing and hauled him to his feet. "You all right?"

"Dude said he wanted to cluck me. What the hell, man? I quit. I quit this stupid job. You can take your chicken suit and your no breaks and your lunch specials and shove them up your ass." He ripped off his chicken head and threw it on the ground.

I glanced back at the diner. Most of the patrons gathered around the plate glass windows, watching the spectacle. Yeah, I was a little over this chicken shit myself.

After we closed, Roxy swept the floor and I poked my head in the kitchen. "Ma, I got a call from Rudy. He wants a truce. We're leaving for his place in five." Then I darted out before she could object.

But on the way to Roxy's car, Ma did object. Quite loudly. "If that man wants a truce, why am I going to his place? He should come to me."

I bundled her into the passenger seat and climbed in the back. "You know how men are. They like to have the upper hand, even when they're wrong."

We drove to Rudy's and parked out front. Ma hiked up her polyester elastic waist pants and sauntered inside. Countrified Christmas carols played over the speakers and a dusty tree, trimmed with red balls, listed to one side in a corner.

Sarah stood near the back of the room. She saw me and winked.

"Well," Ma demanded, "where is he?"

"Let's take a seat," I said. "You can be all relaxed and in position when he comes into the room."

She pointed her finger at me like a gun. "Good thinking, toots."

We all sat down and waited. Four and a half minutes later—I know this because Ma kept an eye on her watch and updated us every thirty seconds—Rudy strode toward us. Sarah trotted behind him.

He placed his hands on his narrow hips, his beer belly stretching the snap buttons on his brown shirt, leaving gaps between the material where his silver chest hair poked through. "I hear you want to talk to me."

Sarah rushed to hold out a chair for him. He sat down, crossing his arms as he trained his narrowed eyes on Ma.

"I hear you're ready to give in," she said.

His brows rose. "Me? The way I hear tell, it's you who wants to end this."

Ma scoffed and wiggled her large frames. "Listen up, sonny—"

"We all want to end this," I said. "It's getting ridiculous. Ma, you're losing money and we're not making any tips."

Rudy grinned.

Ma scowled.

Sarah piped in. "You're losing money, too, Rudy. And I can't keep getting my kid up at five in the morning."

He sneered at Sarah. "If you don't like it, you know where the door is."

"Don't you talk to her that way," Ma said. She bared her teeth at him. "You don't respect anyone, do you?"

"I sure don't respect you, old woman."

This conversation was heading downhill faster than a speeding train with no brakes.

"You need to learn a lesson, mister. And I'm the one to teach you." She scooted back from the table and marched out the door.

As we followed, Roxy popped her gum. "Any other brilliant ideas?"

Chapter 26

"Yeah, I want to confront Marcus," I said. "I want to know why Clay broke into his house and trashed his place and what happened the last time he saw Crystal."

"Next time you decide to investigate, can we go with something like the mall or a shoe store instead of muffler shops and strip clubs?" Roxy asked.

"Yeah, I'll work on that."

We dropped a pissed off Ma at the diner. She wouldn't speak to us and she slammed the door with both hands after she stomped out of the car.

I wondered if I could tick off everyone in my life before Christmas. Fingers crossed.

I climbed in the front seat and Roxy and I made our way to the muffler shop. I toyed with the idea of calling Janelle to join us, but she had her kids and I didn't want to disrupt her life any more. Besides, in the frame of mind she was in lately, she might get more forceful with Marcus than she needed to.

Most of the snow had melted, but dirty mounds piled up on street corners. The temps were in the forties and the sun hung low in the sky.

Roxy pulled into the muffler shop and found a parking space. John, the man I'd spoken to on my previous visits to see Marcus, pushed through the door.

"Hey, you're that girl who was here the other day."

I smiled my most winsome. "Yeah, is Marcus around?"

"I fired his ass yesterday. If you see him, tell him to pick up his stuff or I'm going to get rid of it."

Hear that pounding? That was opportunity knocking. "I'm going to see him later, I can just take it to him."

"Yeah, sure." He led the way through the garage to a row of four silver metal lockers. He pointed to number two. "Here you go. I'll grab you a box."

Roxy stayed behind in the office. She'd taken one look at John and his oily coveralls and scrunched her nose. Didn't want to get her candy pink and white polka dot dress dirty.

I opened the door to Marcus' locker and sorted through the car mags, crumpled receipts, a jacket—I'd check the pockets later—and a pawn ticket for earrings. And it was dated four days ago. This had been what Web Head from the pawn shop wouldn't show me. Earrings.

John walked back with a small cardboard box in his hands. "Here you go. I'll mail his last check to him, minus what he owes me for repairs. And the gas he stole."

"Wait, what repairs?"

"He didn't tell you why he was fired?"

I shrugged. "He said the two of you had creative differences. You know how he is."

"Yeah, I know exactly how he is. And if I were you, sister, I'd run a mile in the other direction. He didn't show up for work twice last week, no phone call, no nothin'. Then Sunday night he takes my tow truck without asking and smashed the front fender. He claims he didn't do it, but who else had a key? This is what I get for hiring an ex-con." He waved his hand and strode off.

Did Marcus run me off the road? Could have been a black tow truck. What had he been doing those days he called in sick? Killing Crystal?

I tossed everything except the claim ticket—which I tucked in my pocket—into the box. I poked my head around the side of the building to get a look at the tow truck, but it was gone. Damn.

Once in the car with Roxy, I checked Marcus' jacket pockets. Gum wrappers and a used Kleenex. Ugh.

Roxy dropped me back at the diner. She said she'd go with me to the pawn shop, but I knew she had a hot date with Tariq. Usually, she kept me abreast of her love life, but she was keeping mum about Tariq. Either she was getting serious about him or they were on a shoplifting spree I didn't want to know about.

It took me twenty minutes to make it downtown to the pawn shop. Web Head worked the counter.

He frowned at the horn on my forehead. "What the hell happened to you?"

"Car accident."

"Are you all right?"

I nodded. "I found the claim ticket." I waved it at him.

He snatched it and skimmed it. "Be right back." He walked to a locked door, took a key from the chain hooked to his belt, and disappeared inside.

He stepped out a moment later. "Here they are." He held up a clear plastic jewelry bag. Inside was a pair of oval diamond hoops, about an inch and a half long.

"How much?" I asked.

"Two hundred and twenty five. But have a drink with me and I'll cut it to one-fifty."

I tried to look sad. "I still don't have enough. I'll just have to come back next week. Thanks, though."

I left and hurried along the darkened street to Axton's car, my head swiveling back and forth to make sure I wasn't being watched.

As fast as the congested Christmas traffic would allow, I sped back to Axton's house, ready to burst.

I tried the door handle, but it was locked, so I pounded on the door and rang the bell repeatedly until Ax finally answered.

"What's wrong?" he asked. "Are you okay?" He took in the bruise on my head. "Get in here. Are you going to pass out?"

Sullivan moved Ax aside and took my hand, pulling me to him. "What happened? What's wrong?"

Stoner Joe stared at the TV without blinking.

Henry poked his head out of the kitchen. "Everything okay, boss?"

I moved in his direction and passed him, tossing my purse on the kitchen table. "I stopped by the pawn shop with Marcus' ticket. I couldn't afford to buy them back." I dug in my purse and pulled out the photo of Brent Crandall and Crystal. "But see these earrings? Marcus pawned these four days ago. Crystal was already dead."

Sullivan took the photo from me. It finally hit me, what had been niggling my brain since yesterday. "Shit, I can't believe I forgot. The money. Crystal found it. She gave it to Kyle to hide."

Henry stepped away to stir something on the stove. Something that smelled delicious.

"Where's the money?" Sullivan asked. He handed the photo off to Ax.

"He said it was locked away." I rubbed my temples. Maybe I did have a concussion that night. Why else would something so important slip my brain?

"Let's go talk to Kyle," Sullivan said.

"I can't. I have to go to my sister's cookie exchange."

"They're all ready and they're delicious," Henry said.

"He wouldn't let me try any. By the way, I found out a little info on Tammy Amsted." Ax handed the photo back to me and walked out of the kitchen.

Sullivan brushed his thumb across the goose egg on my forehead. "Still hurt?"

"Only when you touch it."

"Smart ass. You can't get out of the cookie thing?"

"I would if I could. But my sister will be very hurt, I've already pissed off my mom, and Christmas—"

He held up his hand to stop my flow. "I get it. How about I pick you up at your apartment afterward? We'll go question Kyle then. Axton found his address. He's very good, your IT buddy. I'm thinking about recruiting him."

I slapped my palm on his chest. "Don't you even think about it. Axton controls the force for good. He'd never go over to the dark side."

Ax returned and carried a red folder. "Miss Scarlet?" I asked.

He grinned. "You got it. Everything about Tammy Amsted."

"That was Crystal's real name?" Sullivan asked.

He leaned over my shoulder and read the info. Crystal grew up in St. Louis with her addicted, neglectful mother and a slap happy father who had been to jail three times for domestic assault. They eventually lost custody when Crystal was twelve and she went to live with her grandmother. She'd had a very short, sad life.

Ax also found the trip to California that Martin Mathers had taken. An all-expense, taxpayer-funded trip to some kind of cop conference in L.A.

"I know who owns the Huntingford Motor Lodge," Sullivan said. He leaned against the kitchen wall and watched me.

"Well?" I asked.

"Her name's Annabelle Weiner. She's Stuart's great aunt. Eighty-three years old. She bought it two years ago."

"I take it Clay is the real owner?" I asked.

"I would think so, yes."

"He must have been filming Martin Mathers' and Crystal's little Wednesday afternooners." I pointed a finger at him. "You're not the only one who has dirt on the police chief. He's in Clay's pocket, too."

Sullivan shrugged. "That's the risk you take when you make a deal with a dirty cop. Call me after the cookie thing." He squeezed my shoulder and then headed down to the basement.

"You want some Beer Cheese soup?" Henry asked.

I glanced at my watch. "I have just enough time for a bowl."

He placed a bowls of hot yellow-orange soup in front of Ax and me. The surface was decorated with a sprig of some kind of herb and it smelled so good. Then he plated up thick slices of homemade bread. If Henry wasn't the scariest mofo I knew, I'd get him a job at Ma's.

Twenty minutes later I was on my way to Jacks' house with two huge plastic containers on the passenger seat next to me. At a red light, I pried open the lid and liberated a cookie. It was chocolate mixed with coffee and equaled heaven.

At my sister's house, cars filled the drive and spilled out onto the street. With my hands full, I walked up to the front door and pushed the bell with my nose.

These little get-togethers weren't my fave. My sister's friends all had kids or were pregnant. Sometimes both. And that's all they wanted to talk about. Either that or their doctor husbands worked too hard and played too much golf. But, if it made Jacks happy, I'd make an effort.

She answered the door sporting a Santa hat. She took one look at me and froze. "Oh my God, what happened?" She took the containers and handed them off to one of her friends then pulled me into the house and examined me under the foyer chandelier. "What did you do?"

"I had a little fender bender. No biggie."

She grabbed my chin and tilted my head toward the light. "Did you go to the hospital?"

I pulled my chin from her hand. "I'm fine."

One of her friends, Marcy something, approached. "You should let my husband take a look at it. Just to make sure there's no scarring. Let me get you his card." She examined my forehead.

"Thanks, but really, it's okay."

Another woman in a pair of leather black boots stepped out of the living room. "Wow, what happened to you?"

It was going to be a long night.

Jacks hooked her arm through mine and led me to the living room where eleven women stood and gabbled. "Rose is here," she announced.

One by one, they stopped yakking as they gazed at me in horror. Silence reigned. It was just an ugly knot on my forehead. I didn't lose an arm, for God's sake.

"She had a car accident," Jacks said.

They started talking all at once. 'How are you? What happened? Is the car totaled? That curve's always been dangerous.'

I smiled and tried to answer all their questions.

I always felt out of place at these things. My usual strategy was to stay in the corner or ask someone about a recipe. That usually led to a long, boring discussion about how Grandma Mimi always made this cookie, but it was laden with fat ...blah, blah.

But this year, here I stood, front and center, banged up and bruised, wearing a faded forest green Hanes For Her t-shirt with a coffee stain over one boob.

Eventually talk settled to the familiar. Kids. Husbands. Christmas vacations.

I walked to the kitchen and grabbed a tray for my cookies. Jacks followed. "That was probably a little overwhelming, huh?"

I smiled. "It was okay. Your friends mean well."

She grabbed the containers of cookies and we wandered to the dining room. "You couldn't afford the hospital, could you? I didn't even think about it until Marcy told you to call her husband. I thought, 'Rose can't afford a plastic surgeon.' You didn't even go to the emergency room." She gazed at me with sadness and a hint of disappointment.

I placed Henry's chocolate cookies on the tray. "I would have gone if I'd been really hurt, Jacks."

She grabbed my hand. "I want you to do something for me."

Wary, I pulled my hand from hers and continued stacking cookies. "What?"

"Allen and I want to buy you a car for Christmas. Nothing fancy, just something reliable. I worry about you."

I knew my sister's intention wasn't to make me feel like shit, but it happened all the same. I didn't need her to take care of me. I wasn't poor little Rose. I'd chosen my life. It wasn't perfect. Sometimes it was a crap storm. I had setbacks like everyone else, but I hadn't taken handouts in the last five years, and I wasn't about to start now.

"Thanks, but no. I'll make it on my own."

"If you change your mind..." She looked down at the platter of cookies. "Did you bake these?"

"No, a friend did. And they're delicious."

I snagged a plate and spent the next forty-five minutes chatting and eating finger foods. I wondered when I could break loose without hurting my sis's feelings. As I listened to two women discuss the merits of a drug-free birth, my butt vibrated.

I sighed with relief. I set down my cup of nog and made my excuses as I moved into the formal living room.

"Hey Dane, what's up?" I hadn't heard from him in days. I hoped he was progressing with the case.

"Janelle's been arrested for the murder of Crystal Waters."

Chapter 27

"What the hell? I know of at least four other people who had a motive. Are the police looking into any of that? And what about her kids? Is Sondra with them?"

"Slow down, Rose. Tariq and Roxy are with the kids. I've been to see Janelle. I know there are other suspects. I told my boss I was going full throttle with this case. I know she's innocent. I'm going to do what I can for her."

Tears filled my eyes. I'd failed her. I told her I would find who attacked Asshat, but I hadn't. And in a way, I'd let Crystal down, too.

"She can't stay in there. What's bail going to be this time?"

"I don't know. She barely made bail before and this will be higher since it's a murder case and she's already been charged with assault. The judge may deny bail altogether. We'll have to get a temporary custody hearing so Sondra can officially take the kids."

I sank down onto the tufted sofa.

"Are you still there? Rose?"

"Call me when you learn anything new." I hung up and touched the lump on my head and groaned. Janelle was going to spend the rest of her life in prison. And Crystal's murderer was going to go free.

I sat on the sofa, feeling numb and sick to my stomach, when a blonde whose name I couldn't remember walked into the room.

"Are you all right?"

I shook my head. "No. Not even close."

She sat next to me and grabbed my hand. "You're very pale. Are you having an anxiety attack?"

"Maybe. I don't know."

"I have them all the time. Are you taking anything?"

I felt like I was out of my body as I stared at her.

"Do you take anything for them? Valium, Zoloft?"

I shook my head.

"Here." She opened her Coach bag and pulled out a blister pack. "Hold out your hand."

I obeyed instead of arguing.

"This is the good stuff, Clonazepam. Start with half a pill. Don't take this on an empty stomach or with booze. It'll knock you on your bum." She popped six pills into my palm. "Just take it when you think you're going to die. You're not going to die, by the way, it just feels that way."

"Thanks," I said.

"Do me a favor? Don't tell anyone I gave those to you. I don't want the other girls to think I'm a walking pharmacy. My husband's a shrink and I get requests all the time." She patted my leg and left.

I stared down at the pills. I shoved them in my front pocket and dialed Sullivan.

"Dane just called. Janelle's been arrested for Crystal's murder."

The usual pause. "I'm sorry."

"We have to get her out. She has little kids, she's innocent."

"You know that's not my priority."

"I'm asking you to make it a priority. She's going to need bail money and even though Dane says he's taking this seriously, I wonder if she needs a better attorney. One who's taken on murder cases."

He said nothing for a minute. Then, "Do you have any idea of what you're asking? There's no way you can pay off that kind of debt."

Right now I didn't give a good goddamn how I was going to pay off anything. I just needed Janelle to have a fighting chance.

"I don't care. That's what I need."

"All right. I'm coming to pick you up now. I don't want you to drive."

I pulled myself together and made my excuses to my sister—said I had a terrible headache and needed a good night's sleep. The ladies piled me up with decorative Christmas cookies before I walked out of the house to wait for Sullivan.

He pulled the Mercedes up to the curb and got out, taking the cookies from me and shoving them in the backseat. "Come here." He pulled me into a brief hug, but said nothing—no words of comfort, no platitudes. I breathed deeply, taking in his intoxicating scent before he pulled away and settled me into the car.

By the time we pulled up to Fit and Flex, I really did have a headache. The kind that makes it hard to concentrate on anything else.

Sullivan followed me as I walked to the counter. Zeke smiled when he saw me. "You're back." Then he glanced over the horn on my head. "What happened?"

"Is Kyle around?"

"No, no one's heard from him for the last two days. It's not like him. The boss is worried. Said if he didn't hear from Kyle by tomorrow, he was going to call the police."

I glanced over my shoulder at Sullivan.

"We'll need his address," he said.

Zeke appeared startled at the request. "I can't do that. That's private information."

"Zeke," I said, "I don't know if Kyle told you this, but his sister was murdered this week."

Zeke's eyes grew wide. "I didn't know he had a sister."

"Her name was Crystal." I leaned on the counter. Seriously, I needed a Tylenol or something. I rubbed circles in the space between my eyes.

"Crystal was his sister? He never said."

"We need his address. He might be in trouble."

"Yeah, okay. I'll be right back." He jogged to the office.

Sullivan grasped my nape and gently massaged. "You okay?"

"Yeah." His fingers pressed into the sides of my neck. I closed my eyes and tried to relax my muscles.

"We'll stop and get some pain relievers."

"No, I want to keep going."

Zeke came back with a Post-it note in his hand. "I dug his chart out of the personnel file. Here you go. Let me know if you need anything else."

I smiled and thanked him. I handed the note off to Sullivan.

Back in the car, he glanced at the yellow sheet. "This isn't too far from here."

I nodded.

Sullivan placed his hand on the top of my head. "Let me take you home."

"No."

I closed my eyes and rested my head against the window. The cool glass felt good on my temple.

Sullivan drove to a small apartment complex similar to mine—two stories, probably eight units. Kyle lived on the first floor, in the back of the building. We knocked, but no one answered.

"I'm going to break in," he said.

I rested my hand on his arm. "He might have nosy neighbors." I needed to have Roxy teach me how to use lock picks ASAP. You never knew when that type of crap might come in handy.

I knocked on the door across the hall and waved Sullivan off. He moved out of sight.

I knocked again and finally, an older man, his bald head covered in liver spots, answered. "What?"

"I'm looking for Kyle."

"What?" He peered at me through his thick lenses. "Who are you?"

"His cousin, Jane."

"Who? What happened to your head?" he asked, curling his upper lip.

"My boyfriend beat me up. I need to find Kyle." From the corner of my eye, I saw Sullivan shake his head. I had to repeat myself three times before the old man heard me.

"Haven't seen Kyle today."

"Thanks anyway."

He leaned toward me, ear first. "What?"

"Thank you." I enunciated.

After he shut the door in my face, Sullivan returned to my side. "You're a good liar."

"Um, thanks? Anyway, bust in. This guy will never hear you and there wasn't a light on next door. I noticed the windows were dark when we walked into the building."

He raised his brows at me.

"What?" I asked. "I'm observant."

"Yes, you are." He swiftly kicked in the door.

I dug into my purse and pulled out the last of the latex gloves I'd taken from the diner. "I only have three." I handed him two and slipped one on my ungloved hand.

I flipped on the light switch and Sullivan and I stood in silence, gazing around the room.

"Damn it. I'm always too late for this shit." The place had been ransacked. "This is the second time this week and it's pissing me off."

"Let's go." Sullivan flipped off the light and shut the door. Then he removed the gloves and shoved them in his pocket.

We got back in the car. "You said this was the second time this had happened. Who else?"

"Marcus. Someone's looking pretty damn hard for that money."

"Wished you'd told me this sooner."

"Why?" I glanced over at him. A look of intense anger blanketed his features.

"I think whoever's looking for the money is the person trying to kill me. So Marcus is off my list."

"I didn't know he was ever on your list. And he's still on mine. What if he killed Sheik for the cash? What if he killed Crystal because she wouldn't tell him where it was?"

"Ro—"

"Marcus is my number one suspect. He was with Crystal the night she talked to Freddy Libra about the money. He pawned her earrings the day after I found her murdered and stuffed in her trunk. He took the tow truck Sunday night and I was shoved off the road."

Sullivan clamped his lips tight, took a deep breath. "I have other things to do if Marcus isn't in on this hit. I'm taking you home."

Once inside my apartment, I tossed my phone on the table next to my pink Christmas tree and plugged it into its charger. I didn't bother taking off my jacket before I made for the futon and curled up, my head throbbing so hard, my eyes watered.

Sullivan heated up a piece of lasagna that Janelle had brought. God, Janelle. How could I help her?

"Let's talk this out," I said.

"No, you need to relax."

"I can't relax unless I talk this out."

Before he could sit down, there was a knock on the door. Sullivan froze, then pulled a gun out of his coat that he'd tossed over the back of chair. I should have figured he had a gun, I just never thought about it. Henry, yes, I couldn't see him brushing his teeth without a gun strapped to his side.

Sullivan stared out the peephole. "It's Goedecker." He slid the gun into the back waistband of his pants before opening the door to Mike, who wasn't in a uniform, but dressed in civilian clothes—jeans and a leather jacket.

"Hey, sorry to bother you, but I've got some news." With his hands stuffed in the pockets of his coat, he smiled at me. "How's the head?"

"It's been better," I said, and managed to sit up.

Sullivan opened the door wider to allow Mike to enter the apartment. "What's the news?"

Mike slammed the door shut with his foot and pulled a gun from his pocket. He thrust it in Sullivan's face. "You're a dead man. Hands where I can see them."

"No!" My heart plummeted and I leaped to my feet.

"Sit down, Rose."

Slowly, Sullivan raised his hands.

I sat on the futon. "What's going on?" I felt like I was in a play. Nothing was real except the throbbing in my head.

"Isn't it obvious? Mike's the hit man." Sullivan's voice was cool and calm. I took a deep breath and strived for the same. How could he sound so in control when he had an automatic six inches from his brain?

"Who're you working for? Clay?" I asked.

"Give the girl a prize. She finally figured it out." Mike didn't take his eyes off Sullivan as he patted him down with one hand. "Turn around."

Sullivan slowly turned his back to Mike. "Hands behind your head, fingers laced." Mike removed the gun from Sullivan's waistband, then pulled a pair of cuffs from his pocket and tossed them to me. He slowly stepped back, and kept both of us in his view, the gun trained on Sullivan. "Cuff him, Rose. And don't try anything stupid. If you do, I'll shoot him, just enough to wound him. I'm not ready for him to die yet."

Terror crept its way into my chest. I stood and walked toward Sullivan. He slowly placed his hands behind his back. With trembling fingers, I cuffed his wrists, then squeezed his hand. His skin felt dry and cool to the touch. My palms were a clammy mess.

Mike shoved me aside, grabbed Sullivan by the back of his sweater, and stuck the barrel of the gun against his head. "Here's the plan, we're going to get into Sullivan's Mercedes, and you, Rose, are going to drive where I tell you. If you deviate from the plan or try anything cute, I'll shoot him. Now get the keys out of his pocket."

I kept my gaze locked on Sullivan's as I reached into his front pocket and yanked out the keys. I swallowed the knot that had lodged itself in my throat and raised my chin. We were going to get out of this. Any other outcome was not acceptable.

"Let's go," Mike said. "Rose, you first."

I preceded the men out the door and down the stairs, my head pounding with every step I took. I walked out to the Mercedes.

"Unlock the doors," Mike said.

I hit the button on the fob. Snow flurries dotted the night sky. The temperature had dropped and the wind was biting. Sullivan didn't have on a coat, but I was glad I still wore mine.

Mike opened the front passenger door and did the cop move where he covered Sullivan's head and helped him into the car. "Now your turn," he said to me.

I slid behind the wheel, adjusted the seat and mirror, and started the engine while Mike climbed into the backseat directly behind Sullivan.

"Drive to the cigar bar," he said. "And remember, don't deviate or I'll shoot your boyfriend."

I turned up the heat because of Sullivan's lack of a coat, and because, although I had a bad case of the flop sweats, I was shivering.

Eddies of snow swirled across the road as I drove the speed limit and nibbled on my lip, trying to come up with a game plan. Unfortunately, my head was killing me and I couldn't think straight. I slid a glance at Sullivan, but he kept his eyes forward.

All too soon we arrived at Penn's. By the parking lights, I could see the soot-coated brick near the windows and doors, stained from the fire.

"Pull around back," Mike said.

I did as he ordered, parking next to the back door and shut off the ignition. Mike thrust his hand toward me.

"Give me the keys."

With stiff, icy fingers, I handed them over. Think, stupid brain, think. I hoped to God Sullivan had a plan, because I was empty.

"You get out first, Rose, and walk to the door."

Once again, I followed his directions and stood next to the back door of Penn's. Crime scene tape X-ed the doorway.

Mike got out of the backseat and held open Sullivan's door, waved the gun toward the building. "Nice and slow." He kept his distance from Sullivan, but the gun never wavered. "Tear off the tape, Rose."

I tugged at the tape affixed to the door, wadded it up, and threw it on the ground. Then with his free hand, Mike pulled a key from his pocket and tossed it to me, gesturing to the padlock on the makeshift plywood door.

I opened it and led our little parade inside. In the murky depths of the club, I could make out black debris on the floor. There was definite damage to the place, but most of the lead glass windows stayed intact. The bar stood, but the tables and chairs were scattered, broken, turned upside down. The smell of smoke was overwhelming, and layered over that, was a moldy, damp scent. My breath hung visibly in the air.

"Down the hall to the office," Mike said.

"Did you set this fire?" I asked as I slowly walked.

"No, I had Stuart do it. I'm the one who shot at the both of you that night." His cockiness frightened me.

I opened the door to Sullivan's office and shuffled inside. The round table, where I'd sat with Sullivan, had been tossed against a wall, but the heavy desk stood upright. It was wet and ruined, but in one piece.

I glanced around the room, lit by four portable LED lights that gave off a too-bright glow. That artificial light felt like daggers shooting into my eyeballs. I blinked and held up one hand to shield myself from their brightness. It took a second for my eyes to adjust, but then I noticed we had cellmates. Who weren't moving.

"Walk," Mike said.

Sullivan remained silent as I moved us farther into the room. Marcus and Kyle. Both sported a bullet hole between their eyes and they took a beating before they died. Fuck. Nausea settled in my stomach and I swallowed convulsively as I looked away. We were going to die here. I would never see my friends or family again.

I blinked back tears. Mike said he wasn't ready to kill Sullivan yet. What the hell did that mean? He obviously had no compunction about killing people, so what did he want?

The money. He was still looking for the money. But I didn't know where it was. Could I string him along? Keep Sullivan and myself alive long enough to break out? Mike grabbed an overturned chair and placed it upright. "Sit." He pushed on Sullivan's shoulder, forcing him into the chair. Then he lifted Sullivan's arms up and draped them over the back.

I'd never seen Sullivan's face so impassive. He was devoid of emotion, he wouldn't look at me.

Mike waved the gun in my direction. "Over there, next to Marcus."

I glanced down at Marcus' slack face and took a deep breath of acrid, smoke-scented air.

"Sit next to him. You're going to wind up just like him if you don't tell me what I want to know."

I stepped on an ice puddle—water from putting out the fire had frozen—and slipped as I made my way to Marcus. I sank down on the wet floor next to him, but I didn't look at him, I couldn't. It freaked me out too much. I'd seen too many dead bodies lately. And I was probably about to join them.

Mike gazed at me and smiled. "I want to know where the money is."

My eyes skittered to Sullivan. He shook his head almost imperceptibly.

"I don't know where it is," I said.

Mike tsked. "Wrong answer." Then he bashed the gun handle into Sullivan's face.

I gasped at the bloody gash on his cheekbone.

Mike looked at me with mock pity. "Oh honey, we're just getting started. I will cut off his balls and feed them to him if I have to." His face became a frightening mask. "I want my money!" he screamed, saliva shooting out of his mouth. Then he wiped his lips with the back of his hand. He took a deep breath and regained control of himself. "Okay," he said, nodding. "I see you're going to need a little convincing. No problem." He shoved the gun in his coat pocket as he walked toward me. When he reached me, he jerked me up by my ponytail then slammed the side of my head into the wall. The same side as the goose egg on my forehead.

I thought my skull would burst open, my brain was too big for my head. I was pretty sure I had concussion this time because things were kind of fuzzy. "I haven't been looking for any money," I said.

He pressed his face close to mine and kept hold of my hair. "I just don't believe you, Rose." He threw me to the ground and I landed on my back. Then he stuck his boot on my chest, pushing me down. I gasped for breath, but he kept applying pressure. The floor beneath me was littered with wet, broken pieces of furniture that dug into the backs of my legs.

I tried to bat at his foot, tried to pull it off me, but he reached down and slapped me across the face. "You will tell me what I want to know. If you tell me right away, I'll kill the both of you quick. But if I have to beat it out of you, well, it's going to hurt." His eyes glittered with anticipation. He got his rocks off on this. "It's going to hurt a lot."

Chapter 28

Mike removed his foot, and reaching down, grasped me by the lapels of my coat. He wrenched me up until I was standing once again. Then he backed me up against a wall and placed his forearm across my throat. In vain, I tried to push at his arm. He increased the pressure and my eyes watered from the pain. I gasped for air before he let up a little, allowing me to breathe.

"Where's my money?" he asked, calmly.

I clung to his sleeve, kept trying to push his forearm from my neck. "I don't know," I wheezed.

He sighed. "That's too bad." Making a fist, he let go of my neck and punched me in the stomach, knocking all the air from my lungs. Fire burned in my midsection. I tried to double over with pain, but he held me up. "Yeah, this is going to get really painful."

"Stop!" Sullivan yelled.

Mike released me and I slid to the floor, clutching my belly. "He speaks." He stalked toward Sullivan. "Tell me where it is."

"I don't know why you're doing this, Mike. I would have paid you double on whatever the hit was."

Mike smirked. "It's not just about the money. It's about getting to the top. I would never be anything more than a soldier in your army. But Clay's going to make me a general. When I heard he was putting a contract out on you, I jumped at the chance to prove myself. I do this for Clay, and in return, I get a little extra cash on the side. You have no idea how much a cop's salary sucks."

"I didn't know you wanted to move up in my ranks," Sullivan said. He spoke like he was having a conversation about the weather. Casual. Detached.

"You never asked." Mike circled him, kicked shards of broken wood out of his way.

"Sheik stole your money?" Sullivan asked.

When Mike had his back to me, I struggled to sit up. My stomach cramped from the punch and my head and neck ached with intense pain.

"Yeah, he stole it," Mike said. He made another trip around Sullivan and when he saw me trying to sit up, he laughed. "Is this the part where the bad guy tells all? Well, let me confess my sins. First of all, I hit Sheik." There were equal amounts of pride and derision in his voice. "Right after he argued with that crazy bitch ex of his, I snuck in the back door and he and I had a little talk. But he wouldn't give up the cash. I lost my temper, hit him on the head." He frowned and scratched the tip of his nose. "Going to have to kill him if he ever comes out of that coma," he said, like he was reminding himself to buy a gallon of milk.

He continued to pace around the room. "Then Freddy Libra called Clay, said Crystal was looking for the money, too, threatening to call the police." He shrugged and propped his hands on his hips. "See where we're going with this, kids?"

"I don't understand," I said, my voice croaky from his chokehold. "Why not just shoot them? Why did you hit them?"

He looked at Sullivan, but pointed at me. "Is she always this stupid?"

His eyes met mine and he walked toward me, kneeling down in front of me. "Because those hits weren't planned. See Marcus and Kyle and the great big bullet holes in their heads? I had time to sweat them out, gave them the opportunity to tell me what I want to know. And I have time to get rid of the bodies."

He leaned closer, his face an inch from mine. "But the thing is, neither one would tell me about the money. And I'm obviously willing to kill to get it, so maybe you'll be smarter than either of them. But I'm not holding my breath."

"Why did Sheik have it in the first place?" Sullivan asked.

Mike held my gaze a moment longer before rising. "Stuart put the money in a clean car that I was going to use so you wouldn't recognize my truck. And since you seem to be slow to figure things out, Rose, that's the same truck I used to run you off the road the other night. You were supposed to die, by the way.

"Anyway, Sheik stole my clean car. Dumb luck, huh?"

I didn't know if he was talking about Asshat's bad luck or his own. Didn't really care because I was worried about my own misfortune just then.

Mike planted himself in front of Sullivan. "Now, enough chitchat." He slammed his right fist into Sullivan's nose. "I want. My fucking. Money." He punctuated each phrase with a punch to Sullivan's chin, jaw, and gut.

Sullivan breathed hard through his bloody nose. He finally looked at me, rage and hatred burning from his eyes.

Mike straightened. He ran a hand through his short, dark hair and walked behind the desk. He opened the bottom drawer, pulled out the bottle of brandy, and shook it. "Still here, even has a few swallows left. You always kept the good stuff for yourself."

Before he could uncap it, a ring tone broke the stillness. Mike pulled out his phone and glanced at it. "Shit, I've got to take this. It's work." He seemed conflicted as he looked back at Sullivan. "If you two don't keep quiet, I'll cut out your tongues. And Rose, if you've moved an inch when I get back, I'll turn what's left of your brain into spaghetti." Then he left the room, shutting the door behind him.

"How are we going to get out of here?" I asked.

"We're not," Sullivan said.

That's not what I wanted to hear. I wanted reassurance. Not a death sentence.

I wished I had time to take a couple of pain relievers before I got abducted. Getting kidnapped sucked balls and my head felt like it would split open like a cantaloupe. Oh my God. *Pills.* I had pills in my pocket. The Clonazepam.

My heart pounded, out of fear of getting caught by Mike and excitement that maybe we had a way out. But what if he came back and found me trying to drug his brandy?

Stupid Rose, what the hell did it matter? He was going to kill us anyway. I'd rather go quickly than with a long, drawn out torture scenario.

I pushed myself up against the wall, inch by inch. I'd made it to a crouching position, every breath agony in my chest and head.

"What are you doing, Rose?" Sullivan whispered.

"I'm going to drug him. Hope this works, because this is all we've got."

With every ounce of strength I possessed, I pushed up and forced myself to walk to the desk. Tears pricked my eyes from the lightning bolts shooting through my brain with each step. As quickly as I could, I shoved my hand in my pocket, searching for the pills the doctor's wife gave me. Don't mix with booze or take on an empty stomach, she'd said. With shaking hands, I unscrewed the brandy cap, fumbled a bit as I quickly broke each pill in half and dropped them into the bottle. I recapped it and gave it a shake before staggering back to the wall, where I allowed myself to collapse.

Sullivan watched me. "Rose, I want to tell you—"

The door opened. "All right, let's make this happen," Mike said, striding into the office. He glared at me, but I barely lifted my eyes to meet his gaze. "You ready to tell me?"

I said nothing.

With agitation Mike grabbed the bottle, unscrewed the top, and chugged the contents. He threw it against the side wall and glass rained down the damp, heat-blistered surface.

"Okay, we're going to have to expedite matters." With a sniff, he pulled out a sheathed knife from his inner pocket. He extracted the long, serrated blade and held it up to the portable light. His eyes met mine. "Ever seen a man gutted?"

How fast would the pills work? Why wasn't he calming down? I thought those suckers were for anxiety, but maybe he was too hopped up on adrenalin.

"I know where the money is," I blurted out.

Mike blinked at me. "Oh, do you now? What a coincidence."

"Kyle hid it, but I know where it is."

He smiled. "Really? Because I did some pretty horrible things to him and he never said a word." He rubbed his eyes. "This wouldn't be a ploy, would it? A bid to buy more time?"

Totally.

"Sullivan and I will take you to it," I said.

He waved the knife in front of his own face. "Unh, unh, unh. I don't believe you."

My eyes flew to Sullivan's. Blood still ran from his nose and a bruise was forming on his cheek.

Mike leaned against the desk and rubbed his forehead. "I feel weird." He took a deep breath and straightened. With halting steps he moved to the desk chair and sank down, dropping the knife. "What were we talking about?"

"The money," I said.

His eyes drifted closed, but then he snapped them open. "The money. I want my money."

I sat in silence, waiting to see if the pills were going to put Mike out completely. Nope. He hung onto consciousness.

"Worked hard for that money. Sheik stole it from me." He seemed beyond drunk. A nice combination of sedated and wasted.

Sullivan may be handcuffed, but I wasn't. This was my chance. I shoved myself to my feet and slowly placed one foot in front of another. I stopped to pick up a long, narrow piece of wood off the floor. Used to be a table leg in its former life. The wet splinters dug into my palm.

"What are you doing?" Mike asked, his words slurred.

I took a deep breath, gathered every bit of strength I had, and hit his head as if going for a home run. The sound of the wood on his skull was a sickening thud and I felt the vibration clear up to my shoulders. Mike slouched face down on the desk.

I stumbled toward him, my makeshift bat at the ready, but he didn't move. I grabbed the knife and flung it across the room, then dug into Mike's coat pocket for both his gun and Sullivan's, which I shoved in my own pockets. I found the handcuff key in his jeans, and step by painful step, made my way toward Sullivan.

When I unlocked the cuffs, he swiftly rose to his feet and rubbed his wrists. "Is he dead?"

I glanced over at Mike. His chest rose and fell in shallow breaths. "No."

Sullivan grabbed the wooden scrap from me and raised it above his head to finish what I had started.

I grabbed his arm. "No."

He glared down at me. "I'm going to end this."

I shook my head, almost collapsed from the pain stabbing through my temples. "No. Please. I don't want to decide who lives and who dies. Not this time."

He stared at me a moment, then threw down the wood. After he retrieved the Mercedes keys from Mike's jacket, he scooped me up in his arms and carried me to the car.

The next morning, the news repeatedly replayed Mike's perp walk and the tale of how the crooked cop murdered three people, put one in a coma, and set fire to a local bar.

Janelle got her fifteen minutes of fame. She was interviewed by every local station and full of 'I told those fools I was innocent.' She threatened to sue the police department.

Seems the I'm-sorry-we-accused-you-of-assault-and-murder gift basket didn't quite cut it.

Sullivan insisted I go to the emergency room. Their conclusion? A mild concussion. Rest and take it easy for a couple of days. Didn't need a doctor to tell me that.

At Ma's insistence, I skipped work the next day. But that night, I let Roxy do what she does best—break into Fit and Flex. I figured if Mike couldn't find the money in Kyle's apartment, this was the next logical place.

Armed with flashlights and Ax fiddling with the alarm code, we snuck into the locker room and cut off seven combination locks until we found the bag of money.

We did a four way split: Ax, Roxy, Janelle, and me. But we all agreed that Janelle got most of it because of the kids and her legal fees. Which left the rest of us fifteen thousand dollars each. I tried to give my share to Ax for wrecking his car, but he wouldn't hear of it.

"Dude, if anyone needs this money, it's you. Buy a car already," he said.

A sound plan, but I needed to pay Sullivan first.

Axton had retrieved his car from my sister's house and handed the keys over after our little bout of B & E.

The next morning before work, I stopped in at Rudy's Roundup Restaurant. When I walked in the door, Sarah looked shocked to see me and hurried over. "What happened?"

"I ran into a fist. A few times. Where's Rudy?" She pointed to his office next to the restrooms. Without knocking, I walked in.

He glanced up from his desk. "What're you doing in here?"

"Listen up," I said, "because you only get one chance to do the right thing. I know people in this town and if you don't cut out this breakfast bullshit, I'm going to have you inspected by the health department every week. I'm going to have your license revoked. I'm going to let everyone know that Rudy's is nothing but a mouse magnet. You're not going to have a business at all by the time I'm done with you."

I wasn't sure I could pull any of that off, but I figured Sullivan could. And I was already in debt to him, might as well go for broke. Or broker, in my case.

"You can't do any of that."

I smiled. "All right. But don't say you weren't warned."

I turned to go.

"Wait."

I peered at him over my shoulder.

"Ma would have to give up lunch."

"Of course. Right after you apologize."

I could see the thoughts chugging through his tiny brain. "Fine. I'm about to lose my staff anyway."

I was five minutes late for work. Roxy and Ma scurried around the diner, which was already filling up with customers.

They forced me to work the counter. And at nine, Officer Hard Ass strode in, his eyes scouring every nook and cranny of the place. With his thumbs hooked in his belt, he sauntered up to the counter.

"Miss Strickland, is there somewhere we can talk?"

I sighed. "Sure." I took him to Ma's office. I propped my hip on the desk. "What is it? I've got customers."

"You told me that day at the station to look closer to home to find Crystal Waters' killer. How did you know about Officer Goedecker?"

I hadn't. I'd been talking about Police Chief and stripper connoisseur, Martin Mathers. "Just a hunch."

He narrowed his hazel eyes and tried to stare me down. I just let him and refused to get flustered.

"Well, if you get any more hunches, I'd like a heads up."

I finished out my shift and even helped clean up a little. As I sat at the counter, rolling silverware into napkins, Ma got a phone call. When she hung up, she grinned at Roxy and me.

"That jackass, Rudy, has given up. I win!"

Roxy and I clapped. Jorge and Ray stepped out of the kitchen.

"Is lunch over?" Roxy asked.

"Yeah," Ma said. "We're a breakfast diner. It's worked for almost sixty years, I say we keep it that way."

There was much rejoicing.

I went home and napped. I was exhausted and still sore. Even working the counter had zapped my energy.

Sullivan woke me up when he dropped by around six with a green wrapped package in his hand. A large bruise covered his jaw and his nose was a tad swollen.

"What are you doing here?" I asked. "Clay is still gunning for you."

"It's no longer a problem."

"What do you mean?" I was scared he'd say the words. I didn't want to hear them, but I couldn't bury my head in the sand. Had Sullivan killed Clay?

"He left town and sold me his business interests. And if he wants to live, he won't come back."

"How?"

"Henry and I found the recordings of Martin Mathers. And several other items Clay wouldn't want leaked to the world."

I felt my shoulders relax. "Good." I was just glad that Clay was still breathing. "What about Stuart?"

"Also gone." He handed me the package. "Open it."

I sat on my futon, but he remained standing, his coat buttoned, a blue scarf wrapped around his neck.

Out of the rectangular box, I pulled out the softest pair of red leather gloves lined with silk. I stroked them, tried them on and they fit like …well, you know. "Thanks. They're beautiful."

He pocketed his hands. "I'm starting my business back up."

I felt a twinge of disappointment. "Okay."

"It's what I do, Rose. It's who I am."

"I know."

"I'm not changing."

I stood. "I never asked you to. You're a criminal, I get it."

He stiffened. "I think of it as being an entrepreneur."

I rolled my eyes. "Of course you do. By the way, I have your ten thousand dollars." I started walking to my freezer, but his voice stopped me.

"So, you found the money? Good, keep it."

I faced him. "No, I owe you."

His gold eyes narrowed in irritation. "Why do you have to argue every goddamned point?"

"I owe you ten thousand dollars for Janelle's bail and I'm paying you back."

"The debt's clear. I'm not taking your money."

I raised a brow. "Why? You don't forgive loans. That's not who you are either."

He took three steps forward until he stood in front of me. Cradling my face in his hands, he slowly leaned toward me, his eyes on mine. "I can do whatever the hell I want. Besides, it's Christmas."

And then he kissed me.

Reader's Discussion Guide

1. Rose never doubted Janelle's innocence. Was she right to blindly trust Janelle?

2. Rose denies feeling guilt over killing her stalker. Do you think Rose is feeling guilty? Why or why not?

3. Helping Sullivan is as important to Rose as clearing Janelle's name. What do you think about Rose's dedication to Sullivan?

4. Rose isn't in the Christmas spirit. She claims Janelle's troubles and the threat to Sullivan are the cause. Do you agree?

5. Rose develops feelings for Sullivan in spite of the fact he's a criminal. Should Rose pursue her feelings, knowing what she does about him?

6. In spite of Rose's difficult relationship with her mother, was she right to dismiss her mother's behavior at the Christmas party? How would you have handled the situation?

7. Rose is willing to ask for help for her friends, but not herself. Does Rose's pride get in the way of her own well-being?

8. Did Rose do the right thing by putting herself in debt to Sullivan in order to help Janelle?

9. Should Rose have accepted her sister's offer of a car? What is the difference between accepting Axton's loan of a car and her sister's offer?

10. Tariq sells stolen goods out of his car, Roxy is adept at breaking and entering, and Sullivan is a criminal. Do you view Rose as a moral character? How does she justify the illegal actions of her friends?

11. Do you agree with Rose's final decision at the end of the book? What would you do if your life was threatened?

Terri L. Austin

When Terri isn't writing, she enjoys eating breakfast at her local diner, watching really bad movies, and hanging out with her kids when they're home from college. She lives in Missouri with her funny, handsome husband and her high maintenance peekapoo. Visit Terri at www.terrilaustin.com to see what's next or drop her an email (terri@terrilaustin.com), she loves to hear from readers!

The Rose Strickland Mystery Series

Book One:

Diners, Dives & Dead Ends
by Terri L. Austin

As a struggling waitress and part-time college student, Rose Strickland's life is stalled in the slow lane. But when her close friend, Axton, disappears, Rose suddenly finds herself serving up more than hot coffee and flapjacks. Now she's hashing it out with sexy bad guys and scrambling to find clues in a race to save Axton before his time runs out.

With her anime-loving bestie, her septuagenarian boss, and a pair of IT wise men along for the ride, Rose discovers political corruption, illegal gambling, and shady corporations. She's gone from zero to sixty and quickly learns when you're speeding down the fast lane, it's easy to crash and burn.

Available Now
For more details, visit www.henerypress.com

IF YOU LIKED THIS HENERY PRESS MYSTERY,
YOU MIGHT ALSO LIKE THESE...

PORTRAIT of a DEAD GUY

by LARISSA REINHART

In Halo, Georgia, folks know Cherry Tucker as big in mouth, small in stature, and able to sketch a portrait faster than buckshot rips from a ten gauge -- but commissions are scarce. So when the well-heeled Branson family wants to memorialize their murdered son in a coffin portrait, Cherry scrambles to win their patronage from her small town rival.

As the clock ticks toward the deadline, Cherry faces more trouble than just a controversial subject. Between ex-boyfriends, her flaky family, an illegal gambling ring, and outwitting a killer on a spree, Cherry finds herself painted into a corner she'll be lucky to survive.

Available Now
For more details, visit www.henerypress.com

Lowcountry BOIL
by Susan M. Boyer

Private Investigator Liz Talbot is a modern Southern belle: she blesses hearts and takes names. She carries her Sig 9 in her Kate Spade handbag, and her golden retriever, Rhett, rides shotgun in her hybrid Escape. When her grandmother is murdered, Liz high-tails it back to her South Carolina island home to find the killer.

She's fit to be tied when her police-chief brother shuts her out of the investigation, so she opens her own. Then her long-dead best friend pops in and things really get complicated. When more folks start turning up dead in this small seaside town, Liz must use more than just her wits and charm to keep her family safe, chase down clues from the hereafter, and catch a psychopath before he catches her.

CROPPED to death

by CHRISTINA FREEBURN

Former US Army JAG specialist, Faith Hunter, returns to her West Virginia home to work in her grandmothers' scrapbooking store determined to lead an unassuming life after her adventure abroad turned disaster. But her quiet life unravels when her friend is charged with murder – and Faith inadvertently supplied the evidence. So Faith decides to cut through the scrap and piece together what really happened.

With a sexy prosecutor, a determined homicide detective, a handful of sticky suspects and a crop contest gone bad, Faith quickly realizes if she's not careful, she'll be the next one cropped.

Available Now
For more details, visit www.henerypress.com

Three Interconnected Mystery Novellas

OTHER PEOPLE'S BAGGAGE

by Kendel Lynn, Gigi Pandian & Diane Vallere

Baggage claim can be terminal. These are the stories of what happened after three women with a knack for solving mysteries each grabbed the wrong bag.

MIDNIGHT ICE by Diane Vallere: When interior decorator Madison Night crosses the country to distance herself from a recent breakup, she learns it's harder to escape her past than she thought, and diamonds are rarely a girl's best friend.

SWITCH BACK by Kendel Lynn: Ballantyne Foundation director Elliott Lisbon travels to Texas after inheriting an entire town, but when she learns the benefactor was murdered, she must unlock the small town's big secrets or she'll never get out alive.

FOOL'S GOLD by Gigi Pandian: When a world-famous chess set is stolen from a locked room during the Edinburgh Fringe Festival, historian Jaya Jones and her magician best friend must outwit actresses and alchemists to solve the baffling crime.

Available Now
For more details, visit www.henerypress.com

.

CPSIA information can be obtained at www.ICGtesting.com
Printed in the USA
BVOW022152270513

321756BV00006B/21/P